Educating Nicolas

Tom Fisher

Published by Crusader eBooks, Perth, Western Australia

Front cover image: *Lilith Tempting Adam and Eve*, Notre Dame Cathedral, Paris

Back cover image: *Boy and Bath*, Troy Caperton, detail

Typesetting, Layout and Cover Design by Gil Hardwick

This edition printed and bound by CreateSpace, *https://www.createspace.com/*

National Library of Australia Cataloguing-in-Publication entry:

Author: Fisher, Tom.

Title: Educating nicolas / Tom Fisher.

ISBN-10: 0-98-72987-2-0, ISBN-13: 978-0-98-72987-2-0 (paperback)

Dewey Number: A823.4

Acknowledgements

This novel is personally reflective in many ways, but it is also based on many years of teaching in rural Australia. It is inspired in large part by George Orwell's *Why I Write*, in some part by Kenneth Cook's *Wake in Fright* and Xavier Herbert's *Poor Fellow My Country*.

Style and content, on the other hand, is indebted to a good range of realistic, critical, subversive and coming-of-age cinema including, by date, Peter Brook 1963, *Lord of the Flies*; Leonardo Favio 1965, *Crónica de un niño solo*; Louis Malle 1971, *Le soufflé au Coeur*, and 1975, *Black Moon*; Nicolas Roeg 1971, *Walkabout*; Bernardo Bertolucci 1976, *Novecento*; David Hamilton 1980, *Tendres cousines*; Hector Babenco 1981, *Pixote: a Lei do Mais Fraco*; Bertrand Arthuys 1984, *Tom et Lola*; Fredi M. Murer 1985, *Höhenfeuer*; Jacques Doillon 1989, *La fille de quinze ans*; Goran Paskaljevic 1992, *Tango argentino*; Hugh Hudson 1999, *My Life So Far*; Christophe Ruggia 2002, *Les Diables*; Paula van der Oest 2002, *Moonlight*; Tony Gatlif 2002, *Swing*; Aisling Walsh 2003, *Song For A Raggy Boy*; Isild Le Besco 2003, *Demi-tarif*; René Féret 2003, *L'enfant du pays*; Michael Cuesta 2005, *12 and Holding*; Iván Noel 2008, *En tu ausencia*; and not least Tim McCanlies 2009, *Alabama Moon*, among others too numerous to mention.

I do hope you also get a chance to view these remarkable films.

I am not grateful for the loneliness I endured here, for the
alienation, the contempt, the mediocrity, and the narrow
right-wing provincialism, that always hides a brutality
at its heart.

Dorothy Hewett (1923 – 2002)

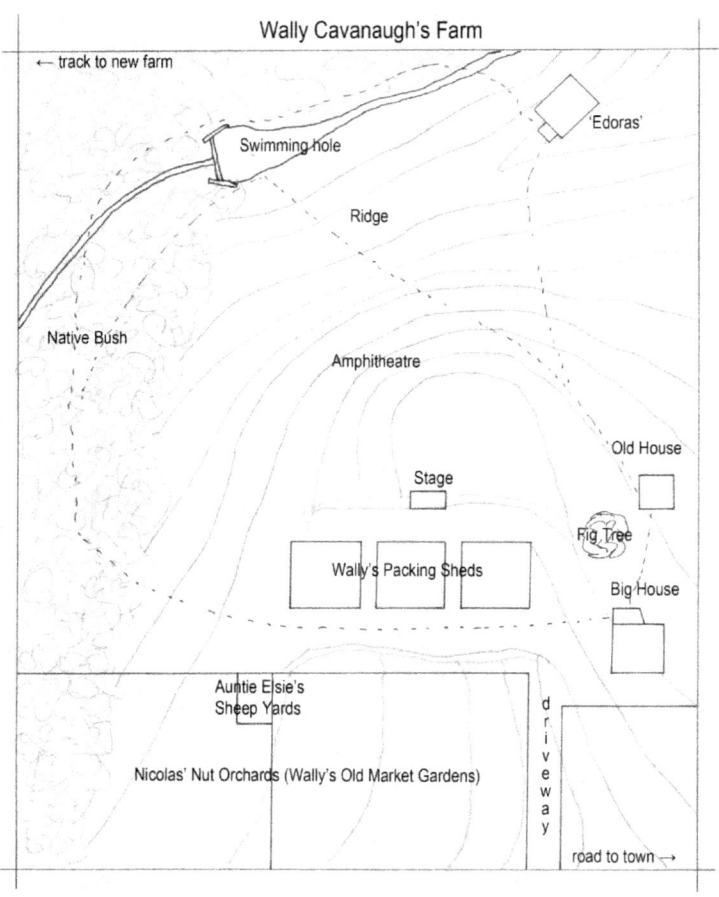

Wally Cavanaugh's Farm

← track to new farm

Swimming hole

'Edoras'

Ridge

Native Bush

Amphitheatre

Old House

Stage

Fig Tree

Wally's Packing Sheds

Big House

Auntie Elsie's
Sheep Yards

driveway

Nicolas' Nut Orchards (Wally's Old Market Gardens)

road to town →

CHAPTERS

Chapter One

The wind was starting to whip up branches as the trees swayed violently and leaves flew. It came upon them suddenly, from over the crest of the hill without warning. Nicolas had never seen anything like it. He kicked himself for not noticing the charged air sooner. The stink of ozone was everywhere, not that it made much difference, he thought later.

Wally called across to him as the cold damp air descended and with it a great wall of dark grey sky flickering with menace beyond the bright clear blue of minutes before, and the first great spatters of rain bombarded the parched dry soil, oddly raising dust among the raindrops which swirled and mixed with steam from the still hot ground.

Nicolas stopped to stare in wonder. The light was electric. The thing was weird, like phosphorescent lights at night, and fairies dancing. His hair stood on end.

Wally called again and he started across, but right then a great thundering crack split the air and he fell over backwards. It seemed like the heavens above had clapped suddenly and he was standing there in the middle, like a great monastery gong had struck inside his head. His ears rung and his head hurt. Slowly he turned onto all fours before struggling drunkenly to his feet. The big old Morton Bay Fig was down, split right down the middle with parts on fire and the rest smoldering. Wally was no longer to be seen.

Chapter Two

Nicolas was vague, they said, a dreamer. He didn't think that himself; it was just that he'd got off at the wrong station, or maybe the wrong planet. On the occasion he thought about it, it occurred to him that he may have missed the boat. Without people like Wally he couldn't imagine how he might have coped.

A school psychologist asked him once, during one of his many visits, what was the earliest memory he had of his childhood.

"You really want to know that?" he'd asked, but the old bloke sat gazing at him until he tired of waiting and shrugged.

"If you want to know my earliest memory, it was my brother getting pecked by a chook." he said finally.

"I beg your pardon?"

"Yes, I was in my stroller on the back veranda, and he went to have a pee down the back yard. He was standing there pissing on the lawn, under the lemon tree, and this chook came up and pecked his dick. Maybe it thought it was a worm or something. Anyway, it made him jump, I was watching, and he started to cry. He came all the way back up to the house with his dick hanging out. It had this drop of blood on the end, bright red; I remember, he walked past me and went inside to show Mum."

"That's my earliest memory," he added after a moment or two.

The psychologist sat staring at him. Eventually he shook his head and sighed resignedly before learning forward to make a note in his little book.

It was like that all the time. It had nothing to do with him. He just happened to have been there, but it was as if he caused things to happen; that it was his fault.

They never wanted to know really interesting things either, like those helicopter trees in the park; the way their seeds flew off, spinning away in the breeze in their tiny battalions, off on some mission, or how scorpions mated. He chuckled at the thought, but the psychologist just sat staring thoughtfully awhile before packing up for the day.

His mother used to say his problem was that he was just too good-looking to be real; what that angry bitch called A Beautiful Boy, as if it were her business, with his classic good looks, dark eyes, rose-petal lips and fine dark curly hair draping in ringlets about his ears. Things got worse after he started passing exams without studying, and then qualified to join Mensa, and they all realized he was incredibly bright as well; just not normal.

His own idea was that when they moved down to Barkhan Crossing from Wallaga when he was four, they wouldn't let him go to school with the other kids. That wasn't his fault either, nothing to do with him really, just something. Children weren't allowed to start school until they turned five. There were only eleven months between him and his older brother but that didn't matter because he was still four, and wouldn't turn five until the end of October.

The twins were two years behind and went to kindergarten, but he was too old to go with them. He had to wait almost until November. Off they all went to school every day while he stayed home. Being new to town they didn't know anybody much, only some of Jack's family, so there he was. Mum was busy all the time, and whenever he complained it was boring she went crook. It wasn't her fault. That headmistress had her rules. That was the end of it.

After that his early childhood memories were of ants, mostly, and birds and insects. He spent hours every day on his backside, or on his knees, watching ants scurry back and forth. There was a big nest near the chook yard that used to raid the kitchen scraps thrown over the fence for the chooks to peck and scratch around. One of the chooks went clucky and Jack built a coop for it while Mum made a nest and set some eggs. Every day after the others left for school Nicolas went and sat next to the clucky chook, watching it sitting there on its clutch of eggs. He watched the chooks, and the ants, and the house sparrows, and as the fruit trees came into blossom he watched the petals fall and the hard green fruit form on the branches, which grew into ripe sweet peaches and apricots.

The trouble with the clucky chook was it kept getting up off its nest, worried, fretting and fidgeting about something. He saw a mouse, and when he lifted the nest to see where it went there was a tiny mouse nest there underneath the eggs, in the warmth from the chook's body, with the tiniest naked pink baby mice squirming helplessly in a little ball of fur and straw there in a hole in the ground. It was awesome. He was gob-smacked. It was the most amazing thing to see, and when the mouse came back it fretted and fussed too so he put it all carefully back together and left them in peace. When he went to bed that night he dreamed about the tiny pink baby mice and the mouse mother there under the clucky chook with her eggs.

Next weekend the kids from next door came over and were playing with his older brother and the twins near the chooks nest, there in the coop. He made the mistake of showing them the baby mice underneath, thinking they'd like to see the tiny squirming bundle of new life as much as he did. They kicked it to pieces, and all the mice babies were squashed and red and bloody splattered on the ground and the mouse mother went hysterical. He was terribly upset about that. It just wasn't fair. It was his yard; his secret, and now all the mice were dead and the warm little nest wrecked, and the chook was cranky so they put her back in the yard with the others.

Next day the ants were out cleaning up the mess, tidying things up, sorting things out, putting the world back in order, and he began to appreciate them even more after that.

Next week Mum went up to the school to see if he could start. He was lonely and upset at home by himself, she said, it would be better if he was at school with the other children, but the spare undernourished head mistress said no he must wait until he turned five, not a day sooner. Those were the rules. It would be another four months, but he didn't tell his Mum he was glad now he didn't have to go to school. He didn't want to play with the other kids after that. He started hiding things, his little secrets, and his treasures, and wouldn't tell anyone where they were. He wouldn't tell anyone after that what was happening in his back yard. He kept it all to himself.

His great aunty Emily told him later, when he was older, that ants were actually fairies. In Cornwall, she said, when fairies die they come back to life as something smaller. Every time they die they get smaller, and smaller and smaller, until they become ants.

Aunty Emily was born in 1877. Her family were on the first boat full of farmers from Devon and Cornwall, and Ireland she said, brought out by

Governor Bourke to replace the convicts. She was a retired school teacher and had been to India, and Europe. She knew things. She was important, and he believed her, but still he said nothing. The school teacher thing worried him.

Chapter Three

The Dad they had when they were little wasn't his real Dad; his or Grant's Dad. That was Frank. He was a good mechanic and still lived up at Barkhan Crossing. The twin's Dad, Jack; Simon and Eric's Dad, was their Dad. He was a painter and decorator, and sign writer and not too bad an artist either. He used to win prizes at the show, and got extra money coming in by doing portraits. He did the most amazing landscapes too but he never showed them to anyone, just kept them in the shed.

Mum was pretty independent, in her own thoughts anyway, and since the war women were starting to assert themselves. "We went all the way through the war without men," she used to argue, "and the drought. They were off overseas, the good-for-nothing lot of them, while we ran the farms and kept the home fires burning, and we still clothed and fed them. We had to make do, so we can do without them now." She was fierce about it. Don't ever start her on the Depression. Anyone tried to reason with her, or argue the point; she'd turf him out and go get herself another bloke to warm her bed, and keep the money coming in. Sperm donors, she called them. Any kids and it was their responsibility. They had to pay for their maintenance and upbringing.

Not long after the twins started school she won a vacant block of land in a ballot, which she sold and used the money as down-payment on another block with a house. She paid the house off with Frank's maintenance, and later when he lost his job she took in a boarder. That was so Jack wouldn't have any claim on it later. His job was to keep food on the table.

Nicolas said to her once, when he was a bit older, that she had four sons. With Frank, then Jack, and the boarder, that was seven of us, all blokes, but it was men she hated not women. It didn't make any sense. He shouldn't have said anything. She came flying around the end of the kitchen table and landed him one right in the ear.

"Cheeky bastard! Spailpeen!" she screamed. "You'll be the death of me, you will, you little bastard. Another mistake like you, mate, Lord only knows where we'd be. You can go to hell."

Yeah, she was like that. It made him think back to the time the chook pecked Grant's dick. He had got up out of his stroller and toddled inside to see what was happening. Mum had his brother's pants down, there in the kitchen, and was on her knees swabbing it with Dettol, or something. It was red and swollen, but instead of crying his eyes had lost focus and he was staring dreamily out the window.

"What are you looking at?" She demanded to know, but he just stood there speechless so she picked him up and strapped him into the stroller on the back veranda, and went back to tending Grant's wound.

He copped it from Grant as well. He was the clever one, and went to school. He'd started school before anyone else, so of course he was smarter. He was a good boy. He worked hard and the teachers were pleased with him. And he was the eldest. By the time Nicolas started, not at the beginning of the year with the other children but right at the end when they were all ready to stop for Christmas, his was a lost cause. Mother was fed up with his whining, and because he made her so unhappy his older brother got the idea into his head that he must be a really bad little boy. Eventually she stopped complaining and got Grant to whack him instead.

Once he started school it was all right, for a while. They started him in the kindergarten class with a pretty young teacher called Miss Martin. He took Miss Martin a bunch of flowers, red and black Sturt's Desert Peas from Mum's front garden, but she didn't get them. One of the other kids in line knocked them out of his hand and stomped on them, saying only sheilas like flowers. What was he, a sheila? He didn't know. There was no time to think about it because next day they moved him up a class.

The new class was Transition. It had another Miss Martin, but everyone called her Miss 1A Martin while the other was called Miss Kindergarten Martin. That was another of those weird things that stuck in his mind. In Transition they made big wobbly spiders out of papier machè, with pipe cleaners rubbed in charcoal for legs, and they made hanging Christmas decorations out of coloured paper that swayed back and forth in the breeze. Miss 1A Martin let Nicolas use the scissors because he was so neat and tidy, and didn't cut himself.

On the way home he was dive-bombed by a magpie. It left a cut on his head and he had blood down the back of his shirt, so a lady on that street took him in to clean it up, and gave him some cake and a glass of milk before driving him home in her car. He got a smack for being late, and didn't get his chance to announce that he was a big boy now and allowed to use the scissors.

Another thing that happened that year was Jack and a couple of his mates laid a cement path up the side of Mum's house. When he got home from school he walked on it by mistake. He didn't know. His shoes sank into the wet mud and left his footsteps behind, so before he went inside he took them off as he'd been told so as not to walk mud into the house. Well, he got a hiding for that too, for making a mess of the newly laid cement.

The good thing that Christmas was that Nanna and Aunty Emily came down. Mum wasn't very happy about it. She and Nanna didn't get along very well so with her being there it was a bit tense. Aunty Emily for her part had done the Grand Tour. That was before the Great War, and before cars, when the family still had money; when they were getting a pound a pound for their wool and the army needed horses, but things were different now.

"Your mother missed out," Aunty Emily explained one day. "Be patient with her."

Meg had been the youngest in her family, and a girl she explained. Her five older brothers broke up the family properties when they came back from the war, after their father died, and went off and bought their own farms closer in, on the irrigation. When she left school there was nothing left for her. Aunty Emily was old and wise and Nicolas believed her. He still didn't quite trust her but he believed her, and held his tongue.

Chapter Four

Now that he had grown up a little, and absorbed a few of life's realities, the next few years slipped by without too much going wrong. The big problem he had was coming first in his class all the time without doing any homework. It just wasn't right. Grant was a plodder; he worked hard, made an effort, whereas Nicolas was always a flibbertigibbet, and a queer; he must have been cheating. He said to him once, after Simon was killed and they were getting pissed together at his wake and he'd had a few too many, that he hated him for it, for being such a smart-arse and causing all the friction in the family, so he and Eric never got a look in. That was why Simon was dead, with nothing to show for it.

"You could be rich, Nicolas, and make a name for yourself, with your ability. What the fuck are you on about? Why don't you do anything about it?"

He wanted to job him, and started yelling and ranting until Frank came over and broke it up, told him to piss off, they were sick of his bullshit.

But that was later. At the time, if anyone had asked him how he did it, he wouldn't have been able to answer. He simply didn't know. He wasn't that interested in school, it was all bullshit. All that trouble over nothing, being marched around and lectured to, and smacked with rulers, when he would rather have been left alone with his ants, in his own back yard, and draw pictures, and write little stories. He wanted to buy a camera but Mum wouldn't let him. She took his money off him and told him not to be so stupid. He'd get no pocket money if he was going to waste it like that. So he did what he was told. He was told to sit for exams like the other kids, and that's what he did. What happened after that was unpredictable, none of his business. They came out and said he came first, so, well, that's what happened.

About that time Jack started getting on the grog. He never drank in the pub with the blokes; he was an artist and didn't fit in there anyway. He'd bring home a whole carton of beer and take it down to the shed where he sucked bottle after bottle while he was painting. He drank it warm. Nicolas had been in the habit of going to sit with him and watch him paint, talking quietly about colour and especially light, except then he started to rave, and his boozy breath stank.

Mum put up with it for a while but then she kicked him out and he took the twins with him. They went to live with his mother away over the other side of town. His Dad was killed in the war and she was on a war pension, so Jack reckoned she was better off getting the money to support the twins than Mum. Some of the other women backed her up. Mum couldn't do much about it, except fume.

Jack leaving had a big effect on Nicolas. He was home by himself with Mum and Grant, and the boarder, and as it turned out Mum wasn't too well liked around town. That was part of the problem. The other part was some of the other kids trying to be popular with him at school when they couldn't figure out why he shunned them. They were getting good marks too, and seemed to think he was one of them for some reason, except he wasn't thinking about school much; it was something he was being made to do, something interrupting the happy times he had away along the river by himself.

The teacher they had that year, in 5th Class, thought he was a spoiled brat and caned him a lot; made him stand in the school foyer by himself until he learned to be civil. An exhibition, he said. The teacher they'd had the year before caned him for not doing his homework, but this time it was far more personal and he began to withdraw into himself. She was a serious bitch.

When he was home he was quiet and subdued, not taking much interest in anything, and that was when Mum started belting him. For not doing his chores, she said. Any time she had a bad report from school she'd lay into him as well, with the wooden spoon. Grant shunned him, locking his door so he could do his homework in peace, he said, so Nicolas used to get away and go for long walks by himself, mostly along the river but sometimes he'd take his bike and ride for miles just to be out of there.

The only good thing around that time was Frank had started a new job, running his own motor repair business and doing quite well at it, so Mum was getting maintenance from him again. She didn't say anything to him about Jack leaving, which was probably better.

Chapter Five

It was Nicolas' next year that was memorable. Like the day he met Wally it stayed with him forever, that year. It was not supposed to have happened, but it did. It started with a problem for the school, being that the headmaster's son was in the 6A class, among the bright kids he normally taught.

The bloke decided it didn't look good, teaching his own son. It looked like he was playing favourites. To resolve the dilemma he swapped classes with his deputy headmaster, Mr. Hill, who normally took the 6B class. Nicolas being so bright and getting first in most exams, and second in the rest, regardless of his inability to get along with anybody, was also in the A stream and got the new teacher as well.

The good thing about it was the new teacher didn't care what sort of kid he was, or anyway reputed to be; only that he could solve arithmetic, and write. He could do all his learning and figuring just by glancing at the blackboard. It sort of went like this:

"Nicolas," he'd say.

"Yes, sir."

"Solve this equation for me."

"That? Eight."

"Not out loud, Mr. Clever Dick."

Turning to the rest of the class he'd say, "The rest of you, I want to see your working out."

After a short while he'd say, "Stop now. Who has the answer? Raise your hand . . . not you Nicolas."

One of the other bright kids would give the answer, "Eight. Cross multiply and divide, and A equals 1,760 divided by 220, which equals eight."

"Are we agreed?" the teacher would ask.

"Yes, sir."

"All right then. Nicolas, what have you got?"

"You don't have to do the long division." he'd explain. "You can do it a lot quicker than that."

"Oh?" he'd be asked.

"Well, we already know there are 1,760 yards in a mile, and 220 yards in a furlong. It's easy, eight furlongs in a mile."

The teacher would gaze at him and ask, "You have no intention to fritter away your hard-earned savings at the races, do you?"

"No sir. I don't have any savings, sir."

"Tell me, why do you not feel we should be working the equation out formally?"

"What? I don't know. How would I know?"

He'd stopped, gazing out the window awhile. Finally he'd turn back thoughtfully, and say, "I can't figure out why we need to be working things out all the time; that we already know. It's like going around in circles."

"To discipline your mind, isn't it?"

"Why? My mind's all right. What are you talking about?"

The class would be watching him by this time, making him feel stupid, and he'd slide back into his seat trying to be invisible.

"Do you understand why we are at school, Nicolas?"

"No sir. It's just something we have to do, or get a hiding."

When it came time for the class to start preparing for the school's annual drama night, Mr. Hill arrived one day with a big pile of school plays sent out by the Education Department. He sat at his desk leafing through them, then plainly at odds with officialdom shook his head and announced that this year 6A would write its own play. He glanced quickly at Nicolas, who glanced back, for the first time with a glimmer of interest.

Nicolas didn't say much at the start. He knew he could make things. If they were going to do their own play maybe he could help with the stage set, or something. Jack had left some stuff in the shed, and he'd spent enough time down there with him to have a few ideas. If he could get past Grant and Mum he'd have a chance.

But it wasn't his family who ended up being the problem. First they had to write the play. He hadn't thought of that initially, until Mr. Hill called the class together to come up with a few ideas. The plot they came up with was stupid. He couldn't believe it. After the first session he sat at the back with his nose in a book. For two weeks they ignored him. One day Mr. Hill came over and asked him what the matter was, but he just looked at him, then glanced at the other kids and went back to his book. After class he made him stay back for a talk.

"What's the matter, son?"

"Nothing."

The teacher sat watching him awhile, and then sighed. He shook his head. "All right, look, just for now, let's pretend I'm not your teacher, eh? Let's pretend, well, ... no, let's just pretend."

"Pretend what?"

"Pretend we are out of here. Where would you be if you weren't here right now?"

"Home. Getting yelled at."

"Really? Where else might you be?"

"Down the river by myself. I go swimming, or just walk around, or ride my bike."

"Would you now? Could you write that down for me? What you'd be doing?"

"What for?"

"Just as a favour, all right? Don't tell anyone about it, and I won't say anything either."

On his way home Nicolas thought and thought about it. Mr. Hill wasn't so bad, not like the others, but he was still a teacher. What was he to do?

The issue was decided for him, more or less, once he got home and Grant was there calling to their mother that he was home finally. Instead of waiting for her to start yelling he slipped past the house and went down to the shed to be by himself. He knew what Mr. Hill was getting at. The new play was awful. It was hopeless. There was a cupboard there with some of Jack's old stuff, so he took a black drawing pencil and some blank sheets and started writing. It was nearly dark when Grant arrived to tell him his dinner was on the table, and getting cold.

Next day when the teacher came into class there was a neat folder on his desk, which he slipped quietly under some books before starting his lessons. Next week he started feeding bits of plot to the class, and some of the characters. Within a fortnight they had a story about this boy who got lost, and following an ant trail found his way to a fairy kingdom. The fairies did not normally allow humans to live with them, because in general they were so nasty and killed things, but this boy was the exception. The trouble was his parents and brother missed him so much, but the only way they could rescue him was by being nice, by having good manners, and by asking instead of demanding. You couldn't get anything from the fairies by yelling at them. You had to be nice, and say please and thank you.

From then until the end of the year the whole class busied itself getting the script typed up on a real typewriter, and making fairy costumes and ant costumes, and tree costumes and small bush animal costumes, and children and grown-up costumes. They finally persuaded Nicolas, on the teacher's prompting, to play the lead role. He seemed such a natural for the part, almost as if it had been written for him.

As chance had it, about the same time the local newspaper ran an essay competition for primary school pupils and he entered and won. The essay was not at all about fairies, or ants, or anything like that. It was about children being punished twice; getting the cane at school, for something or other, then getting a hiding when they got home for being in trouble at school. He didn't think it was right or fair, and he said so. Maybe grownups should talk to each other a lot more, and sort it out. A lot of the other kids liked him after that. As the play night drew near they started coming over to help make costumes in the back shed. Jack had left some florescent paint in tins in the cupboard, and they used it to paint ribs and spots on the fairy's wings so when they started coming onstage, out of the dark shadows, they would glow. The effect was brilliant.

Their play won. It didn't just win, it stole the show. Nicolas was awarded Best Actor, and his next in line Best Supporting Actor. The class won Best Play, Best Script, Best Set Design, and Best Costumes.

Next day at school Eric came up behind him and started telling him not to get too big for his boots. Nothing changed as far as he was concerned. Nicolas made the mistake, just at that moment, of being pleased with himself. He had this silly idea in his head that he'd achieved something. He told his younger brother to take a running jump at himself, and leave him be.

That started Eric yelling, of course, which attracted a crowd and along with it Richard, the headmaster's son, who also happened to be a prefect. The crowd with the prefect trying to maintain some semblance of order drew the attention of a teacher on playground duty who grabbed Nicolas by his shirt collar and pulled him out of the melee kicking and yelling.

That was enough. The teacher got a sharp kick to the groin, which made him let go, and once free Nicolas made a beeline for his bike and mounting up rode off. He rode and he rode. The next town was Berriwal, almost exactly thirty eight miles away by road, and he reached the post office there at around ten o'clock that night. He knocked on the door of the telephone exchange, which was the only building with lights still burning, and told them he had run away and could they ring his family and tell them where he was.

Jack drove over to pick him up. The girls on the exchange bought him fish and chips and an ice cream, he was so hungry, and he had just finished eating when his lift arrived. When they arrived back in Barkhan Crossing Jack simply dropped him off home, before going on home himself without saying anything. Grant didn't say anything either. He was already in bed asleep. Neither did his mother, who sat at the kitchen table glaring at him as he went through to his own room. Nicolas had a bath and went to bed.

Next day at school he was dragged sullen and beaten before the headmaster, and after a long boring lecture given six cuts, three to each hand, which hurt like hell.

Chapter Six

More trouble began for Nicolas when he started High School. It seemed to him much later there was some sort of correspondence between the two headmasters. Of course they were in regular contact, but at that age it was something that had not yet occurred to him. His first day thus found him standing outside in the corridor waiting, and waiting and waiting. He waited forever, it seemed. After nearly an hour the big, balding old man poked his head out the door.

"Come in, Brick," he said.

Nicolas continued standing there.

The headmaster was plainly looking at him.

"Me, sir? No, it's Brook. Sir."

The other glanced up and down, then abruptly cocked his head and bade him follow. Inside the office he sat wearily at his big old mahogany desk and shuffled through a folio of papers while Nicolas stood waiting.

"B, r, u, i, c," the headmaster recited eventually. "County Kerry. I dare to venture Clare and Galway. Your family is Irish. The word is Gaelic, and pronounced Brick," he looked up, "the same sound on the tongue, boy, as in 'building'."

Nicolas stared at him a moment, astonished.

"No sir, excuse me, it's Australian; Australian as you and me."

He stopped, confused a moment. "It doesn't matter, it's Brook, like 'bruise', not 'building'. You can say it the way you want, except most people who get it wrong say 'Break'. I never heard of 'Brick' before. That's just silly."

"You argue with me, child! You defy convention; make your betters out to be stupid! That's the way it's going to be?"

"No sir, but it is my name. I can pronounce it anyway I like." He found himself genuinely confused. "Why would I want to argue about that? I mean, what are you talking about? Who are my betters, anyway? What does that mean?"

The headmaster leaned forward slightly to write something before glancing up once more, and leaned back in his chair.

"I read your essay, Brick," he began slowly, "think you're clever, do you?"

Nicolas froze, and stood listening intently while the other went on, "My considered view is that you are a brat, and I cannot abide brats. I read your report. You are lazy and a time waster. You think you can set yourself up as a ringleader, in my school, don't you? You think you can make a name for yourself, among the hooligan elements, instead of applying yourself to your studies; a boy with your obvious talent and potential. Well, young fellow my lad, let me tell you, it's not going to happen. I will break you, boy, do you hear? We will avert this tragedy, avert it; nip it in the bud. Have you got that? You are here to work, and you will work."

He watched Nicolas' face as he spoke, watching for a reaction, but none came. He leaned forward again and wrote something further, then abruptly closed the file and got up from his chair. Stepping over to the corner he selected some canes from an umbrella stand and turning back to his desk laid them out.

"Which do you prefer, Brick?"

"Brook, sir."

"All right, as you will."

The headmaster picked up a long thin whippy cane and flexed it before bringing it down whistling past Nicolas' ear. He didn't flinch.

"This one is a stinger, boy. You won't like it. Not one little bit."

He picked up another, only slightly thicker. He flicked the tip over his shoulder and it made a light humming sound, harmonious, not at all hard on the hearing.

"This one I call Cassius. It sounds pretty, doesn't it? But mark my words, it hurts, boy. You won't like it either. Not one iota."

Placing the cane back on his desk he picked up another, heavier cane and flicked the tip past his ear again. It made an unpleasant drone, like an angry bee, and Nicolas involuntarily jerked his head away.

"Ah!" The headmaster nodded to himself, eyes not leaving Nicolas' face. "We arrive at an understanding. All right then, back to your class."

In a daze Nicolas wandered back to his class, or tried to. In Primary they had the one room all the time, but here the class moved around depending on their subject and he had to sit and consult his timetable to discover where he was supposed to be. Even then he had to go back to the headmaster's office for a map so he could locate his classroom in the maze of buildings. It was little use. He felt sick. For the rest of the day he sat stunned, and the moment the bell rang he simply stood and left without saying anything to anybody.

Chapter Seven

On the way home an old truck slowed and pulled up beside him, so he stopped his bike to see who it was. It was Jack's Uncle Wally. He knew him because he had a market garden and often used to bring in potatoes and vegetables when Jack was living with them with the twins, before he got on the grog.

"Put yer bike in the back, son," he called across. "I'll give yer a lift home."

Nicolas obeyed, but before he drove off Wally glanced across, looking him up and down.

"Drivin' past 'n saw yer leave school. Yer didn't look too happy, did ya. Thought I'd better catch up wiv ya." He paused a moment. "Y'all right are yer, son?"

"Not really," Nicolas said slowly.

"What 'appened?"

"Ah, that bloody headmaster, he's just a bastard, that's all. What are they, stupid people they are, prison bloody guards or something, bloody concentration camp?"

The old fellow looked away and sighed, then started the truck again and drove off.

"Tell yer what," he said eventually. "Why don't yer come up 'n see me Sat'dy. I'll give yer a job, eh? You c'n dwive me twacta for me, eh? You'll be right, bit a money in yer pocket, 'n them cunts c'n get fucked."

Nicolas looked sharply up at him. "Really?"

"Yeah, it'll be right. Been gunna call in to see yer, but never got 'wound to it. We know what's goin' on, evwybody does, wiv yer Muvva 'n that. Been a bit too busy meself, that's all, 'n yer a good lad, I c'n see that, just doin' it tough."

Wally paused, glancing across thoughtfully. "Jack read yer letter to me, yer know, the one yer had in the paper. Thought it was spot on, meself."

He stared out the window, lost in thought, then sadly shook his head and said nothing more until they got home. Once Nicolas had his bike down off the back of the truck the old bloke simply said, "See yer Sat'dy, all right?"

Nicolas nodded and the truck drove off. After he put his bike in the shed he fed the chooks then split a good pile of wood for the kitchen stove, and for good measure filled up the bin at the side of the house though it would not be used until winter set in. It was all right, good. The steady swing of the axe and the muscle rhythm of his body working relaxed him and took his mind off the day. The job done he returned to the chook yard where he cleaned their water troughs and collected the eggs.

When Saturday came he rode off early after breakfast, worrying that old Wally might have forgotten him and gone out. The place was five miles away and it took him half an hour to get there. The old bloke was as good as his word, however, and was waiting for him there at the house. He must have been keeping an eye out for him and came out onto the front veranda to meet him as he rode up. He chuckled to see the boy arrive bright-eyed and breathless from his long ride.

The old place was huge, rambling, overgrown with creepers covering half the front of the house, with remnants of lawn uncut and old rose bushes straggling to form almost a hedge amongst the kikuyu leaving worn foot-beaten tracks in and out. A few sheep wandered about, keeping things more or less in trim. Inside it was dim; cool with an old, dry, musty, lived-in smell like the place hadn't been aired in fifty years, but not uncomfortably so. It felt like it had been lived in, that old house. Along one side against the setting sun was a tall shady bamboo grove, equally unkempt.

Two small boys came out onto the veranda, neither wearing pants but the older of the two with a grubby t-shirt, quickly followed by a remarkably handsome woman who shepherded them both back inside while Wally came down the steps to greet his visitor. Taking him by the arm he led him around the back of the house along a rough track toward a row of large sheds.

There was nobody else around. Nicolas thought the place must be busy, it was so big, but no sound of work or machinery disturbed the quiet. As they drew closer Nicolas noticed cobwebs and dust settled everywhere, like a film of neglect and disuse over what looked at first glance like busy packing sheds. He stopped, confused.

"Where is everybody?" he wanted to know.

"Give 'em all the sack, eh," Wally drawled. "We 'ad ta close evwyfing down, 'n put it under quawanteen. Suspected bloody infestation of some fing or uvver, so they weckon. Doesn't matter, just can't sell me vegies for a while, that's all."

Nicolas stared at him before turning on his heel to gaze about, frowning.

"You said you wanted me to drive your tractor, and earn some pocket money. I rode my bike all the way out here."

"What? No, you'll be wight. We're gunna have a folk festival. You're just the lad. You can wite letters, and put on plays, just what we want, eh. Jen's gunna sort the music, get a few people in, and Bob's yer uncle!"

"Come on, ye c'n get started stwaight away," Wally went on happily. "Ye c'n dwive a Fergie, can't ya? Good little twacta."

Without another word he stepped across to the first shed, Nicolas at heel, and together they went inside. There was a little grey tractor with a good flat-bed trailer, but Nicolas demurred, less confused now than astonished at the suddenness of events.

"Maybe we should go back to the house and talk about it a bit. Don't you think so?"

Wally stopped. "Yeah, righto, 'ave a nice cuppa tea, eh?"

With that he turned straight around and strode back toward the house.

Back in the big main house Wally led Nicolas through a large glass-covered observatory converted from what once must have been a back veranda, along a short passage and into the big old homestead kitchen. The lady was there with the two boys, bathing them in a tin tub on the floor, and a girl about his age was helping her with them; plainly her daughter they looked so alike, except a little gawky in her early adolescence. She would be a fine looking woman like her mother with long dark hair, high cheekbones and flashing dark eyes. He'd seen her at school, but he being so shy hadn't anything much to do with her, or anyone much. He was always in trouble, and she glanced up shyly as he came through the door.

Wally went over to the stove and put the kettle on, and pulling a chair out from the dining table for Nicolas to sit busied himself with cups and saucers. That done he turned and said affably, "Yer know evwyone I s'pose?"

"No, I don't, not really."

"That's me daughter Jennie," he said first, "wiv the boys, Kennie and Owen. And that's me grand-daughter Emma. This is Nicolas. 'E's gonna be 'elpin' us wiv the festival; dwivin' the twacta, and whateva else 'e can do. Gunna be good, eh?"

Jennie glanced up at her Dad, smiling affectionately, then across the table to Nicolas.

"We've heard a lot about you, Nicolas. It's very nice to meet you finally."

Emma glanced away, her face crimson, then back slightly before bending to scold the boys. She took a towel and grabbing the little one by both arms lifted him up out of the tub and onto a towel on the floor, and kneeling head down out of sight began drying him.

Jennie smiled again, refusing to be distracted, but glanced curiously at her daughter before continuing.

"Dad does need someone to help around the farm, but that's not really so important. He can do it himself if he wants, except we thought it would be a way for you to earn some pocket money. I really wanted to know more about your writing."

Nicolas flashed at Wally who was back at the stove by then, busy with the kettle.

"I was going to stop writing," he ventured cautiously, "not do it any more. It's too much trouble. It gets me into too much strife all the time."

Jennie's mouth dropped. She leaned forward, across the table, and took his hand in hers.

"No, don't you ever dare think such a thing. How could you? You have a gift. No, it's not possible."

She stopped, looking at him intently, and her face clouded. Her eyes narrowed, frozen, angry.

22

"Tell me, what are they doing to you?"

Nicolas sat back, stunned. "No, it doesn't matter. It's all right. I can get by. It's just not worth it, that's all."

Wally turned as well to watch his face, confused. "Don't talk like that, son. No, yer gotta live yer own life. Fuck 'em. Learn to tell 'm to get fucked."

"Yes, you must," Jennie took over. "Put it out of your head. Nobody can live like that, else we go crazy and they'll have won. That's what they want."

He paled at the thought. As they watched him Emma looked up as well. Everything rushed in on him and he started to cry. He didn't move. Externally he sat frozen with only his eyes glistening while tears ran down his cheeks. Inside a storm raged. Thunder cracked as lightning tore across his thoughts, shredding his resistance, undoing the years of stillness he'd nurtured within himself. Eventually he went pale and started trembling, but sat there without moving until after a while he heard voices and realized they were arguing about him. He felt Jen take his head in her hands to hold him against her breast, crooning softly as if to a baby.

"Listen to me," she said quietly. He couldn't tell whether the words came from her mouth, or from her heart straight through into his head. It didn't seem to matter. Nobody had ever got to him so directly before so he just sat absorbing it.

"Don't worry about your mother," she was saying. "We'll look after her. She'll get what for. I'll see to it, by God. You come and live with us. Dad will take you home in the truck, all right? Today, right now, as soon as you're ready. You pack your things, and that will be the end of it."

Eventually he nodded, ever so slightly, almost to himself so the others wouldn't notice, but she felt it and let him go. He stood and only briefly turning to Wally went back out through the observatory and around the house to the front where he got into the truck. Wally came out the front door.

On the way back into town neither spoke. When they arrived home Wally simply followed him inside the house, to stand guard at his bedroom door while he packed his few things. Grant came out to see what was going on, but catching Wally's eye thought better of it and ducked back into his own room. His mother was in the kitchen. She must have seen them arrive but said nothing.

It didn't take long. Nicolas simply folded his clothes and packed them into a cardboard carton with his school things in another and the rest of his junk, his few toys and games, his little bush treasures mostly, in another again. Wally took two in his arms while Nicolas carried the third, and that was it.

Back in the truck the old fellow sat a moment, glancing across at him as he had a few days before.

"Y'all right, are yer?" he asked abruptly.

Nicolas simply nodded.

Chapter Eight

While he was away from home, things didn't change much at school. Not for some time at any rate. The headmaster had it fixed into his head that Nicolas was a serious trouble maker, and determined to make an example of him. That resulted mostly in his being made to stand in the corridor outside his office for hours on end while the rest of the students trooped back and forth to their various classes, and recess and lunch. Finally he would be called in and given six cuts with Cassius, rarely with the stinger or the drone except when headmaster was really angry, or agitated about something or other.

There was little point attending class for only brief periods, and when he did he sat at the very front saying nothing while the teachers simply worked around him. When it came time for exams he consistently failed, except of course credit passes in English and French, but that was not for lack of apathy. He simply didn't care anymore. More correctly, he simply didn't care any more about school, or whatever it was school represented. It was getting beyond him.

Wally was good. Rather than make him ride his bike five miles out every day he came into town to pick him up; he and Emma. They got the bus in the morning, but the bus went around a long circular route in the same direction morning and afternoon. That part of the district was fairly closely settled with a lot of small farms and market gardens; with a lot of kids to pick up and drop off again, and by the time it arrived back past Wally's gate of an afternoon it was late.

Toward the end of the year, they were in town one Saturday morning to do some shopping. People started looking at him and whispering, until somebody came over to Wally and spoke quietly in his ear.

"Fuckin' 'eadmaster of yours died, last night, eh," he turned and said. "'Eart attack they weckon."

Nicolas glanced up briefly before turning away. He walked off a few steps then shrugged, face blank, and shook his head.

"No, fuck him," he muttered under his breath, "fuck the lot of them."

Out loud he simply said, "None of our business, is it? It'll be all right now. Next year I can leave school anyway."

One of the women walking past overheard him and called out, "Don't you mind about that, Nicolas Bruic! It was you wasn't it, you little shit, smart-arse little bastard. Took us years to get someone decent way out here, with an education, give our kids a chance, but you were the death of him. He was a good headmaster until you arrived!"

She reached forward suddenly and took him by his shirt collar, shaking him like a pup and throwing him off-balance as she yelled furiously at him.

Wally moved with surprising speed. Grasping her arm firmly he placed himself directly in front of her, glaring angrily and without a word. She let Nicolas go and looked away, unable to hold his gaze.

Nicolas stood a moment dazed before reaching up to take Wally by the hand, who had slowly eased the woman out of reach before letting her go.

"Come on, Wally, leave it. Let's do the shopping and go home."

Avoiding Wally she called after him as they turned away, "You haven't heard the last of this, Nicolas, you mark my words!"

When he ignored her she turned and after a brief exchange with some of the other women went over to a car, and getting in drove off toward the school.

"Who's she?" Nicolas wanted to know as he and Wally walked along to the grocery.

"Mrs. Kulinski, Vicky Kulinski" Wally said. "That's Steve Kulinski's missus. Steve, you know, from the pwimary school. But she's English, maiden name was Briggs, used ter be a coppa of somefing like that, back in the old country."

"Oh yeah, I know him," Nicolas said after thinking a moment. "That real quiet teacher who doesn't say much. He's all right, but she left him. She's living with Andy Gronault, the retired SAS bloke who sells life assurance down at the estate agents. She's got a kid who's a real shit, that Dinky Kulinski, you know. He's got a lot of mates who suck up to him now because his step-Dad's an ex-commando, except they're all bastards. He takes them out trail-bike riding. They cut up the bush real bad with their motorbikes, back over the other side of the river where we had a big colony of red-tailed cockatoos, and numbats, used to anyway. They all reckon they're hell tough. Grant and Eric hang around with them sometimes."

He glanced up at Wally. "They all think I'm stupid, but I notice things. There isn't anything that happens in the bush I don't know about."

Turning back for a moment frowning he watched the car disappear around a corner at the other end of the street.

"They don't just rip up the bush, they bomb whole cities and countries, don't they," he said, looking up at Wally.

Chapter Nine

The regular monthly meeting of the Barkhan Crossing High School Parents and Citizen's Association began promptly at 7:30 pm. Faces were drawn and the room was tense. The first item on the agenda was a notice of condolence to Mrs. Klein and her family at the sudden and tragic loss of their husband and father before discussion turned to a replacement headmaster. The deputy, Mr.. Werner, while taking over school administration in the meantime had already declared his interest in maintaining a professional focus on his science teaching and would not be applying for the job.

At that point a list of names put forward by the Education Department was tabled, which bought a sharp rebuke from several of the mothers present wanting to discuss the state of the school and how to manage the number of errant students in the town who placed a burden on successful school administration. They argued that they placed their own children at risk of poor academic performance, in particular the example set by one Nicolas Bruic who had no family to speak of, and cheated in exams, and came and went as he pleased. This is a decent town, with a good school being dragged down by single mothers and riff-raff.

The deputy at that made a point of order about naming individual students and their family circumstances in a public forum, and put a motion that the department's list of prospective headmasters be considered as a matter of priority. He argued that student care was already well serviced through the school psychologist, nurse and chaplain, and it was not part of the teaching role to enquire into their students' family circumstances. The police sergeant Mick Lewis sat back listening. His wife was school secretary and because she was on the staff had no standing in the P&C. They had two girls there so he sat in for her, if only to give power to her views, not that it mattered as it turned out. Finally he leaned forward and seconded the deputy's motion, at which the three women stood and walked out.

That left the meeting without a quorum. The chairman shrugged, shaking his head, and quietly folding his papers declared the meeting invalid.

In the local paper that week a notice appeared announcing the formation of *Bold Hearts*, the Barkhan Crossing Child Protection Society, with a date for an inaugural general meeting to be held in the Shire Council chambers, on Tuesday the week following.

Two weeks later as the school P&C met again to consider the application for the job of headmaster, twenty three new members arrived *en masse* and put a vote of no confidence in the chairman, who promptly resigned leaving the position vacant. Vicky Kulinski was then duly elected to the chair with an overwhelming majority of twenty six votes to four.

Chapter Ten

Back out on the farm preparation for Wally's folk festival sort of puttered along when they found time to get things done. By this time the family decided that Easter next year would work out all right. The two big sheds furthest from the house looked out over a more or less natural amphitheatre, which had given Wally the idea in the first place, at the back of which the broad saddle of the hill above was fairly flat allowing plenty of room for camping, while the sheds on their graded embankment could house the food stalls, and markets for whatever people wanted to buy or sell.

Gradually over winter they cleared all the old vegetable gardens, and the potato patches along the low ground where it was poorly drained and inclined to waterlogging over winter. They sowed grass there they could mow later so it would be green right up to the front of the stage. Wally had been a very good farmer, and his father before him. Over the years they had terraced the gentle slopes to stop soil erosion and retain water up in the higher ground longer; plowing along contours instead of up and down like everybody else. Nicolas became adept at manoeuvring the little tractor back and forth, occasionally with the trailer but as time went by increasingly with a blade attached to the three-point linkage so he could level the ground and even out the bumps.

At the back of the hill ran a broad stream from which they pumped water using a really old fashioned hydraulic ram that clacked endlessly, driven by the flow of water itself to deliver a steady dribble up into the big tank on the crest of the hill, and down again to the big house. The gardens higher up had been watered by a big slow thumping old three-cylinder Southern Cross diesel on an iron sled further downstream that drove an ancient piston pump through a gear box of sorts. It had been dragged into place with the tractor, and left there at the top end of a big pond formed by damming the creek with sacks of sand and cement that went hard in the water, but that too had been shut down to save fuel when the quarantine was imposed and Wally lost access to his vegetable markets.

It was very pretty there. The family had constructed a short diving board and made it into a swimming hole and picnic area, and they thought it would make a nice recreation area during the festival where people could relax and have their meals away from the clamour. When there was nobody else around Nicolas would go down there for the peace and quiet, to be by himself with his thoughts, and commune with the place as he thought about it.

Very early in the morning was the best time, as the sun came up. The old diesel engine with its workings sat there in the early light like a garden sculpture. Birds came in to drink, and kangaroos occasionally to nibble the fresh green grass. As the day warmed the ants were busy, and insects humming and buzzing in the still air, somnolent, until late morning a breeze would spring up from the southwest and the place would change and freshen. The varying mood of each day entranced him.

Coming into summer it grew warm. About mid-morning one Sunday the sun had a sting to it heralding the hot weather ahead. Without thinking he stripped and waded into the pool. It was colder than he thought, causing him to suck his breath in as it came up to his waist, but once into the deeper water he dived and swam a short way, underwater, marveling at the soft dappled colours from the rays of light slanting through from the surface. Just ahead of him a big green turtle slipped off a snag and made its ungainly waddling way off into the gloom, and he turned again back from where he had come as his head broke the surface for air.

He froze. Emma and the boys were coming down the hill. Glancing back he kicked with his feet and moved slowly back against the far bank, hidden slightly by the reeds. It was no use. She saw his clothes there as they came down onto the grass and stopped, glancing around for a moment before ushering the boys down to the water's edge. As they tugged at their shirts she bent to help them, but they managed their pants themselves and were quickly in the water splashing about.

Emma stood there only briefly before disrobing. Nicolas swam out a little so she could see he was there, but she only smiled and continued to undress. He was going to say something but Jennie coming across the grass behind her caught his eye so he just stood there in the water waiting to see what would happen next. The mother took in the scene at a glance, and striding over to her daughter set down her picnic basket and began to undress as well. Both naked, mother and daughter, they waded into the pond, gazing intently at the growing young man there in the water who swam back a little, shy now, but she called across to him.

"You are very welcome, Nicolas. Welcome to our little family. Dad will be down shortly, he's just tidying up that last bit of leveling you did yesterday."

Emma flashed her eyes at him, smiling shyly, then without warning swam right across to him and began splashing.

"Hey! Cut it out," he spluttered, but she giggled and came at him. He launched sideways away from her, protesting.

"Emma," he cried, "I'm not ready for this yet, all right."

"Why? We always come here swimming."

He looked at her. "It's your family, isn't it? I'm not your family, not really, it's different."

She stopped, gazing steadily at him. Her eyes met his and held there for a long moment.

He plucked up his courage. "You're so beautiful, Emma, that's the trouble. You're not my sister, but, and I can't help myself."

She took a deep breath and said slowly, her skin breaking into goose bumps and eyes not leaving his face. "And you are far too handsome, Nicolas Bruic."

He flushed, awkwardly, his body stirring, and swam back away from her a little. From a safe distance he turned only partly toward her and said softly, "Well leave me be then. Not here. Talk to me later."

There was a long moment when the air seemed completely still, as a spell woven, but he shook it off and swam back past the boys frolicking there oblivious; back across to the other side where he stepped up onto the bank and picking up his shirt began to dry himself, not trying to hide himself but at the same time not looking back at her either, maintaining his dignity. He dressed casually, then turned and walked promptly back up the hill toward the house. Halfway up he ran into Wally coming down, who'd taken in the situation from the top of the hill and smiling quietly to himself went on down to join his family.

Just before Christmas Jen's husband Chas, Emma and the boys' father, came home. He'd been working cattle way up in the northwest and brought a big mob of stores down with him into the southern districts, and leaving them there on agistment decided he wanted to spend the summer with his family. His given name was Charles, but he hated being called Charlie. He considered it flippant, disrespectful. He was a quiet man with little to say; just did things and got on with it, so of course he and Nicolas hit it off immediately.

Nicolas had decided for himself by then to keep away from Emma. He was gentle with her about it, taking her for a long walk around the property, not even holding her hand or anything like that but in his own quiet way asked her to be patient with him; to wait for him, and let him find his feet before they went any further. They were far too young as it was, but that wasn't really the point he wanted to make; he simply didn't want to talk about it, so when they arrived back at the house she leaned in close and kissed him on the lips before pushing him away. He stood there as she went inside, musing awhile, and then turned on his heel and strode over to the shed to prepare the tractor for the next day's work.

What they decided to do finally was sow the entire amphitheatre with lawn grass, not just the bit at the front, and fire up the big diesel pump every other day to water it using sprinklers.

Wally had a little mower attachment for the tractor, not quite up to the task but adequate, which he'd once used to keep the grass down between his neat rows of vegetables. Every week Nicolas got the job of running it over the terraced hillside, and down again in decreasing circles and back and forth in front there where the stage was going to be.

Chas played guitar. He was very good, and when he brought it out of an evening Wally would get down his old banjo and Jennie her fiddle. Emma played flute and a penny whistle. They tried to get him to join in, learn to play something or other, but he demurred saying he would rather sit and listen; let him be their audience. Wally and Chas usually brought a few bottles of home brew up from the cellar and settled in for the evening. Chas would lean over with a small glass for Nicolas, but he drank only little, until once the rhythm set in the four of them together would launch into some of their favourite old American Bluegrass, broken up with Irish two-steps and the occasional Cajun jug-stomp when they insisted he at least blow an old earthenware jug for them. That was about as far as he wanted to go musically, but it was fun, and the close family atmosphere he'd never experienced before softened him and got him smiling.

After a week or so he began writing again.

Chapter Eleven

Emma persuaded his brother Simon to come out and rehearse for the new play when it was ready. He was as keen as mustard and argued all day with Eric trying to get him to come too. Eric was a bit too much like Grant and their mother, practical and down-to-earth; no nonsense they said of themselves, so Simon gave up finally and took sides with Emma. It hurt him to break with his brother because they were twins and so rarely apart, but when Jack decided to come out as well that sort of decided things. Nicolas found himself quietly pleased they had a professional sign-writer who could paint scenery and back-drops, but Wally went on with the job as if it were all coming together as planned. It was in a way, but without fuss or being too obvious; the whole family it seemed having something to offer.

Simon's grandmother Elsie was Wally's sister; Jack's mother, and when he saw the old brother and sister with their heads quietly together he began to appreciate Jack a lot more. As they worked neither said much to one another, not from dislike only that there was not much to say, especially about his mother. It was awkward so they avoided it and got along, Nicolas trying to get an image of the play in his head while Jack stayed off the grog and followed him patiently around pointing out to him the available options. Chas for his part enjoyed himself immensely. The old property was coming back to life, people coming and going constantly like the stations up north, and a real sense of community beginning to develop which went beyond family ties.

The idea for the play itself, however, came about because Emma refused to leave him be. Every time he turned around she was there. Try as he might his concentration failed and he'd turn to notice her watching him. It bothered him no end, though he didn't say anything to her because there was a tension building in him he realized went beyond the way his body stirred at the sight of her. One night after dinner they were all tired so instead of bringing out their instruments Chas played some records on the gramophone. Nicolas was playing around with some ideas in his notebook, head down with Jack at the kitchen table, when his ears pricked up and with it goose bumps and a tingle up and down his spine.

"Chas, what's that you're playing?" he wanted to know.

Chas passed the cover across. "That's *'Dark Eyes'*; *'Les Yeux Noirs'* in French. Django Reinhardt."

"Really? Can you play it again for me?"

"Sure." Chas reached over and gently shifted the needle back to the start of the track.

This time Emma flashed through his mind, and as the music played he turned to see her watching him, as she did every day now, and he realized what it was she was doing to him, and how he felt about it. It that moment it fell into place and head down he started writing furiously. The record finished and everyone started off to bed, but when Jack nudged him he waved him off and sat there scribbling with his pencil.

Next morning as they straggled in for breakfast he was still there, sound asleep at the table with the stack of papers neatly there beside his head. Chas picked him up bodily and taking him to his room stripped him down to his underpants, not bothering with pyjamas, and tucked him into bed. He didn't emerge until mid-afternoon, woken by people talking in the kitchen, and when the back door slammed with Wally coming in from the shed for his afternoon smoko he jumped out of bed and dressed hurriedly to go apologise for sleeping in. He said he forgot, but when he got to the kitchen they were all there smiling at him, his play scattered about with everyone reading their various parts.

Emma was radiant. She stood there defiant as Nicolas hurried around grabbing the sheets of paper, mumbling that it wasn't finished yet he still had a lot of work to do on it, and, no it wasn't about anyone he knew it just came into his head and he hadn't quite worked it all out yet who was going to play who.

No, it's just an idea I'm playing with, it's not ready, leave me alone.

She wasn't fooled, however, and toyed with him until frustrated and angry he put all the sheets back on the table and went out the back through the observatory to get away from them.

"It's too late, Nicolas," she called after him. "It's not yours any more, it belongs to us. If you behave maybe we'll let you be director."

He stopped, turning on his heel to face her. She watched his face.

"You haven't read it yourself, have you," she declared suddenly, and started to giggle. "You don't even know what it's about, do you?"

He stood there, helpless.

"Well, anyway Nicolas," she went on, "You're not playing the prince. Simon is. He'll be perfect."

It all started coming back to him in a rush. He frowned. "I suppose you still want to be the princess, Emma. I don't have any say about either, do I?"

"Of course I do," she grinned, "and of course you don't have any say about it."

"Is it that bad? I thought it was all right. It's all right, isn't it? It doesn't need to be fixed up that much, does it?"

"Nicolas, it's brilliant. It's very, very funny."

He turned to walk away but she called after him, keeping his attention, "You can play the Greek statue, the one in the garden. Not David, I mean the other one, Adonis, you're so beautiful. The boys can be cherubs."

"What? There isn't any Greek statue. What are you talking about?"

"Not yet there isn't, but we can soon write one in. You'd perfect for it, just exactly right."

"You mean you want me to stand there nude, right through the play. No. I mean, having a statue in the garden's a good idea. I never thought of it, but Jack can paint a statue when he does the scenery, all right?" he paused, "With a fig leaf, Emma. Agree?"

"I agree. So long as you stop avoiding me, Nicolas."

He gazed steadily at her now, but resisted. "No cherubs either."

"All right, no cherubs. Just tell me if you love me or not. Stop doing this to me."

"I love you very much, Emma, too much," he glanced away and back again. "It's hard for me, you know."

"Well, all right, we've got that far. What makes you think it's easy for me, seeing you here every day? Do you want me to start yelling at you? I can be a real bitch, you know."

He sighed. "No, I didn't know. It's not something I would have thought about. I don't think you're like that, not really, you've been good to me and your family's nice."

"I've been good FOR you. You've come out a lot since you've been here with us. But I haven't been good TO you. Not yet. I haven't even started being good to you yet, Nicolas bloody stupid Bruic, when you won't let me. You're just like other boys. That thing between your legs gets in the way, does it?"

"What? You shouldn't say things like that. That's not right. You're hot for me just as bad. Girls aren't so different."

"Well why are you so embarrassed about it?"

"I'm not. No, I am not. That doesn't bother me, not the way you think . . . . I just . . . ," he flushed, angry. "It's not fair, Emma. Girls have something there too, between their legs, but not so obvious, and you get away with lying about it. Boys cop it. We have to deal with it."

"No, that's not true."

"Yes it is. What you said to me, you got that from school, didn't you. The girl's toilets are a lot worse than the boys, the stuff on the walls. Girls have really dirty minds, not like boys at all. That's the problem, and you get away with it while boys get the cuts, or get a hiding."

"Stop, yes, Nicolas. I'm sorry, it just came out, but I'm not like that. I know some girls are, but not me. I'm not. I don't know. Sometimes I just don't know, things, but you shouldn't think about me like that."

"Well I didn't, did I? I never thought about you like that. Don't talk like that, all right?"

"All right. So what else is going on? You still haven't said why you keep avoiding me."

"Nothing. I don't want to talk about it. Not to you or anyone. But it's not what you think. I do love you. I told you I love you. But if you love someone you respect them, and think about them, and take them the way they are. Maybe I should just show you sometime, what I'm about, and then you'll believe me. But I'm not going to try and explain otherwise you'll think I'm loony like everyone else does."

"Go on."

He looked at her, then without hesitating further stepped in close and kissed her lightly on the cheek, then her lips, holding her close, lingering until she let herself go. Taking her hand he led her back inside to the kitchen where he announced, simply, "All right, we've decided what we're going to do. Simon has the main part and Emma will play the princess. I'll be the director, because I know how it's supposed to be. Jack can do the stage. We can get anyone else we need, maybe put an ad in the paper for actors, or something."

The title for the play was to be, they finally decided, 'The Prince in the Cooking Pot'. Emma was right, it was really very clever, and very funny; a satire on having to grow up. Nicolas had turned it into a farce, with everyone onstage rushing around worrying about preparing their handsome little prince to become the next king. They were boiling him up in a big pot with vegetables, trying to make him jolly, fat and red-faced, enough at least to succeed as their next monarch, but he made out to be having a nice bath until a beautiful dark-eyed princess arrived from a far-off kingdom. She saw what was going on and turned everything topsy-turvy.

Chaos ensued. The Grand High Chancellor didn't like it, and ran around with his walking stick trying to bring order to the proceedings. He didn't like his kings undercooked, not one little bit. Kings had to be hard-boiled; tradition demanded it. The Dowager Duchess was even worse. She wanted her princes baked to a crisp in a hot oven.

None of it made a lot of sense, but it was still very funny. By time they had rehearsals under way Nicolas decided that he would play the High Chancellor with Jen putting in an appearance as the Duchess and Simon in the cooking pot, while Emma slipped into her own role the way she wanted it to be. It became difficult to know whether the princess could actually see what was happening, or thought something else entirely. In the end she decided she simply wanted to rescue the prince and take him away with her, to a land where in her own eyes at least things were the right way up, where they followed musical rhythms instead of rules, and princes didn't have to become monarchs but live happily ever after.

The stage settings were fairly simple. There were only two scenes, one inside the palace and the other in the garden. Nicolas really wanted the music to be just right so the thing had a lilt to it, a rhythm and cadence to engage the audience and get them involved in the story as it unfolded. Once Jack had his work orders sorted out they started rehearsing, which was when Emma showed Nicolas how she wanted things to be between them, keeping him at a distance while she and Simon acted it out. Poor Simon didn't have a clue what was going on, until about a week later after they'd finished for the day Emma and Nicolas began to slip away together.

Chapter Twelve

The upshot of the play itself was that it proved to be a major draw card for Wally's festival. Through contacts among the musicians they'd managed to get flyers up to the university and some of the teachers' colleges, and it became something more than a straight-forward music fest. This was more radical, drawing quite a lot more than the usual run of traditional, folk, jazz, and blues fans. As time went by enquiries came from far and wide for accommodation and travel details.

What Emma came to realise about Nicolas was that he found himself in early adolescence unable to take anything seriously. All the years they'd been worrying so much about him, then his attempt at running away, he'd resigned himself to the notion that the world was inherently stupid rather than threatening or dangerous; flat when it should have been round, and having inured himself to pain couldn't help but dream up alternate, what-if scenarios populated by the same pompous and ridiculous people. He simply failed to apprehend what other people called reality. Everything was make-believe. Maybe he'd been touched by the fairies, or at least the mental health equivalent, but what else could he have done?

When they went swimming together, after the day's work, he was like a wide-eyed little boy full of wonder at the shapes and colours and textures of his world. He'd spend long quiet moments with her, getting her to sit still with him long enough, naked together in the clear water, to really listen, to enter his world of insects and all the magical tiny creatures, and take in the flowing, breathing rhythm of life.

Only once they made love, there in the soft grass. Once past his initial nervousness he was so nice, so gentle, patient and still with her it diffused their passion, but he added afterward that they should wait to have a baby. It wasn't just that they would get into trouble, being so young; it wouldn't be fair for their baby, he explained. The world wasn't right.

She didn't say anything, simply leaned over and holding a finger to his lips kissed his cheek.

After that Emma had a long serious talk with her mother and she consented that they share the same room, with two single beds and that would be the end of the matter as far as she was concerned, although being such a big room they moved another desk in as well. What swayed Jennie was the simple fact that they were both so handsome, together and apart, each in their own way attracting undue attention, so it was better if they were together and kept an eye out for one another. Both being spoken for would make life easier all round.

By early February they all had to start school again. Nicolas was admittedly nervous the first day, worrying what the new headmaster would be like. He needn't have worried. Nobody took any notice. Apparently they'd written him off, so he thought, so after the first week he decided he might as well just be himself and pay no attention to them either. He did what he needed to do to get by, until late October when he could walk out of there a free man. But that was a fair way down the track.

The two weeks remaining before Easter they spent marking out the farm, setting aside camping areas, digging toilet pits over on the far slope away from the creek, rebuilding the stage which they had to move out of the middle shed where Jack was working, and generally tidying up. They would rent space to the stall holders on a first-come, first-serve basis, and leave the catering to them.

What they did not expect was nearly 3,000 people showing up.

Neither did they expect the police to arrive, or for leaders to emerge from what became an unruly crowd by Easter Monday. Wednesday and Thursday went by calmly enough with early arrivals settling in well, and an atmosphere of excitement and anticipation infusing the place as instruments were brought out, campfires lit, and music and laughter echoed across the gentle slopes. By mid-morning Friday as cars and trucks, vans, utilities, crowds of people lined up at the gate waiting to get in, however, chaos reigned.

Wally drove the tractor around with the trailer on the back helping out where he could, taking luggage and camping gear, giving children rides, enjoying himself immensely until the queue began to grow and grow and grow. About mid-morning their neighbour from across the road drove through wanting to have a little chat, but before it got angry someone came up asking whether his front paddock was available for camping and Wally simply put it to him that maybe he could make a few quid charging camping fees. He was sorry he hadn't thought of it before but nobody expected this many people, and they could come over later and help dig a toilet pit.

Once that was organised people themselves started redirecting traffic, taking the pressure off their own driveway. For the rest of the morning and early afternoon there was a fair team effort. When the police arrived things were in fairly good order so once they had given a few instructions on traffic control they went off somewhere, and the few left standing out on the road started to group together until someone took them their meals and someone else cracked a carton of beer.

That second night music again sprung up from everywhere as campfires were lit and the smell of cooking wafted across the two farms, while a revelry started out on the road, linking the whole into one mass of festivity. The night was sheer magic. Nicolas and Emma with Simon in tow did the rounds, happily greeting everyone and handing out leaflets for their play tomorrow afternoon, and before long a few kids their own age began to tag along.

On the way back they ran into Wally, who'd come out trying to get the road party moved into one of the big sheds, but by then police had returned as well to check that the crowd was peaceful and there were no problems as far as they were concerned. They too joined in the effort to get the party off the public road on the condition that they leave two officers there to manage traffic, and that settled the road crew loaded their gear onto the trailer and Wally took them up the track with children skipping and laughing along behind.

At the shed a big long-haired man in a kaftan came up to Nicolas and introduced himself. He was Marcus. He and another bloke Karl had been out on the road all day, watching them back and forth wondering whether he was the famous Nicolas, the radical playwright.

Nicolas grinned sheepishly. He liked the big man straight away, but shied away when Karl came up and introduced himself as a school teacher. It turned out his daughter Sarah had been hanging around with them all afternoon, however. When she saw the way Nicolas reacted to her Dad she stepped in. Her mother had died of leukaemia when she was little, she explained, and Karl raised her by himself. He was cool. He taught mathematics but played dulcimer and guitar, and banjo in a folk/jazz ensemble, and wanted to quit teaching to become a full-time muso. That was why they came to the festival.

Marcus watched them closely, starting to engage Nicolas on tomorrow afternoon's play, but Nicolas was already distracted by an idea. He hadn't been happy with Jennie playing the Duchess, and with the way the flow of the plot was interrupted with her disappearing off the stage to rejoin the musicians. It would be much better for the Duchess to be onstage all the time, as a looming threat.

Marcus was ideal for the role; he could dress up in drag, would he do it? He'd already asked Sarah to play the Princess's Lady-in-Waiting; he'd been thinking about that, and if Karl liked he could join the band. If he could get a few more people to make up the palace crowd and create mayhem while the Prince climbed out of the pot and eloped with the Princess that would be just great.

All agreed he went back across to the house and wrote in their lines, then came back with clear instructions on how he wanted their characters played. They had time for rehearsal in the morning so with that he went to bed while Emma stayed out a while longer with Sarah and some of the other girls their age.

Chapter Thirteen

Saturday morning began overcast, though Wally thought it would clear by lunch so he went about as normal. Cool change, he said, won't hurt a bit. The market stall people in the two big sheds were out early with their wares on display, and soon after breakfast the crowd started to filter through. Nicolas let his actors take a break early so they could mingle, but after final dress rehearsal behind closed curtains he made them do the rounds in costume while he went off for a long walk by himself.

He was feeling uncomfortable, kicking himself for taking the part of the High Chancellor and doing to Simon what the headmaster had been doing to him. He didn't think it was right, but how else could he show people what it was like to be treated like that? On top of all that Emma was playing her own game, and bringing Marcus in had shifted things quite a lot so he thought maybe he could manage for the audience to hate the Duchess instead. But that wouldn't be fair on Marcus either.

By time he got back the amphitheatre was starting to fill. The different folk groups had taken over the stage and were keeping them entertained so he took his time and went over to the house for some lunch. Emma found him there at the kitchen table with a cold meat and tomato sandwich and cup of tea, and told him to hurry up.

He needn't have worried. When it came to the actual performance Marcus followed cue as if he'd been reading his mind. Once the Duchess started on the Prince, just as the Chancellor finished reading the Riot Act, the audience began to scream their displeasure. It went beyond pantomime. Marcus in his hair curlers and flouncing gowns amped it up more and more until even the Chancellor threw up his hands in dismay, and when the Princess instead of waiting went over and tipped Simon out of the tub in his singlet and underpants the crowd went wild.

Once through the great palace doors and a quick set change into the garden children began to stream onstage, blocking the Duchess and allowing their escape. Off they went, right around the amphitheatre from top to bottom, while Jen thought quickly and brought the band onstage so that by time the lovers returned the music was in full swing. They literally returned to a land of rhythm and started to dance. The Duchess stood howling and screaming from up the back, prevented from coming close by the press of the crowd, while Nicolas left out of it by this time couldn't help but fall to the ground laughing his silly head off. It was excellent.

Finally they let Marcus through. He took Nicolas by the hand and marched him up to the stage, where begging forgiveness they went on and joined the dancing. The moment it began to slow he stopped the show and called for applause, and the crowd roared a standing ovation. After that, taking over as MC he called for quiet and promptly began organising the next round of events, including music the rest of the afternoon and a big party that evening.

The sky failed to clear until late afternoon though it remained hot and humid. Once the play was over quite a number of people retreated to the swimming hole on the other side of the hill, and when they checked later Nicolas thought there must have been five hundred people cavorting there naked. As he glanced smiling at Emma she shrugged and grinned shyly, and then when Sarah arrived with Simon in tow they decided to join them. Why not? It was hot anyway and so nice there in the water, nobody seemed to worry until Marcus arrived and promptly stripped, and with a running jump bombed right in the midst of the bathers.

The party that night got a bit wild.

Next day, Sunday, only a few stragglers were up early enough to be noticeable. Nobody else emerged until the sun was well up and the new day began hot and humid. Wally roused Nicolas and Chas early to help him draw a big canvas tarpaulin over the stage to provide a bit of shade for the musicians, and while they were at it rolled up the painted backdrops from the play to allow what breeze there might be to come though.

As they worked Grant and Eric arrived on their bikes wanting to know what was going on. Eric had ridden across town to Grant's and stayed the night, and they left together as soon as they got out of bed to come out while it was still cool. Chas quickly had them both up on stage to help with the work, then with the job done they went back to the house for breakfast, where Simon was still asleep. Eric went in and tipped him out of bed amid angry shouting and complaining that woke the whole house.

Chas started serving breakfast, counting kid's heads and serving up bowls of porridge with fresh milk and honey for the lot of them, then went to work on toast, chops, eggs and bacon for the grown-ups. While they were eating Emma nudged Nicolas, who looked up to see Grant glaring at him from across the table. He didn't say anything but went back to eating his breakfast, glancing up occasionally trying to think what might be the matter.

Chas leaned over finally and said quietly, "Say what you need to say, young fella."

"I don't have anything to say. I'm just eating breakfast. Ask Grant, why don't you?"

"Mum wants him home," Grant said abruptly. "It's no good for him out here. Who knows what he'll get up to?"

Chas looked back across to Nicolas, who said quietly almost to himself. "Too late, I've been adopted already. She can't make me go back. Why would I want to anyway?"

"'Cause that's where you belong," Grant replied, speaking directly to him now. "You need looking after, and we can do it. They don't know what's wrong with you, that's all, and if you get into strife they won't know what to do to help you."

"Oh, I think we manage well enough," Jen broke in. "You tell your mother, Grant, that Nicolas is in my care and if she has anything to say she can talk to me about it."

Grant sat back in his seat, sullen, then leaving the remainder of his cereal in the bowl got up from the table and left. He stopped briefly at the back door to check with Eric who at that moment was busy with Simon, and nobody paying him any attention slammed the door on the way out. After breakfast Eric went looking for him, Simon in tow, finally locating him up on the saddle of the hill watching people skinny-dipping in the pool below. After that, it seemed to Nicolas at any rate, they just hung around together without joining in much while he and Emma with Sarah and some of the others their age joined in the music and dancing.

Late morning it started to get hot again, with a low sky but still no sign of rain or anything else much, so they all went off to the creek and spent the afternoon there swimming and mucking around. Eventually Wally came down, calling them to come and help start packing and cleaning up since some of the crowd were going home already, though by the time he'd dressed and got back to the big shed the other three had already gone. Chas and Jack were both worried about them getting mixed in up in the traffic on their bikes, especially Eric wanting to dink Simon all the way back into town, so they caught up with them on the road and gave them a lift home in Wally's truck before returning to help out with the cleanup.

Chapter Fourteen

Maybe he should have been paying more attention to his brother, but at the time Nicolas had too much else on his mind. He'd been so used to dismissing Grant's evil rants anyway, shedding them like soiled clothing, and when the big party started up again that night he and the girls simply went out to enjoy themselves. By dark they found themselves back at the big tent Karl and Marcus were sharing. Inside was like a great eastern harem, with carpets and embroidered cushions scattered about. There were quite a few people there; the air infused with a sweet spicy odour as they lay about smoking and laughing among themselves.

As he entered with the girls a place was made for him while somebody passed him an oddly shaped cigarette with pinched ends, one end alight, but he turned it away. It was weird. Everybody seemed to off somewhere else, not looking properly at one another but chattering almost to themselves. It was like nothing he'd expected after the excitement of the weekend. The atmosphere made him light-headed and dark shapes began to appear at the edge of his vision, so before long he went out again into the fresh air.

Whatever it was had shifted his consciousness of himself. Emma followed him out and asked what the matter was, but he only gazed at her and shrugged. He looked up, glancing about then back at her, shaking his head. "I might go home," he said. "I'm not feeling very well."

Sarah came out behind Emma and the two girls had a brief exchange before turning back to Nicolas standing there waiting, then stepped up and said they'd go with him. It was one of Karl's mull parties, Sarah explained. They'd still be at it next morning and nobody would get any sleep. Maybe they'd just go and listen to the radio or something, if there was nothing else happening. She was right. He hadn't noticed before, but the remnant crowd had broken up into small groups each doing their own thing, so he shrugged again and led the way.

Past the big shed approaching the house Emma asked if Sarah could stay the night, and without thinking he said it was OK with him what she did.

But then Emma asked, "Do you like her?"

"Yeah, sure, she's nice," he went on, oblivious.

"She likes you."

"Does she? She likes you, too. She's nice. I already said that."

"Nicolas! Don't say that."

"What? What did I say?"

Emma turned to Sarah. "See what I mean? He's hopeless."

Sarah giggled and pushed her way in between Nicolas and Emma. She took his arm to hold him close, leaning in to kiss his cheek, and then suddenly licked his ear.

"Hey, stop that!" he said.

"Why? You said you like me."

"What? Not like that, I didn't mean like that. I'm with Emma."

"But she can't, not tonight."

"Can't what? What are you talking about?"

"Shit you're dumb. Em, you're right, he's real dumb."

"Wrong time of the month, silly," Emma said.

Nicolas just looked at her before turning and walking off, back to the house. Inside he went straight to their room and plonked himself on his bed. He picked up a book and was leafing through the pages when they came in, watching him closely, and when they sat on Emma's bed he threw the book down and removing his shoes and socks took a towel and went off to the bathroom hoping for a bath and a bit of privacy. That was a mistake.

They waited until he'd run the bath and was in the tub before following him in and calmly undressing got in with him, Sarah at one end and Emma in behind him pushing him toward her, so he promptly took the wash cloth down and covered himself.

"The real trouble, Nicolas," she said, quietly, "is you're not just beautiful. It's not just your body. You really are such a nice boy. You're so decent, and you're so thoughtful. You don't even think about yourself much, and I can't do a thing about it. It's hopeless, really."

"What? Not hopeless. It's my body, isn't it? I can be the sort of person I want to be, can't I? Without being molested?"

"Oh, you're being molested are you?"

"Yes, I am. Leave me alone."

"What if we did? What would you be doing? What would you be thinking about?"

He stopped and half turned to look at her. "I wouldn't be thinking about anything much. I wasn't thinking about anything, just being happy. I was just happy, that's all."

"Sarah can make you happy."

"I'm already happy, or was. Shit!"

Emma sighed, leaning against him, and after a moment turned her back to him and said, "All right, you can scrub my back for me then. Sarah can scrub your back while you're doing me, and when we've finished we'll turn around and you can scrub hers for her. Will that be all right?"

Then he sighed in turn, "Yes, all right then."

He took the cloth from his lap and started washing Emma's neck and shoulders with it, but as he did so Sarah came in close and instead of washing his back started to caress him with her fingertips. Nicolas froze as Emma giggled and leaning back slowly pushed him into Sarah until he could feel her nipples against his shoulder blades. Her hand came around his chest as she reached down to hold him, slowly and gently like Emma had that first time in the grass, and he stirred and closed his eyes. She licked his ear again.

An hour or so later they heard the back door slam and somebody in the kitchen, and Emma jumped up all wet to snib the catch on the bathroom door. The back door slammed again and there was quiet, so she stood with the door slightly ajar to listen before picking up her clothes and disappearing down the passage to their room. Just as quickly she came back and beckoned them to follow. Nicolas pushed Sarah out before turning to empty the bath, and wrapping a towel around himself picked up their things and with a last look to see he hadn't forgotten anything made his own way down the passage.

In their room he dried her with the towel them himself, but then pulling on his pyjamas pushed her across to Emma's bed and lay down on his own watching them both.

"It was all right, Nicolas, wasn't it?" Emma asked quietly.

"Hhmmm, yes," he almost whispered. "Too good," then louder, "it was too good, Em. I don't know what to do now."

"Why don't you just love both of us?"

"What? Both of you? Two girlfriends? Me? No. Sarah has to go home."

"No, Marcus and Karl are coming to live here, with us. They're going to live in the old house, fix it up, didn't you know?"

He stared at them. "Is that what this is about?"

"What? No. That's got nothing to do with it. Sarah really loves you; we didn't trick you, not about that."

"Well, why me? There are plenty of boys out there; plenty of fish in the sea. That's what they say, isn't it?"

"No there's not. Not like you. They're ignorant, and they're rough. Girls don't like boys like that. We don't, anyway, but we already talked about that."

Nicolas looked away, gazing into the distance before saying quietly, almost to himself again, "What, are you going to line girlfriends up for me, are you, because they can't find a nice enough boyfriend? How am I supposed to feel about that?"

"No, not too many, just us to start with," Sarah broke in. "You still like me, don't you?"

He looked down, then back up at her.

"You came between me and Emma, when I didn't expect it, when I was happy with the way things were, but now I don't know."

He glanced at Emma, and back again, "I really don't want to lose her because she's a lot more than a girlfriend to me. She's like a sister as well, no, more than a sister, like family I mean; she's my best friend. If she hadn't pushed me into this I wouldn't have even thought of looking at you, like that I mean. You've got me all mixed up."

Emma watched him closely. After a moment she came over to his bed and lying down beside him took his head in her hands.

"But we're different; Sarah and me, and you're bigger than other people. You're way too bright. You're too much for one person. You're too much for me by myself. But if we do it together, she can do things for you that I can't, and I can do things for you that she can't. I mean, I don't see my Dad very much but she doesn't see her Mum. She knows about boys like I don't. So it'll work. We thought about it a lot, and I really wanted to tell you first but, um, Nicolas, it was a sort of embarrassing thing to talk about and I really didn't know what you'd say. The best thing to do was the way it happened, all right."

He thought about that a moment and glancing across to Sarah on the other bed nodded quietly. He pushed Emma slightly aside, and patting the bed next to him made room for her, but as she got up he said turn the light out first.

Before they went to sleep he murmured, "All right, but you've got to let me have a bit of time to myself. I need to go for my walks else I go crazy. You have to agree. Sometimes I'm not so nice, what they did to me, and I get angry and I don't like it so I have to get away from people and be by myself. I never told anybody, even Emma, 'til now, but lucky I didn't shoot that bloody headmaster. Lucky I didn't kill someone. I felt like it often enough. You're never to say anything to anyone about that, promise, not anybody, ever. Better for people to think I'm a bit cuckoo."

They didn't say anything, just moved softly against him; one on either side, except before he dozed off Sarah whispered, "We'll come with you."

Chapter Fifteen

When they came to breakfast next morning Jennie gave them a dark look. "That's not what we agreed, Emma," she said quietly.

Nicolas glanced around the kitchen, at Chas first then Wally and the two boys, then back up at Jennie before sitting at the table while the two girls stayed blocking the doorway.

"Um, sorry," he said. "I should say it was my fault, but it wasn't, not really, except I feel I'm responsible. Other than that it just sorta happened. It was good; I'll say that, it helped me understand something. Sometimes things just happen; it's not the worst thing. Please don't be angry."

Jennie leaned back against the sink while the others sat quietly. Nobody said anything, so he went on, "It wasn't the first time, me and Emma, but Sarah yes it was. We had a long talk about it. They really only wanted to help me wake up a bit; come out of myself, because I can be such a dead shit sometimes, so they're not bad or anything. Don't think we're bad. We're pretty good actually, considering."

Jennie studied him for a moment. "We don't think you're bad, Nicolas."

She paused a moment, glancing back and forth between the three before continuing. "This morning you can help Chas with a bit of a cleanup, and Dad with what he wants you to do. You girls are grounded until we've had our little chat, if you don't mind."

At that moment the toaster popped so Chas got up and started buttering toast before going to the stove to load up the plate with eggs and bacon which he placed on the table before Nicolas. "Eat your breakfast, son," he said, before glancing eyebrow raised at the girls.

"Just cereal for us," Emma said, "please."

"Tea?"

"Yes, please."

"Nicolas?"

"Yes, black please. And Chas, thanks."

"What are you thanking me for?"

He sat quietly a moment. "Well, everything, I mean, not belting me. You had a right."

The adults glanced at one another before Chas went back over to the stove to pour tea while Jennie simply indicated to the girls the cereal packet there on the table, before turning to the sink to continue washing up.

"Anything else you want to say?" Chas asked from the stove.

"No, not really, I just wanted to ask you something; something else."

"Yep?"

"Is it true Marcus and Karl are coming to live here, on the property?"

"Oh, we've been talking about it, yes. If you want to know, the problem is we don't want you leaving school. We're thinking about home schooling from here. Where you are is not good for you, but giving it away altogether is no good either. And we have to do something about the farm, change over to livestock or something. Anything you want to say about that?"

Jennie by this time had turned around and was watching his face. Wally just sat there all the way through listening and nodding occasionally.

"No. I mean, I don't know. I wasn't even thinking about school."

"What were you thinking about, Nicolas?" Jen wanted to know.

"Um, well, Sarah will be living with us too, won't she? That's what we've been talking about. That's what happened, last night I mean."

"You're too young. You're all too young. It's getting out of hand, don't you think?"

"Maybe we are, but it's too late isn't it. I can't help it now. If you try to stop us we'll just run away, or something." He stopped, shaking his head. "Anyway, it's not out of hand; only twice, in all this time. Shit, that's not fair. We've been really good, you know."

"All right I get your point, without going into detail. You've become a young man. You're not a little boy any more, and they are no longer girls. We have to reckon that in. Maybe we weren't thinking about that enough. Maybe things could have been better, but they're not. I understand that."

Jennie glanced at Chas and back again. "What we will do, young man, is move you in with Dad and the two girls can share your room. That way you can still see one another and we can have some peace of mind, until Chas finishes up north anyway, and while have regular money coming in. Beyond that we can't promise you anything."

He thought about that a moment, somewhat relieved in fact, and nodded.

"Yes, all right. Anything else you want me to do?"

"No. Yes. Only one thing, Dad has some money for you, your share."

"What? Share of what?" he was confused. "I didn't do anything for money, did I?"

"It was your play, Nicolas. That's all yours. We took the gate and the market, and the camping fees on top of that, but it was your play."

"Really? How much?"

"Well, we thought two dollars a head, but then we rounded it up so you can pay your own people. We charged ten at the gate to cover the play and our own costs, but the play was a big thing for us so we thought maybe twenty percent would be fair, or something like that. Six thousand dollars, is that all right?"

"Whooa!" he said, "Really! Six thousand dollars. That much? I didn't expect that much. I really didn't expect anything."

He looked around, dazed, furrowing his brow. "Yes, everyone helped, didn't they? How much do you think I should pay them?"

Chas leaned across. "Have a yarn with Jack later, all right. He knows these things. Come on, finish your breakfast. Mum wants to talk to the girls."

Outside was a mess. The crowd was starting to stir again, and with quite a few empty bottles lying around a lot of people had hangovers. Others were wandering about stoned and glassy-eyed, while down at the creek a few bodies were scattered about and more again in the water laughing and splashing. This lot appeared sober enough so they started down there and began herding them back up the hill, cleaning up after them. Wally carefully placed the bottles in a big crate on the trailer, while all the paper, cardboard, food scraps and rubbish they raked up into piles to burn.

Nicolas skirted the tractor around the few remaining tents, knowing that Marcus and his crowd would still be asleep and not wanting to disturb them, but hearing the engine close by he came out anyway, yawning and stretching.

He pulled up and called across to him, "You coming to live here are you?"

Marcus pricked up, "Yeah, maybe. What do you think?"

Nicolas looked away across the paddock and back again. "Yes, good, that'll be good. You going to help me with school, aren't you?"

"Maybe I will. Interested in Classics?"

Before he could answer; to ask what that was, Chas called him to keep up, so he started off again with only a backward glance to acknowledge the question. As he turned his head he saw the girls coming out the back of the house with Karl, Sarah's shrill voice carrying across the distance in the still morning air. They were plainly arguing, though Karl seemed to be coming out second best when he turned and walked away, leaving them standing there. Emma took Sarah's hand and led her back inside. Karl came up the slope toward the tractor and Nicolas sat waiting for him.

"Sorry," he said as he approached.

"Ah, there's nothing for you to be sorry about. Good luck to you, mate." He paused, "Just be careful with her, eh? She's willful and stubborn like her mother, but she could have done a lot worse. That's the end of it, eh? I don't want to talk about it."

"All right. Can I ask you something else then?"

"Fire away."

"Are you coming to live here, to give us home schooling. That's what they said."

"Yes, maybe, we'll see. Thing is, Nicolas, everyone's worrying about you. You're far too intelligent to be wasted. You have real talent but nobody seems to be able to get inside your head for some reason. We'll talk about it later, all right."

"I'm all right, Karl," he protested. "It's not me, it's them; they're all stupid. They just come at you and yell at you, and cane you all the time, and give you these long boring lectures, but I haven't got a clue what they're on about. Why don't they just say it; whatever it is they want? Then I'd know. Then I'd be able to understand, wouldn't I?"

Karl stood watching his face, perplexed, then after a long moment sighed, adding, "Maybe you're right. Maybe it isn't you that's the problem. But it is you in it, isn't it? You're the only one who can do anything about that, mate, without changing the whole world."

Karl stopped there, watching his face. "Or maybe you can," he said finally.

Nicolas simply nodded, and with only a brief pause put the tractor into gear and went off after Chas, who'd gone a fair way ahead by then. Only Wally stood patiently waiting for him, ready to load more bottles into the crate.

By time they got back to the house for lunch, Jennie and the girls had moved a bed into Wally's room for Nicolas, while Sarah discovered there was only a partition between the two rooms. Without saying anything she had his bed placed against it and contrived to sleep there that night to be close to him.

Most of the crowd outside was beginning to dissipate, and Nicolas began to appreciate the quiet, patient efficiency in the way Wally got things done. He'd thought it was enough that they had the place ready in time, working as they had over the week or more, but the speed with which the place was cleaned up after everyone had gone astonished him. He thought a great deal more about both Wally and Chas after that, and especially looked at Jennie with new eyes.

He was away up the back helping to fill in the cesspits when Sarah left with Marcus and her Dad in their van, which he thought later was better else she would have made a scene in front of everyone. Emma told him she was sitting in the van crying while they packed up the tent, but he simply nodded. They were allowed to spend time together after dinner so they went for a long walk, just the two of them, hand in hand, though even then they didn't say much; just did what they were asked to do, and went to bed early for school the next day.

Chapter Sixteen

What happened next surprised him, though nobody else seemed to have thought it was anything out of the ordinary; not for him, anyway. For some reason or other the Education Department decided to carry out a state wide survey of intelligence quotient in their schools, and when they got off the bus next day instead of going to class they were all herded into the school gymnasium and made to sit at desks with papers in front of them.

Nothing much was explained; only that the government was carrying out a compulsory survey and they would be advised of the results later.

The moment they were told to start and he turned the paper over, Nicolas was engrossed. He'd never seen anything like it. The flow of equations and questions and patterns completely transported him, until the pages stopped suddenly and disappointed he looked up to see everyone else head down, and the whole room quiet. He sat, head up looking about until a teacher came up to ask if there was anything wrong, and he said he'd finished. She took his paper then led him outside and shut the door, leaving him standing there in the quadrangle by himself.

Eventually another teacher came along and asked what he was doing there, and he said he'd finished the test so the teacher sent him outside. The other looked at his watch, then said go sit in the library, and walked away. He went across to the library and nobody there he took a book down and sat reading it. After a while other kids started streaming out of the gym and he glanced up to see Emma out there, looking about, so he got up and went to the window and waved to her.

After that, and for the rest of the week and into the next, people started avoiding him more than ever. It wasn't something he noticed especially; he was tripping quite a lot on the puzzles and patterns, and started doing drawings and scribbling notes in his exercise book, but even at home they trod carefully around him as he worked away. Eventually Emma persuaded her mother to let him back in his old bed, in their old room, at least until Sarah returned. Jennie talked it over with Wally and Chas, and finally they agreed.

A month later when Karl moved onto the property things were more or less as normal, as they had been before Easter. Sarah didn't say anything when they moved into the old house, past the sheds, and when Nicolas saw her there as Wally drove them in from school he simply caught her gaze and turned away. Two days after that Emma came into their room and asked him if there was anything wrong, why he didn't want to see her. He looked up without saying anything so she took him by the hand into the kitchen. Sarah hadn't come right into the house but stood there at the back door waiting, so the three of them trouped out and rather than hang around there headed across in front of the sheds toward the bush block on the other side of the farm where he liked to go for his walks.

Once clear she took his hand, tentatively, almost shy like it was the first time they'd been together, but he only smiled and taking Emma's hand in his other led them both down to one of his spots quite a way downstream from the swimming hole. Settled there on a fallen log he put his arm around her and finger to his lips motioned for her to be quiet and listen. Presently a little family of fairy wrens appeared, the tiny iridescent blue male flitting from twig to twig like a jewel sparkling in the sunbeams, while three drab females hopped about among the fallen leaves and grass. They came in quite close and Nicolas held Sarah still so as not to frighten them, until eventually they flitted off and he gazed about for something else to show her.

They sat that way for an hour or more, then getting up followed the creek back up again to the pool. It was getting too cold for swimming so they lay on the grass on their backs awhile watching the clouds, soon making out patterns and shapes which turned into a game and they started to laugh and giggle among themselves, until Sarah sat up and taking his hand undid her shirt and had him cup her breast. She was wearing nothing underneath, but he didn't want to go any further than that beyond caress her, to re-establish contact with her and renew their affection while she slipped her hand under his belt. He stopped her there, so she leaned down to kiss him before rolling over and doing up her shirt snuggled in close to him.

That evening she moved back into the house with Emma while Nicolas took his own things back to Wally's room.

A copy of the school's newsletter arrived in the mail the next week, declaring that it had some of the top students in the state and admonishing parents and teachers to consider the special needs of gifted students, but when Nicolas read it he screwed it up and threw it into the bin. Outside he went over to Karl's house and knocking briefly went inside to see him there at his desk in the front room.

"Hey, Nicolas, what's up?"

"Nothing much, just bored. I wanted to ask you when we're starting home school. And when's Marcus getting here, anyway?"

"He won't be here until the end of semester. He's back lecturing this year."

"Really, what does he lecture?"

"Classics and Ancient History, but that won't help you much; not yet. To answer your question, yes, we can start any time you want. We've been waiting for you. What about Monday?"

"Yep, all right, good," and with that he turned on his heel and ran back across to the house where he burst into the kitchen to tell everyone they could leave school, and be home all the time now with Karl. Jennie made him slow down a bit, not talk so fast, and anyway they had to get them all registered with the Education Department. By then he was no longer listening. He went and spent the rest of the afternoon with the girls in their room.

Things weren't to work out the way he thought, however. The shock came when Monday went by then Tuesday and Wednesday, when they hadn't been to school police arrived on the property accompanied by somebody from the Family Services Department to investigate a complaint that the children were being neglected, were truant, with girls being sexually molested and in danger of further abuse. The five of them were promptly bundled into two police cars and driven into town, Nicolas in the front car between two officers, the girls in the second car with Kennie and Owen closely followed by Wally in his truck bringing Chas and Jen with him, and behind them Karl in his van.

Wally was fuming. He pulled up at his solicitor's office while the others went on to the police station, and storming into the building called out, "Tom! Get out here! Bloody kids've been awwested! That bitch's fuckin' dobbed 'em for somefing! Get yer arse out 'ere!"

The poor girl behind the reception desk tried in vain to stop him but the silk came out anyway and taking Wally by the arm led him back out onto the street. He held his hand up for quiet before heading for the police station. Wally turned, walking backward a few steps as he caught Chas's eye and waved at him to bring the truck.

When they arrived Wally proved to be right on the money. The moment he saw Nicolas' mother sitting there he said loudly, "Margwet, knew it was you. Jesus Bloody Chwist, woman, what's fuckin' got into you, eh?"

He needn't have bothered. Jen had already said her piece and the atmosphere was electric. Sergeant Lewis sitting behind the desk looked on bemused now, scratching his balding head while the fat lawyer waded straight in demanding to see the children. Nicolas was being kept separate in a holding cell while the others were in the reception area with a police woman who was giving them ice cream and sweets, so he dismissed her and sat talking to the girls a short while before he came out demanding to talk to Nicolas. On his way through to the cells he paused to speak briefly with the sergeant before escorting the boy into an interview room, and sat there gazing at him awhile before saying anything.

Nicolas hadn't reacted at all, just sat there quietly until Tom said suddenly, "You're being charged with carnal knowledge, Nicolas. That's the old term, but it means the same thing; you have been engaging in sexual activity with the two girls. Do you know what that means?"

"Yes."

"Are you guilty?"

"No."

"The girls both agreed. They said you'd been together."

"Well, we have. We do a lot of things together. The whole family does."

"Have you had sex with them?"

"Yes, only once. I mean once each. But that's all."

"When?"

"With Emma, last year at the swimming hole, and with Sarah a month ago in the bath. But we owned up; we didn't tell lies about it. We all talked

62

about it and then we agreed to behave. They shifted me in with Wally and Jennie had a talk with the girls, not me. It wasn't me who started anything."

"So you don't think you've done anything wrong, committed any crime, anything like that?"

"Why are you questioning me? It's no use talking to me. I said I'm not guilty. I'm going to plead not guilty. I don't feel guilty, and I'm not going to plead guilty. The girls won't come out and say anything, not in public, and neither will anyone else. We love one another. We're the same age, not even eighteen months apart, and we're good together. I don't have a clue who complained, or what they're complaining about. It's nothing to do with anybody."

"All right, but the girls were examined by a doctor and they're going to charge you anyway. You will be under a prohibition order until the hearing, which may be months away. I'll try to get it expedited; you're all children, but you have to stay away from the girls, and from Simon. What do you feel about moving back with your mother in the meantime?"

"What? Is that what this is about? Bloody Mum! Shit! Grant, I bet he did this, I didn't even think. It was him talking to Simon, him and Eric, now he's a witness is he? But he doesn't know anything. Nobody was talking to him about anything; he's just a little kid. No, I'm not going back there."

"Where can you go, to stay for a while at least?"

"I can stay with Auntie Elsie, that's Wally's sister, but Eric and Simon live there with Jack. Better if I stay with Karl in the old house, but we were starting home schooling there."

He sat thinking for a moment. "What about I stay there with him and come in to the High School every day, and the girls can still do their schooling with Karl. That'll keep us apart; that'll be all right, won't it? How long will it take?"

"Well, we'll see. The magistrate will hear the matter this morning but it may not go to trial for months. Let's see what he says before we make any rash decisions, all right? Are you happy to stay in the cell until we call you?"

Nicolas looked down, then shrugged and without looking at him stood ready to leave. The lawyer opened the door and handed him over to the policewoman standing there waiting for them. Back down the bare corridor he went and the cell door slammed behind him. He gazed about at bare painted concrete with a steel sink in one corner and toilet in another, so he paced around awhile then lay down on the hard bench and closed his eyes.

Eventually the same hollow crash echoed down the corridor and he sat up as footsteps rang and his own door swung open to the rattle of keys and bolts banging loose, and they took him out the back through the yard into the court house next door.

Chapter Seventeen

Deciding to stay at school was hard, especially without Emma coming in with him every day. Wally picking him up of an afternoon kept his spirits going, and as the days went by he slipped his mind back into his own space and began to daydream. Jennie brought his meals over herself every evening, and sat with him awhile talking gently with him, but he rarely said anything much to her. On the weekends she took the girls' place during his walks, and for the first time wondered at him, and understood finally their devotion to him.

Hurting him were the newspaper headlines, "Local Boy Arrested", and "Boy Charged with Sexual Assault", with lurid details of his alleged affairs without actually naming him because he was still a child. There were extensive interviews with the *Bold Hearts* Convener Vicky Kulinski endlessly quoting his mother and brother, expressing her ongoing concern about mental health, and children at risk in their town, and about time something was done about it. There was no escape. Other kids tapped on the library window when he was there reading, tripped him in the playground, and wolf-whistled all day. He was glad Emma wasn't there, though mostly going through his mind by then were ideas about meeting up with Marcus.

The old books he read were mainly on introductory Oriental and Western philosophy and English grammar; that's all they seemed to have there aside from the kids' stuff, but with some digging around he found more on law, political rhetoric, semantics and formal logic.

Emma watched him from a distance, and sat talking to her mother about him worried that he might be slipping away again, and what she could do to keep him, while Sarah sat simply listening. When Jennie came over to see him she'd bring little gifts, or meals they'd cooked, and once a postcard with a lovely photo of three fairy wrens which he placed on the table next to his bed.

About that time Karl came in to talk to him about starting his studies anyway, at least with what the girls were doing and what he wanted to achieve with them, so when this silly other business was finished he'd be on track. Realising that was not going to happen to plan, one day he drove his van into town to see the headmaster and talk with some of the other teachers about what they'd been doing in class. When he discovered that Nicolas was paying nobody any attention at all, even their psychologist, he suggested they recommend some reading as if that would make any difference, and simply leave him there in the library. Returning home he rang Marcus and asked him to come down for the weekend.

Nicolas was off walking when he arrived, making his way up the far slope through a tangle of undergrowth. He took his time studying every little insect trail and where they went back and forth, and the birds flitting about chirping and challenging one another, yet when he came out onto the top track over the ridge and saw Marcus standing there he simply took his hand and ducked back with him into the undergrowth. Back along the contour he stopped there at the fallen log where he'd been with Emma and Sarah, and coming to life sat Marcus down and sat next to him.

"What do you want to say to me, lad?"

"Nothing."

They sat together for a while before Nicolas piped up and said, "What I mean is, I don't mean nothing I only mean I don't have to say anything to you, because you know already don't you."

When no answer came he stood and undressed, stripped naked; "Explain this to me."

Marcus looked him up and down and said, "All I can say is you're a very handsome boy. You look so good, supremely well-proportioned and attractive; every part of you. You're also exceptionally intelligent. Civilisation has worshipped boys like you for millennia and it has become an embarrassment. They don't know what to do about it."

"So they beat me."

"No, no, put your clothes on."

"I don't want to. Why don't you answer my question for me, Professor of Classics and Ancient History? Why did you take over my play, and make it work right? You knew, didn't you!"

Marcus reached across and took his hands, pulling him in close. "You're a threat. Nicolas, please listen to me. It has nothing to do with your play,

I'm sorry I got carried away. It was a lot of fun, a catharsis, and I'm glad we did it. But this has nothing to do with you personally; it's only something going on in their minds, in the way they think about you. If it makes you feel any better, the Sufis say that human desire is nothing more than man's yearning for God, though I'd have to add that this secular society we live in dishonours the ineffable, so you cop it."

Nicolas pushed himself away. "All right. So what you're saying to me is they make things up to attack people because they're scared of them, but they're not really scared of the actual person they're only scared of some fancy idea of them, scared of God, or some God concept they have, but in their own minds, like, it has nothing actually to do with anyone real, but I have to live with that. Like being in a prison all my life, but it's not my prison it's their prison, a mental prison, and I'm in it not them. That makes sense?"

He dropped to his knees and head down started to cry, sobbing to himself. Marcus took him by both hands and picking him up drew him in close. Reaching down he took his clothes and turning him half around like a little boy leaning against him picked up one foot after the other and pulled on his underpants, then his trousers, before turning him around front again and pulling his shirt over his head buttoned it up.

"What happened?" he said in his ear. "What have they done to you?"

But Nicolas just cried. He settled a little finally as Marcus sat watching him.

"You never had a childhood, did you, just running around with other the kids, having fun; learning to be a human being," he said eventually, thoughtfully. "You've had to cope from day one. Bloody miracle you're still sane."

He stood; taking his hand to lead him back home, though instead of going back down the slope toward the sheds Nicolas led him instead along the ridge contour and down the other side to the swimming hole where he went with the girls on his walks. They spent the best part of another hour there before Jennie came looking for him.

Chapter Eighteen

Tom Lynch succeeded in having the charges against him dropped for lack of evidence, the fact that the three were the same age, and the unreliability of the sole prosecution witness who he showed had been interfered with, and that done drove out to the farm to let him know.

The girls were in the kitchen when he arrived and took him over to Karl's house. Nicolas was taken aback when they ran in on him suddenly with the lawyer right behind, banging the door and calling out to him, so he stood waiting to see what he wanted.

He was more annoyed than relieved and turned away when he heard the news. Tom sent the girls outside so he could talk to him a moment.

"Do I owe you any money?" Nicolas wanted to know, distracting him.

"Eh? Oh no, what! It's a pleasure. Let me help you, son, I know what you've suffered. I'd rather you tell me how you've been."

Nicolas watched him for a moment before asking whether he'd like a cup of tea, and when he nodded yes went over to the bench and busied with the kettle.

"How's Simon," he turned and asked suddenly. "Is he all right? Can I see him?"

"Yes, any time you want. But it's not about him, is it? It's about you."

"It's always about me, and I'm sick of it. Why don't they leave me alone?"

"Is that what you want?"

"What I wanted was to go to court, so I could tell everyone what was really going on, but now I can't."

"Ho, brave lad! System doesn't work like that. Get on with your life!"

He didn't reply, just turned back to making tea and that done brought the cups over to the table, then went back for sugar. Settled finally, he said quietly, almost under his breath, "If it's that bad, what sort of life do we have?"

The old man leaned forward and said as quietly, "Nicolas, you have two quite stunningly beautiful girls who love you with a passion, and a good family taking care of you, and a fine intelligent mind. It's not about what life is going to do for you, but what you can do with these wonderful gifts? The rest doesn't matter, does it? All those people out there, we're really only trying to stop them all killing one another. But that's not your business, is it? Forgive them, and move on."

He sat sipping his tea, watching him, but Nicolas didn't answer. Finally he put down his cup and stood taking his leave. He left his card on the table, and at the door turned and said, "Let me help you, lad. Call me any time." Then he left.

Nicolas heard him say something outside as he left, and straight away Emma and Sarah came rushing in.

Chapter Nineteen

Wally snored all night, and farted and mumbled in his sleep after a few beers, and with Sarah scratching at the wall keeping him awake Nicolas decided to stay sleeping there in the old house with Karl. When they were out on the tractor together they all joked and laughed, though at dinner Jennie insisted the two girls stay where they were in Emma's room.

Marcus and Karl got together to nut out a study program for him based on University level outcomes-based curricula. They decided to take him off the standard High School curriculum altogether, provided he demonstrate steady progress in the core skill areas because that's what they had to report. Even then Marcus refused to contemplate early matriculation and set him on a slower course toward mature age entry later when he could gain a place as a legal adult through scholastic aptitude. That left him time to play and have a bit of fun, mature naturally; maybe just be a kid awhile if that were at all possible.

All this they discussed with him at length. One after the other they took him by the hand and gave him time to think about what it was they were asking him, and heard his arguments while Wally simply went about his own business keeping a steady eye on things. What they hadn't properly considered was Nicolas' unconscionable naïveté; his simple and absolute failure to apprehend the world on their terms, which Wally had recognised long before and never doubted.

Karl for his part wanted to know why he'd shied away from mathematics, and he replied that he didn't know why children should be forced to learn how to plot projectile curves, just so when they grow up they can kill other people with missiles from a such long distance away. Why didn't all those people just go talk to one another, or beat each other up if that's the way they felt? Or bite each other's noses off, whatever. If they really wanted to study things, be a student, why didn't they plot a butterfly trajectory and learn something real, and beautiful? Wouldn't that be a lot more interesting?

Chas asked him why he didn't go riding; there were plenty of horses they could bring over. He said you haven't said anything about it. Wally didn't ask me about driving the tractor; he just said you drive the tractor, "dwive the twacta", so I did. He said I can write a play for his festival, and I did. What he didn't say was I could make a lot of money doing that, and I didn't even guess, so he's smarter than me. What's wrong with that? Chas, you haven't said anything to me about horses.

Marcus watched. Emma and Sarah watched. One day Nicolas was lying on an old bed at the back of the old house and the two little boys came and sat with him. He was reading Mark Twain's "*The Adventures of Huckleberry Finn*" when Owen appeared at the top of the steps with Kennie on his heels. He leaned back to accommodate them and kept on reading, but out loud once they were there, telling the story. When Jennie came out looking for the boys she found the three of them curled up in a ball asleep like three puppies.

The only rule Karl made in the new school was that the girls sit separate from the boys and do their own work otherwise they'd be leaning on Nicolas to help them. Instead he made him defacto preparatory teacher. Kennie was already in Fourth Class while Owen had yet to finish Second. They mainly needed coaching with their spelling and grammar, arithmetic and geometry while Karl came across occasionally for history and social studies, and to help them with their little science experiments.

For the first time Nicolas actually took an interest in the lessons, asking so many questions and making Karl grumpy trying to keep the others on track. When the boys finished he'd take him aside and argue it out with him, not trying to prove him right or wrong merely probing the nature of his arguments and other ways to think about the question being posed, and how to go about methodically to find answers.

After they ended lessons each day the boys would hijack him to come and play, and read stories to them, until eventually the girls started noticing.

One night just after dark he heard a slight tink at his window, and peered out to glimpse both of them out there beyond the porch; tossing pebbles to attract his attention. The moment his face appeared they skirted the house and waited for him under the big old Morton Bay fig tree at the front, and when he came out they grabbed him straight away and hurried behind the shed out of sight. They were both cranky with him, but he didn't say anything just took them both up through the amphitheatre and down again to the swimming hole where he lay down in the soft grass and pulled them down with him. They undressed each other and he made love to them both, one after the other, and twice again without saying a word.

Only then as they lay watching scudding clouds play hide and seek with the stars, and the waning moon rise to light up their edges with glistening silver did he quietly mention Chas bringing some horses up, and maybe they could go riding after he finished playing with the boys and Jennie called them in for their bath. But he was definitely staying with Karl, not going back into the big house; it was too hard otherwise, and anyway they'd better get back before somebody noticed them missing. They lay back watching the clouds again.

"Dad's going back up north next week," Emma said finally, "there's enough time for a trip south to get them, and Wally can drop him off there to pick up the droving plant, then you and he can come back with the horses. Why don't you go with them?"

"Anyway," Sarah butted in, "you're going to be a good Dad yourself, Nicolas. Don't worry about the boys. We're not jealous, really, we just miss you an awful lot. We like to see you play with them, and Simon can come out with Jack sometimes. Chas is going away again, and Karl's not interested he's had enough of teaching, so that'll be good. Grant and Eric can go to hell, and your Mum."

He stood and started dressing, pulling his pants up then his shirt, and gave her a sly look.

"Not too soon."

The three glanced at one another. "No, we can take turns," she went on. "You'll be safe. We'll talk about it, all right? Agreed?"

"Do you agree, Em?"

"Yes. Yes, of course, silly."

"Well, you go first. Go around the front of the house and when you're clear I'll go home past the sheds."

They dressed quickly and slipped away, and he watched them disappear into the dark. He stood awhile then as the moon came out from behind the clouds, skipping pebbles across the still water before heading back up along the track around the amphitheatre to come through the far shed, and from there straight home.

When he got back Karl asked him if he'd seen the girls; Jennie was just here looking for them, but he said nothing and went to his room where he undressed again and wrapping a towel around him headed for a bath.

Next day Wally pulled up beside him on the tractor as he was walking back past the sheds to do a bit of cleaning up, and said, "Wait 'till we get some ov these ponies back up, son; ye'll see what I mean. You're a colt yerself; fine figure of a boy. That's what we want." Then he drove on. Jennie wouldn't quite have agreed with him, but she saw his point and went along with it.

Chapter Twenty

Marcus arrived at the end of Semester for a month's break, and declared his wish to see a commune established on the property. There were a lot of people wanting to drop out; take time out at least from the way things were in society, numbers of his students among them, so over the next week Wally had a think about it. He was worried about commodity markets and the farm business. Even had the quarantine been lifted vegetable prices were nowhere near where they should be, and lamb wasn't much better. If he purchased another farm and turned this place over to Community Title, then sold shares in a private, unlisted holding company giving members residential entitlement and with it a right to build their own house, the family would still come out all right.

As he went about getting his jobs done he'd stop and chat. One after another he gleaned everyone's ideas and opinions until one evening at dinner he looked up suddenly and uttered, "Yeah, why not? We'll give it a go, eh? I'll give Tom a call tomorra an' get it sorted." That was that.

Next day he and Nicolas were planting rows of potatoes in the basin at the bottom of the amphitheatre, working quietly together as they did, without talking much. Marcus came down to let them know he'd be on campus for a few days and back by the weekend, and would they mind if he brought a colleague back with him to look the place over; a landscape architect with experience in group housing and what he called intentional communities, which made Nicolas prick his ears up.

"Ask him if we can build a permanent theatre. Do you think we might be able to do that, if this works, I mean?"

Marcus looked at him curiously, then with a shrug said, "Why don't you ask him yourself? Why don't you come with me; come for a drive?"

"Oh, we need to get these spuds in, two more days."

Wally glanced sharply at him. "Nah, off ye go. We'll be wight. On the way past the house tell those pretty young fillies of yours to get their fannies down here. They can give me a hand wiv it."

Nicolas laughed at that, and leaning his spade neatly against a post turned on his heel to follow Marcus. After he'd showered and changed, and packed a few clothes, on the way out he saw the girls there at the fig tree and called out merrily from the car window, "Hey, you pretty young fillies; Wally said get your sweet little pussies down there and help him with the spuds."

They giggled, calling back to him, "Where are you going?"

"Off to Perth with Marcus for a few days."

He was going to call out something else but Jennie appeared at the back door so he ducked, grinning, and told Marcus to get him out of there.

Marcus glanced across at him and smiled. "You've come a long way suddenly. What have you been up to?"

"Nothing, Marcus, I'm not telling; you or anybody. It's none of your business." He paused a moment before adding sheepishly, "Well, thanks for helping me, anyway."

"No problem. Tell me, how are your studies?"

That started them on a long drawn-out debate all the rest of the way. It was late afternoon by time they arrived and threatened rain, but Marcus took him out for dinner regardless and continued their debate.

When they got to his apartment finally he saw it was a total mess; books and papers everywhere, but without much ado Marcus cleared the couch for a bed and went to get a pillow and some blankets. Nicolas wanted to watch television for a while so Marcus showered before turning in early, leaving a clean towel for him on the way through, and said good night.

Rising the next morning he found him there asleep at his desk, a pile of books next to his head. He stared in amazement. Nicolas had skipped over the classics, even Euripides, and Graves, and gone straight for Morris Cohen's *An Introduction to Logic and Scientific Method*. It was open before him, there next to Descartes' *Principles of Philosophy* and *Discourse on the Method*, and Kant's *Critique of Pure Reason*. He'd torn up bits of paper and scribbled notes on them before bookmarking the pages, but at some point sleep caught up with him and he'd stopped abruptly.

Marcus shook him partially awake, enough to steer him over to the couch where he tucked him in and drawing the curtains turned off the light, and went to the kitchen to make himself breakfast, shaking his head in wonder; he was just a kid. It didn't seem a good idea right now to do anything much so finishing coffee he went shopping and let him sleep.

Nicolas woke before lunch and staggered off to the toilet, but when he came into the kitchen and started on Cohen Marcus shut him up and made him sit quietly at the table while he made him something to eat.

"What are we going to do with you?" he asked finally.

"What?"

"You run so far ahead we can't keep up with you, and then when we think we have you all sorted out you're like a small child. That's what."

He gazed across at him, holding his attention. "You want to talk to me about that?"

"No, not really," Nicolas answered cautiously. "It's not me. What are you talking about? I'm steady; me and Wally, and people like that. It's the world that's mad, or something."

"OK, I can follow that. But tell me, why don't you want to be part of that world?"

"Why? It has nothing to do with me. And it hates people. It sort of, says, um, we are helping you, but the way we help you is march you around, and cane you and beat you up, and have you arrested, or something, the minute you actually start to think, with your own brain. And if you don't like it we'll declare war. But then I read these beautiful books I sort of think, why don't people read them? Why don't they see the beautiful things; the little birds and animals, and flowers, and such lovely words they make my heart sing, and be part of that instead? It seems a much better way to do things, don't you think? But instead of doing things like that they want to destroy them all the time, as if everything was ugly."

Marcus watched him closely.

"What is your experience of reading those books, Nicolas; sitting up all night like that? They told me when you wrote the play you sat up all night with it, out of the blue. What is it?"

Nicolas looked away, thoughtfully, trying to find something to say about it. Finally he shrugged.

"It's like the words take me there, no, not there, but like, opening a window and dragging me through. It's like, I'm talking to them, and they are talking to me, but in that space not this one."

"Is that right?"

"Yes."

"Forget Cohen for a moment, but Descartes died in 1650, and Kant in 1840."

"No, they didn't. That's not possible. I was talking to them."

"Who else do you talk to?"

"Lots of people, and birds and animals; every time I go for a walk or open a book they're right there, and they stay there so I can keep talking with them; after I've closed the book I mean."

He leaned forward earnestly. "People, I mean ordinary people, a lot of them anyway, they're not like that are they? They think everything is like, dead or something, and it doesn't matter if they kill it or not. It's not whole and beautiful and alive; just a dead thing. When they arrested me for carnal knowledge I looked it up and it said "flesh"; knowledge of flesh. That's Latin, you know."

"Go on."

"Like I was rooting dead meat or something, like it was bad; not something nice with the two people I love most in the whole world, sort of. Not like Wally, I mean, the way I love him, but the girls. But that's the way people look at things. They think I'm some sort of dead body, but I'm not, but they arrested me for it anyway. Then they made the girls undress and show them, like they were meat, and I was doing something bad with it, but they never said anything about Sarah with her hand on me like she had, stroking me the way she did, in the bath, and how beautiful it was, when I didn't even expect it, or imagine what it would be like; how anything could possibly be like that. But they didn't examine me at all, only the girls, or ask any of us what it was like to be together like that."

"But you've changed the way you deal with that, haven't you? You're facing it now."

"No. Us, yes, but not them, the way they do things. Isn't there something wrong in all that? Doesn't that matter?"

"What does matter, Nicolas?"

"What matters is why they don't go for walks, or read books and learn things, or sit and listen, or talk to anyone, or love one another like we do; just go around yelling at them and telling them what to do, treating them like they were just . . . things . . . I don't know . . . . , really I don't. They're scary."

Marcus gazed out the window a moment. "Don't you think, Nicolas," he said thoughtfully, "that just maybe they have problems and we are trying to help them deal with those problems, and you just happened to get in the way? Don't you think you might forgive them and get on with your own life?"

"Well, Mr. Lynch said that to me too. I don't know, but if I do that I won't have anyone to talk to, about anything real; only deadshit stuff all the time."

"You have the girls, and Wally, and your family, and I'm still your friend I trust."

Nicolas giggled slightly as he thought of the girls, then flashed across at Marcus and pulled his face straight. "Yeah, but it's not the same, as you and me I mean. I don't want to sound like I don't love them because I do, very much. It's just so frustrating sometimes when I can't have the same sorts of conversations with them as I have with you, except for Wally, because when I'm out with him nothing needs to be said, like he already knows, like he loves me even more than Em or Sair, or Jennie, or Simon or Jack, or Chas, than anyone else on earth. Wally's just magic, he can't even read but he listens to every little thing, you know."

"All right, come along then and we'll see what we can do to fix that, some of it anyway."

In the car again they drove awhile through fairly light traffic, until Marcus pulled off into a side street and finding a big car park drove in. He parked the car and went over to a machine to buy a ticket, and that sorted he led him past a big three storey sandstone building then across a lawn past a great spreading fig tree and under an arch. There was a big stone seat there next to a pool, with an engraving on it which read, "Verily by beauty it is that we come at wisdom."

Nicolas looked around. "This where you work, is it?"

"Yep."

Marcus gazed about and shrugged, while Nicolas stared curiously at him, eyes bright and head cocked to one side.

Chapter Twenty One

Before they left to return home Marcus booked Nicolas in with a Mensa Proctor, who made a place for him in the next round of entry tests in two weeks' time. On the way out of town they called by to pick up Ted Ashcroft, the landscaper, and Marcus sat him in the back seat with Nicolas allowing them to get to know one another. Ted for the first time in his life took him into discussion of space and the way people negotiate space, in their moving about day by day but also in their settling somewhere and making a place for themselves, which he felt were two quite different things.

What Nicolas wanted to know was whether he was talking about real spaces or spaces in people's minds, and what was the difference. The conversation then turned to imagined spaces and how they affect the way people perceive real spaces, and engage them, and on to how real spaces might be represented in art, or theatre.

Nicolas said, "Yes, but on stage you have to have backgrounds, and costumes, and a script. I mean, you have to have a play, don't you? Someone has to write the play, and you have to have characters, and a story, and an audience. If a stage is only a space, or a space is a stage, what are you talking about?"

Ted answered quietly, "If we are talking about the big stage, the universe, a lot of people would argue that God wrote the play. I don't want to go there with you. What I mean is that together, as a society, we construct a reality for ourselves. How good it is, how well it meets our expectation of what is real and what isn't real, or how well it reflects our beliefs about what is real; how intuitive it is for us to negotiate, is what sustains it. We are the actors, all of us, but at the same time we are our own audience. If you are what we call 'embedded' in your own space you may not actually be able to see what's happening. But if you step out of it; go somewhere else, into some other space, and then come back to it, you can see it. Between one and the other are what we call boundaries, and between those boundaries there may well be in-between spaces; in a ritual context, for example. Technically those are referred to as liminal spaces, where quite a lot else can be happening."

"That's where you went, Nicolas," Marcus said quietly, "as part of the trauma you suffered; somewhere you were safe, and kept you sane. Isn't our mind the most wonderful thing?"

He thought about that, saying nothing as they drove along, until eventually he looked up suddenly and said, eyes in open wonder, "That means we can create new spaces. That means we don't have to be bothered with old spaces, where everyone is so unhappy, and afraid. We can do better than that, can't we? We can make the world the way we want. It's true then."

Ted glanced across, and Marcus at the wheel turned his head to look back at him, a hint of a smile on his face.

For the rest of the journey Nicolas sat and fidgeted, starting up now and then to gaze about in confusion before settling restlessly back into his seat. The moment they arrived home he jumped out of the car and ran straight across to Karl's house, and going to his desk grabbed pencil and paper and started writing. At dinner they brought his food over to him there at the desk but he ignored it. When he finished his own meal Marcus came over and sat with him, and as the evening progressed ate his dinner for him, and sat waiting and waiting and waiting.

Finally Nicolas started to slow, so watching him closely Marcus reached over and took the pencil, and leaning him gently back in the chair tidied his pages. Nicolas stared almost from a great distance at what he was doing, but seeing things tidy nodded slightly and Marcus picked him bodily up. Taking him to his room he started helping him undress but Nicolas impatiently fobbed him off and stripping off his clothes tucked himself into bed. Marcus went out and without glancing back switched off the light.

Nicolas woke suddenly to loud screams outside his window, and jumping up ran outside to see what was happening. It was broad daylight and Jack's ute was there. Jack was standing beside it with Simon and Eric watching Sarah taking to Grant with a cricket bat. Emma came running out of the big house, and taking up one of the wickets from the lawn where the boys had been playing came after Grant as well, both yelling and hitting at him as he tried to duck around behind the car. Nicolas ran over and grabbed Sarah, taking the bat away, and holding her by the wrist turned to take the wicket from Emma. She held on to it grimly, resisting him, paying no attention to the fact he was naked but glaring pure malice at Grant, so instead he dragged her away by the stick. Sarah was beating at him with her free hand, still screaming, until he stood and yelled, "Stop! Stop it! All right!"

He held them and held them, and didn't hit back, accepting it until they calmed a little. The moment they did he went straight around the car and swinging an almighty punch with his right fist knocked his brother flat to the ground. He stood over him but Grant didn't move; only his hand to his mouth wiping away blood, so taking both girls in hand took them across to Jennie standing there at the back door. Returning to the car he picked Grant up and shoved him bodily toward Karl's house. Sitting him in the kitchen with a stern glance not to move an inch he came back out onto the porch, but then suddenly realising he had no clothes on went back inside to pull on some shorts.

"What?"

Nobody said anything so he sat down on the steps. Jack came over, making him look up.

"What, Jack?"

"Your mother died, Nicolas."

"Yep. When?"

"She killed herself. The doctor told her she had cancer and she couldn't face it apparently, so she went home and got pissed on a bottle of whisky, and overdosed on sleeping tablets."

"Yes, but when?"

"She got the news yesterday afternoon. Grant found her during the night."

Nicolas looked away, and back again. He stood and went back inside. He looked at Grant there at the table and asked him, "You all right, mate?"

Grant sat there blubbering. Nicolas gazed at him curiously and frowned. Shaking his head he went back outside. He walked over to the car and gazed at each twin in turn. Eric pushed him away, but Simon came in close and without looking up put his arms around him.

"Yeah," Nicolas thought to himself, and saying nothing took Simon across to the girls and turning around shrugged at Jack.

"You right with Eric?" he wanted to know.

"Yeah, he'll be right."

"Maybe Grant can go back up to Wallaga and live with Frank for a while, maybe get him a job up there; after the funeral. Dad'll give him a job." He stopped, distracted for a moment before continuing. "That house, it's his and my house isn't it; Mum's house that you helped pay for, you and Frank, and that boarder, Terry, but it's ours."

"Yeah, it's your house, probably. There's no will that we know of. What the fuck."

"Oh well, maybe we could sell it I mean, or let it to someone, doesn't matter, it's a good house. Or you could live in it yourself, nice big shed. What do you think about that? Better for someone to be living there, wouldn't you say? When I get a bit older maybe I'll live there, or maybe not; depends."

Marcus stood back stunned. Later in the afternoon he went across to the desk and rifled through the stack of papers, but all he read was a script for a play about time-warping from space to space, and fixing things that were wrong; making things right, and asking for help when you need it. Whatever else happened in the writing of it was completely lost on him.

Chapter Twenty Two

Nobody said anything much at the funeral, apart from running into a number of long-lost uncles and cousins who promised to try and keep in touch, cracking old jokes on the way out about having to meet like this, only ever at weddings and funerals; maybe they should catch up some time, before disappearing into a haze of cold dry dust kicked up by their own wheels.

Frank came down from Wallaga and didn't say much. He'd take Grant on as an apprentice he said; he was going on fifteen already, and after a bitter round of arguing that almost ended in another fist fight they too drove away.

On their own way out of the hall where they'd put on some food and drinks for their guests they ran into a local Aboriginal family from the reserve north of town who stopped, gazing at Nicolas, and started talking among themselves before moving on. Nicolas turned to stare after them before noticing Wally wave to them and an old man waved back.

"Do you know them?"

"Went ter school wiv 'im, old Jim. They come from out our way, in the old days, and those fellas used ta come fishin' on our place, down the creek there. When I was a kid, eh? That old fella helped build our dam, yer know that?"

"Did he? Why don't they come out any more?"

"Ah, lots of reasons; the war, and the Welfare mostly. Just lose touch, don't ya."

Nicolas gazed at the old man a moment, then back down the street where the others were just then turning a corner out of sight. Marcus stood watching him.

In the car on the way back home he turned to him, wanting to know, "What are you up to, Nicolas?"

"What? I'm not up to anything. What are you talking about?"

"Things have shifted a bit, and I don't know who else to be looking at right now."

"Me? No. The only thing happening with me is I learned something I didn't know before, so I've been thinking about it a lot; about how the world might be better."

"Is that so? How might the world be better?"

Nicolas looked across at him, thinking. "Diotima said," he recalled finally, "'Then at last man will behold beauty with the eye of the mind and will be able to bring forth not mere images of what is good for men but realities. Would that be an ignoble life Socrates?'"

"Well, no, it wouldn't, young Puck, but Plato also cautioned, 'but this can only come about after patient instruction and much hard study.'"

"Why?"

"Why not?"

"We've already tried that." He glanced across, dismissing the idea, "Anyway, why did you call me that; Puck, or something? I'm not a Puck, or a Bottom either."

"No," Marcus glanced back. "You're not so common, are you? I apologise. You're Eros and Adonis and Angus and Oisín all rolled into one. No wonder those girls have trouble dealing with it."

"No they don't. Anyway, who's Oisín?"

"He is the son of the greatest of all heroes, Fionn mac Cumhaill. His mother Sadhbh was a princess who'd been turned into a deer by Fear Doirich, who was a druid. Fionn changed her back and married her, but the Druid changed her back again though she still gave birth to a human boy, their son Oisín. Oisín when he was a young man was seduced by a beautiful girl, Niamh of the Golden Hair, and taken away by her to Tír na nÓg, which is the Land of Eternal Youth, from which they never returned."

"That's a good story. Is it a real place, do you think?"

"Aha," Marcus exclaimed,

Delightful is the land beyond all dreams,
Fairer than aught thine eyes have ever seen.
There all the year the fruit is on the tree,
And all the year the bloom is on the flower.
There with wild honey drip the forest trees;

The stores of wine and mead shall never fail.
Nor pain nor sickness knows the dweller there,
Death and decay come near him never more.
The feast shall cloy not, nor the chase shall tire,
Nor music cease for ever through the hall;
The gold and jewels of the Land of Youth
Outshine all splendours ever dreamed by man.
Thou shalt have horses of the fairy breed,
Thou shalt have hounds that can outrun the wind;
A hundred chiefs shall follow thee in war,
A hundred maidens sing thee to thy sleep.
A crown of sovranty thy brow shall wear,
And by thy side a magic blade shall hang.
Thou shalt be lord of all the Land of Youth,
And lord of Niamh of the Head of Gold.

"Wicked! Do you think we could make such a place, for our commune maybe?"

Marcus glanced across, adding,

And if the Babe is born a Boy
He's given to a Woman Old
Who nails him down upon a rock
Catches his shrieks in cups of gold

"Why did you say that?"

"That's William Blake. Just so we don't get too carried away, all right?"

Chapter Twenty Three

Nicolas began to feel somewhat confused by the sudden change in their lives, and spent a lot more time out walking by himself again. Everyone thought he was grieving for his mother and left him to it, without realising that he'd never really thought much about her aside from keeping clear of her as much as he'd been able. In a big sense he was relieved that he didn't have to do that anymore, or be worried about her coming after him, but the world Marcus was opening up to him was also big.

Sometimes he'd go up onto the ridge and wait for his fairy wrens, or kangaroos to hop by, and sometimes that big old goanna that stopped to flick its long forked tongue at him.

He had a shadow on his top lip and after a long swim he'd lean forward exploring himself, wondering over the hairs starting from his scrotum. Grant had hairs growing from the V of his groin, and so did the girls except they didn't have a moustache, but his was growing from his scrotum like an old Chinaman's skimpy beard. He thought maybe he'd ask Wally about it, and about the bumps growing on his chest, under his nipples, when he thought only girls grew breasts. Maybe he could find a book about it somewhere.

He didn't know why anyone would be worried about such things, or what made him think about it apart from the change it made, or why nobody seemed interested in explaining them to him regardless of anything else. Maybe it was the time when they were little, when that chook pecked Grant's dickie that stayed in his memory, and the impression it made on him, and that school psychologist wanting to know so much about it.

It was all a bit too much to think about, with Euripides, and Kant and Descartes, and now Adonis and Angus and Oisín, and God knows how many more of these new people he'd have to get to know if he was going to cope with them all. It was starting to get enough to deal with already, with so many at the festival, and wanting to move onto the farm.

A week later Marcus drove him back up to Perth for the Mensa test and despite his protest paid the fee. Again Nicolas became mesmerised by the questions, and the shapes and patterns, and when finished he handed over the paper in something of a daze. Shaking hands with the woman on the way out, he smiled shyly without saying anything.

Marcus then took him back across town to the University campus where they spent the rest of the afternoon exploring the grounds, and arguing over busts and inscriptions gracing the old buildings. Eventually they found their way along an open second storey gallery at the end of which a carved stone panel portrayed nude boys in puberty, in procession with girls draped in gossamer. They stopped to look at it without saying anything. They didn't even exchange glances.

There was little else to do after that so they went out for dinner in a real restaurant before going back to Marcus's apartment.

Chapter Twenty Four

Next day they arrived home just before lunch. Nicolas sat in the car while Marcus took their bags across to Karl's house, but before he returned got out and went over to the big house; through the conservatory and into the kitchen where Jennie was busy cooking. Simon was at the table going through his homework but he ignored him to stand beside Jennie.

"Hello stranger," she said quietly.

He didn't say anything straight away, just touched her and slid his arm around her waist.

"Nicolas," she said, "If I were Emma I'd be head over heels in love with you myself, and I do love you. You're a beautiful boy, in many ways. I don't want you to misunderstand me."

He thought about that a moment, watching Marcus unload the car through the window, then turned more directly toward her.

She sensed his movement. Turning away she put the knife down and went over to wipe her hands on a towel before turning back to him. She cocked her head.

"I can't do it like this," he said simply.

She turned to Simon and said, "Simon, please go and do your homework in your room."

Simon stood and taking up his books glanced back with a cheeky grin. At the door he bumped into Sarah, but pushed her aside and disappeared down the passage. Sarah stood staring at Jennie and Nicolas there at the bench before turning on her heels to follow Simon. Within the minute she returned with Emma in hand. Jennie looked from one to the other and nodded. Neither of them blinked as she set a pot of tea, occupying herself arranging cups and saucers, and sweet biscuits on a tray. She leaned against the sink, back toward them waiting for the kettle, hand to her forehead, and when the water boiled she made tea and picking up the tray carried it out.

She went out the back door into the conservatory and sat at the garden table there, turning only slightly to expect them, the three together, and they didn't disappoint her. She nodded as they sat, respectful but determined. They didn't move while she set the table then sat down to pour tea, until Emma leaned over and said, "Mummy, it's nearly lunch time."

When she failed to reply Sarah piped up and said, "We know what we're doing. There isn't any problem."

Nicolas said nothing.

Tea poured finally, Jennie sat back with her cup and said quietly, "Simon will move into your room. He needs a bit of space, and somewhere for the boys to play. You will move into the old house, into Nicolas' room, and he will move into the sleepout. Karl will keep an eye on you. Do you understand me?"

Nicolas sat back thinking, then nodded. Sarah and Emma had no choice but to follow his lead. He was relieved in a way that the matter was out of his hands, though the way Jennie dealt with the two girls fascinated him. He sat sipping his tea while the women continued to exchange pointed remarks, watching Jennie's face change from annoyed to exasperated to sad and back again in as many seconds, then finding his cup empty stood and excused himself.

Wally was in the kitchen, having come in through the front door and noticing the meeting in the conservatory ducked out of sight to start getting lunch ready. Nicolas went across to the bench to help, looking for a distraction.

"Don't twy and figure it out, son. You'll be wight," Wally said quietly, and then louder, "Ted's comin' up this arvo wiv a surveyor. You can give us a hand, eh? Do a bit a measurin' for us if yer like. How'll that do?"

"Good, yes; that'll be good," he said, distracted, but turned suddenly. "Can the girls come and help? Emma's really good at maths, better than me, really. And Sarah can help."

Wally leaned back a moment watching his face before replying, "Yeah, righto, get 'em outa the house. Do 'em good, eh?"

Nicolas turned away with a pile of plates to start setting the table, smiling to himself, but when he turned back for knives and forks Wally was right behind him, bumping into him, and he shoved back affectionately. Wally poked his head out the back door, calling the girls in to help with lunch while Jennie caught his glance and quickly turned away.

He waited a moment then came out to sit with her, and poured himself a cup of tea.

When lunch was ready Emma called Simon and the boys before poking her head out the door, smiling shyly, inviting her mother and grandfather to join them.

Immediately they finished and washed up the two went and packed their bags, and without ado lugged them across to the old house. They took Nicolas's few things and hung his clothes in the dusty old lowboy and his smalls neatly in a chest of drawers, before stacking his books and papers neatly on the floor for want of a desk and shelves. Sarah gave her father a hard glare on the way through but Emma giggled and putting a stop to it pushed her out the door.

Out in the yard Marcus pulled them up and started to say something, but at that moment Ted arrived with the surveyor in his truck and he turned to greet him so they slipped away. Nicolas come looking for them and found them inside tidying their old room. He poked his head in the door and said Wally wanted to know if they could do a bit of figuring, and if they could why not come and help the surveyor; get your sweet little pussies into gear, and walked out again chuckling to himself.

Back outside he went across to the truck where they were standing around maps spread out across the bonnet, talking about the job to be done. As he came up Wally made a place for him among their elbows and shoulders and he gazed intently at the drawings. The bloke noticed and moved aside for him a little further.

"Hey, young fella," he said. "Can you read a map?"

Marcus introduced them. The surveyor's name was Graeme Little and Nicolas took a liking to him straight away. He leaned in to study the map, then up and around. He creased his brow. "Where are we now," he wanted to know, looking down at the map again. He followed their fingers to a marked spot before cocking his head to point with his left hand up across the amphitheatre. "Is that there the same as the top of the hill over there?"

"Yes, you've got it. The saddle runs that way, you can see. There's the creek line down the other side, and there's the dam."

Nicolas gaped. He leaned closer in, pushing his way through, running his fingers up and down the lines on the paper.

Chapter Twenty Five

When the girls came up he shoved the men aside to show them the map and explain where they were on it, before looking up again to ask what they wanted him to do.

"Well, get some gear off the truck first. Then you can sharpen your axe and cut some pegs for me."

"Righto, good, Sarah can help, can't she? She's a pretty good worker." He turned toward the back of the truck before swinging back a moment. "Emma can help you, will that be all right?"

"Yeah, sure," Graeme turned to Emma who glanced up, smiling, and rummaging through his brief case presented her with a note book and some pencils. He looked across to watch Nicolas with the gear, selecting an axe to swing and balance in his hand before trying another and another, until he had the one he wanted.

"There're a couple of files and a stone in the bag there, mate."

Nicolas glanced up and nodded, but first helped Sarah select an axe before picking up the tool bag and started walking over to the shed with it.

"Back of the truck, Nicolas," Graeme called after him. "Come here, I'll show you."

Briskly he took the axe and holding the head on the back tailgate gave its edge a few quick swipes with the file, then spitting on the stone rubbed it back and forth to finish the job with a polish.

"If you keep your gear in good order, son, it only ever needs a bit of maintenance. No need for constant repairs; we don't have time for that." He paused, looking down slightly. "But you did pick a good axe. It's one I use myself."

Nicolas nodded; eyes wide. He turned to take Sarah's axe to try his hand but she resisted, holding onto it.

"I can do it," she said.

Nicolas leaned forward to take another axe, but stepped back as Graeme helped Sarah with the file strokes, watching while he explained the correct angle, and how to attack the edge with the stone to get a good sharp finish quickly so as not to take too much time holding up the job, while the others stood around waiting for her. But when he was done he let Nicolas sharpen the other axe. As he finished he took it and gave it to Sarah, saying that was the better axe than the one she had in her hand. He swung them both and had her do the same thing, taking care she held them right and not cut her leg or foot on the way down.

Nicolas watched that too, but stepped forward to say no, that first axe was better for her because it was lighter, and fit better in her hand; he was watching how she had to work her body more with the slightly heavier axe, not so relaxed.

The surveyor nodded, bemused. "All right," he said, "let's see how good you are."

Wally and Marcus both looked up, glancing across at Nicolas then Graeme who handed him the spindle of measuring tape and a graduated stick, and hoisting the theodolite over his shoulder led the way down the front track to the gate. Scratching around in the grass beside the road he uncovered a peg in the ground, and setting the instrument over it checked his position with the plumb.

"See that fence post at the corner of the big house," he said, "there's another peg just like this one. Go and find it for me."

They ran on ahead but he called them back. "Run the tape up for me, eh?"

So Nicolas came back and giving Emma the end walked backward with the tape unrolling as he went. When they got to the post Sarah kicked around in the grass until she found the peg, and straightening up Nicolas ran the tape onto it. This looked like fun. They watched as Graeme had Emma look through the theodolite. She nodded and ran up, sending Sarah back to look, then she came back and taking Nicolas by the hand led him back down the track to the front gate.

"All right mate, let me show you something. Look through here."

Nicolas did so while Graeme explained the horizontal and vertical axes, and the length of the tape, and the result he had Emma jot down in her note book.

Nicolas looked at him curiously. "Why that peg," he wanted to know, pointing down.

"Well, that's the marker peg."

He rolled out the survey map and pointed to it. "We have a fix on it from when this old road was first surveyed. That work has already been done. When the farm was first laid out and the house paddock established that other peg was fixed, there, you see. All we're doing right now is checking that original work before we do anything else."

"What else are we going to do?"

"We triangulate from these two points; then set up a grid allowing us to position the new house lots. That's about it."

"But where; I mean, where are the houses going to be?"

"Ted's already designed that. That's his job."

"What job?" Nicolas looked around, confused. He marched back up the track and across the yard to the front of the shed where Ted and Marcus were still looking over plans laid out across the bonnet of the truck. He stopped, waiting.

"How's it going, kid," Ted asked.

"Where are the houses going to be?"

"Oh here, look," he stood aside to show him the design, pointing with his finger, "and here and here and here, taking advantage of aspect and slope. What I mean is, to catch the sun and shade, and still have a good view. We'll have another enclave there in the bush, once we do a bit of clearing; on the east facing slope to catch the morning sun, and another overlooking the dam facing south. Together we achieve a balance of sustainability and diversity within the one overall site plan. That'll yield the results we want."

Nicolas frowned, peering intently at the drawings. He turned to the girls as they came up, and before they drew near took them both by the arm and led them across to the corner of the shed.

"They're going to knock down our bush to build more houses; over there, not just here," he whispered. "And they're going to build houses over at the swimming hole."

They exchanged anxious glances before turning to face the men standing there watching them.

"Don't you like the idea?" Marcus wanted to know.

Nicolas stared at him, frowning. "Where's our theatre going to be, and our art gallery?" he paused, querying, "and why do you want to get rid of the fairy wrens, and the bandicoots, and that old kangaroo that lives up there? And anyway, what happens if people want to go for a swim, and all the neighbours are watching? That place should be private; I mean, set aside for everyone, not in someone's back yard. If we are going to do it right we should have clusters of houses, with shared laundry and things like that; and play areas for the kids, like we had all the tents pegged out for the festival. That worked just great!"

Wally chuckled. "Told ya!" he exclaimed.

"Told them what?"

"Better ask you kids, that's what I told 'em."

"We're not kids."

Marcus gazed at him soberly. "No, you're not, are you? More's the pity." He turned to Ted. "All right, back to the drawing board."

"We can keep surveying for today, can't we, at least those houses closer in?" Sarah butted in.

Graeme had come up the track by then to see what was causing the holdup, and hearing the argument decided to call it quits for the day. There was no point his wasting time fixing pegs that might have to be shifted anyway, he said, then come back again to do an entirely different job.

Nicolas nodded. He hadn't finished yet, now that he'd found his feet. "And another thing, while we're all talking about it," he went on, voice rising, "why can't we have a decent school finally. To be allowed to learn anything we have to be bussed in to a prison camp and marched around all day, and yelled at, and given the cuts, or we get holed up here in the old house like refugees. That's not right either."

The men all stared at him speechless but he simply shrugged. "You could have asked first; you never ask," he muttered, before turning to walk back over to the house. Sarah and Emma in unison spun into place behind him.

Chapter Twenty Six

"Nicolas," Ted began as they sat around the big table in the kitchen, "We'll never get your ideas approved. That's the problem."

"Why not?"

"Well, basically because Barkhan Crossing is the gazetted townsite for this district. The old outlying stations are still gazetted, but that's only because merging those old green titles takes far too much time and effort, and sets precedents no minister wants to face. So they are left as they are."

"What?"

"Put simply, we cannot initiate a whole new settlement here. We are close enough to town, and this area with the old market gardens is marked for subdivision, but it must be presented as residential subdivision not as a separate town centre."

Nicolas gazed at him curiously. "Well don't then," he said finally. "Don't tell them."

Marcus leaned forward. "We can't simply break the law, Nicolas, and do anything we want, and we cannot secede from the Commonwealth. It's not like that."

"What does secede mean?"

"No, it doesn't matter. I'll explain to you later."

"It does matter. We get beaten up all the time and have to live out here, and stay away from town otherwise we're in trouble, for some reason I don't know. We have to have somewhere we can live and be ourselves."

They sat watching his face as he struggled with the argument, but then he piped up and said simply, "No, don't tell them. I mean, what can we tell them? What can we say to them so we can get approval? If we just build more houses it'll be the same as in town, and we'll have to move away again; go somewhere else to live. That's not fair. It's really not fair. Why can't we build something good here, for ourselves and people like us?"

Ted sat back, twiddling his pencil thoughtfully. Eventually he leaned forward, and taking his map started penciling in his thoughts. Nicolas watched while he rearranged things.

"No, not there," he said finally. "Use the two big sheds. We already have the sheds, haven't we? We don't have to knock them down, do we? They can't make us knock them down, can they?" he went on rapid-fire. "Yes, that's it, Ted. Just build some houses, there and there and there. That works, but it'll look like we've just got people here and they'll think that's good business, good for the district, whatever they want to think."

"Anything else, while we're at it?" Ted was plainly annoyed.

Nicolas looked up, startled by the tone, before leaning forward again undeterred. "Keep the spuds and vegetables there, I think. That can be made into a big garden, for everybody, as it's easy to water, and we should get some more chooks, and ducks. If we keep the horses up there in the top paddocks over the other side of the creek we can bring them down occasionally, but we might as well run sheep with them, and a dairy cow over on this side, for milk."

He glanced around, smiling, and nodding to himself rose from the table and left. Emma followed him outside, asking where he was going, and he said for a swim so she ducked back into the kitchen and taking Sarah by the hand dragged her out, leaving the others sitting there bereft.

They stopped by the old house to grab towels, and ran happily up the slope and down the other side, getting up a sweat and laughing. While the day itself was warm the weather was late autumn and cool. It was still mid-afternoon as they stripped and jumped into the pool, but the water was cold, a shock after the hot run, and they didn't stay in long, just enough to show off. When they finished their swim they had to dry quickly to avoid the chill. Dressed again they came back down through the amphitheatre to see another car coming up the track from the front gate.

By time they arrived back at the house everyone was inside and they stormed in to pull up abruptly at the sight of another boy there, handsome like Nicolas but with blond curls in place of his own dark brown, with a startlingly pretty girl standing next to him.

Ted looked up.

"Nicolas, this is my son Robbie."

Nicolas stepped up to shake hands, smiling, braced and fresh from his swim in the cold pond.

Robbie turned and mumbled, "This is Laura. She's my girlfriend."

"Really?" He turned to Emma. "Emma, this is Laura. She's my girlfriend. And Sarah, she is as well." He blushed at that, while Marcus and Ted glanced away and Wally stood beaming, grinning from ear to ear.

"Father!" Jennie broke in, but by then it was too late. "Nicolas," she said, "take your new friends outside perhaps, or over to the house. Before you do, you should introduce yourself to Robbie's mother Elizabeth."

"Liz," the other came forward, smiling. "I'm very pleased to meet you, young man. I've heard a lot about you."

"Really?" He glanced away, embarrassed.

She chuckled with a merry tinkle and Nicolas took to her. "Nothing bad, young man; a rising star I should imagine."

He watched her face curiously as a thought struck him. "Are you thinking about moving here, with us? Buying one of our houses?"

"We may very well do, as a matter of fact."

"Well, we're not knocking down any bush, all right? And nobody's to build near our swimming hole, that's for everybody."

"Nicolas, bugger off!" Ted burst out angrily. "Out! Out, out, out! Scat!"

He stood back in astonishment. "I only meant, apart from that; it'll be good. It'll be good," he turned smiling toward Robbie and Laura but by then the girls had them both in tow and out the door. He swung around disoriented and tripped over a chair sticking out from the table, which went flying. The girls giggled while the adults stood glaring at him, there on the floor, except Wally who'd disappeared already down the front passage.

"No, before you go, Nicolas," Marcus interrupted the melee. "Tell me, what made you think of a school associated with your theatre and art gallery?"

"Um," he struggled up from the floor lost for words. "I only thought," he said after a moment, catching his breath, "what we needed to do was find a way to help us get into your university, where you took me to show me around. I mean, that's a different planet from what we've got here."

"Is that it?"

"No, um, what I mean is, I always thought I was on the wrong planet, until then, and it made me think maybe I am on the right planet and all these other people are from somewhere else. What we could do is connect, maybe."

Marcus simply nodded. "All right, off you go, eh?"

Robbie watched Nicolas closely as he brushed past and led the way through the conservatory and out the back door, before leaving last to follow them out.

They didn't hear Ted ask Marcus, "What do you think?"

"He has Asperger's Syndrome. I have no doubt of it, though I'll wait for the Mensa test results to come through before we take it any further."

Marcus turned to Jennie, adding, "I think we can help. He's coming along quite all right, and if we keep him settled and catching up with his studies we might see about a special entry for him."

Chapter Twenty Seven

When they got back to the old house Karl was at the kitchen table with a beer, and after making their introductions suggested firmly that he'd better go across to the big house and help with designing the new school; Ted was working on it now.

Karl went to the fridge taking a couple of bottles with his half-empty glass, but on the way out bumped into Simon on the back porch, spilling it. The spill went over Simon's shoulder so he ducked under his arm and came inside with only a brief glance back to see what happened. Sarah caught his arm as he approached the table where they'd sat to talk, telling him to go back across to the house and tell them Robbie and Laura would be staying here the night, then come straight back.

Emma called after him to tell Mum to look after the boys.

By time he returned the two girls had a meal cooking, Sarah had taken some of her Dad's beer from the fridge and poured glasses all round. She wouldn't let Simon have any until Nicolas interjected and poured him a small drop in a vegemite glass, and when he sat down put his arm protectively around him, not thinking that he hadn't got to know him very well yet even though he was his brother, or how unexpected events might unfold. Emma glanced across at them curiously before getting up to help the other two girls at the stove, leaving the three boys to sip their beer.

"When are you starting your new house, Robbie?" Nicolas asked, breaking the ice.

"I don't know. I didn't even know we were moving here."

"Really? Don't you like the idea? It's great living here; real good. When we get all this stuff done it'll be wicked." He paused, "Um, what do you do?"

"Muck around mostly, go to school, go home, and hang with Laura. It's boring really. Ah, no, she's not boring; I didn't say that, but it's the same old stuff all the time."

Sarah turned away from the stove and said, "Why don't you boys go have your shower and we'll call you when we're ready?"

Robbie glanced at Nicolas, who simply shrugged. "Ah, we share bathrooms here," he explained. "We go skinny dipping anyway, so it doesn't matter."

"Cool," Robbie replied, "doesn't worry me."

"You go in first then, and I'll go get you a clean towel. Simon can have a bath, can't you, mate?"

"No, that's all right," Robbie countered. "We've got stuff in the car that we'll need to bring up anyway. I'll go get it. You go ahead, eh?"

By time he got back Simon had poured himself a bath and Nicolas just about finished his shower, so Robbie simply came in and not thinking either stripped off his clothes waiting for Nicolas, leaning against the towel rail making conversation until he noticed Simon. Nicolas got out of the shower and made way for him, but Simon there in the bath caught his attention as well. The two older boys exchanged glances.

"Simon, don't do that," Nicolas said.

"Is he queer?" Robbie asked from the shower cubicle.

"What's that mean?"

"Homosexual. He likes boys, not girls. He was looking at me when I got undressed."

Simon went a deep red so Nicolas put his towel back and got into the bath with him, but by then he'd taken the washer to cover himself as Nicolas had done that night with Emma and Sarah.

"Do you like looking at boys?" he asked him gently.

Simon nodded, bursting into tears.

"What about Owen and Kennie? Do you look at them like that?"

He shook his head vigorously.

"Me?"

"No."

"Robbie? I mean older boys, thirteen or fourteen?"

"Yes. If they're nice looking," Simon said barely audibly.

Nicolas turned around. "Do you want him to get out of the bath, Robbie, and leave you alone?"

"No, it's all right. I know another kid like that; it doesn't matter, not to me anyway. But you better look after him though, or one day somebody's going to beat him up."

"Eric already did," Simon said miserably, "and Grant. They know."

"Is that right? Is that why you wanted to live here with us, after Mum died?"

"Yes."

"Anything else you want to say?"

"Jack's queer too. He has blokes coming around sometimes."

"Really?" Nicolas looked away, confused. "What does Eric think about that?"

"He doesn't live there much. He stays over at Sean's place, you know, Sean and Lewis. Their Mum's really strange, and their Dad works up north somewhere. They never see him anyway so Eric just sort of lives there."

"What? Hell, I didn't know. I don't know anything about all that. So Jack's by himself in that big house, Mum's house, is that what you said?"

"Nicolas," Simon burst out, choking back his tears. "You're so bloody dumb. You never see anything that happens, but that's why you're good too. I don't know. You'll hate me now you've found out. I don't want you to hate me, I love you. If it wasn't for you I don't know where I'd be, maybe dead."

"Don't say that. Don't think like that. You never did anything to hurt me, and I loved it when you came out here."

By then Robbie had finished showering and was drying his body. He stopped suddenly with the towel up to show himself, looking Simon directly in the eye making him blush. He smiled, reaching down to scruff his hair saying, "Bad luck, you can't have me anyway. I'm with Laura."

Nicolas looked up at him. "Don't speak too quickly. I was with Emma, but Sarah jumped in the bath too. She did, just like that, and that was it."

"Maybe I'm bi then," Robbie chuckled, thrusting his hips forward.

"What's bi? What does that mean?"

"Both ways."

"What?"

"Shit you are dumb. But I'm not, Simon, so still bad luck."

"Dinner's ready," Sarah poked her head in the door, and smiled at catching Robbie there in that pose. He flicked the towel at her and with a sharp squeal she ducked out again.

By time they'd donned their pyjamas and were back in the kitchen the girls were giggling among themselves, and looked up as they came in.

"What?" Robbie looked deadpan innocent.

"What are you up to?" Laura demanded to know, glancing briefly at Simon and Nicolas.

"Nothing. Simon's queer, that's all. Or thinks he might be."

Emma turned to gaze intently at him, nodding quietly to herself.

Nicolas picked her up. "What do you know, Em?"

"What do I know? Shit you're dumb, Nicolas."

"What's that supposed to mean?"

"Half the flamin' family's homosexual, you idiot. Jack is, and Uncle Edward, and so's his cousin Arthur. Granddad's younger brother Ben was a bit queer too, but he died. In the old days the family was sort of quaint, that's the way they used to talk about it."

"Is that why you were worried about me?"

"Well, we did wonder, at first, but turns out you're something else entirely," she gave Sarah a nudge.

Nicolas gazed about the room, studying their faces, before sitting at the table to toy with the napkin. "Maybe nobody will want to come here, if we let it out. Maybe it'll cause trouble for us."

"No more than usual," Emma replied. "Who do you think all Wally's friends are, and Karl and Marcus? What do you think's going on here?"

He looked down at the table, studying the pattern on the cloth before looking up finally. "I really don't have a clue," he said simply. "I haven't got any idea what people think, or what they like or don't like, or anything."

He looked up. "Why did Jack and Mum get married then? What was that about?"

Emma just looked blankly at him, so he turned to Simon. "You all right, mate?"

Simon nodded, and then leaned in close to whisper in his ear, wanting to know if he could sleep with him tonight instead of going back to sleep in the big house; maybe move in with him.

"Sure you can," he answered as quietly, "just do it, but. Don't tell anybody, all right?"

Then more loudly he turned to the others and said, "Well, now that we know everybody's grubby little secret we might as well celebrate. How much beer did Karl leave us?"

"Bloody fridge is half full," Sarah said, "as usual."

That was the first night Nicolas became really very drunk. He woke next morning with a blinding headache, dimly remembering Simon tipping beer down the sink and taking him by the hand, but not much else. He was in bed with him, with Robbie tangled in blankets on the floor. He staggered out to the toilet, and on the way back poked his head into the girl's room. They were far worse. Sarah threw a pillow at him and when he ducked his head spun as if his brain had sloshed from one side to the other, and he nearly collapsed on the floor. Maybe it had. He made his way gingerly back out to the toilet and vomited his heart out.

By late morning they all began to stagger out, and being another hot day ventured over to the swimming hole for a quick dip in the cold water to sober up. Shy Simon stayed close by Nicolas until the girls came around behind and grabbed him, throwing him bodily into the pool and jumping in after him. Sarah began tickling him until he cried out, and when Nicolas and Robbie leaped to the rescue there was a free for all.

When they'd had enough and clambered out exhausted onto the bank Nicolas collapsed on the grass and failed to notice Sarah taking Simon aside until he looked up to see him in her arms, laughing, trying to escape.

They fell, rolling naked and giggling away from them while everyone looked on chuckling.

"What are you doing, Sarah?" he wanted to know.

"You boys!" she cried, letting Simon go. "I know about your mother. All you need is love and fun with nice girls like us, not ugly women with hang-ups like that. Sorry, I know she was your Mum, and she's gone now, but you have to get over it. He's not queer. Simon's not queer; he's just turning twelve that's all, look!"

Simon spun away from them, embarrassed, but Sarah kept after him trying to turn him back around and prove her point.

Robbie and Nicolas ran over and grabbed him, jostling Sarah out of their way before throwing him back into the water.

"Well, that's no big deal so you'd better cool off, Sarah's my girlfriend," Nicolas called after him, but then Sarah came behind and grappling with him took him straight into the water with her. She held him under until he came up gasping, but she held onto him, relaxed now, no longer fighting but gentle and soothing with him.

"Jealous." she said.

"Yes. So what? He has to find another girlfriend."

She wrapped her arms around him, holding him close, whispering in his ear. "We'll only ever love you, Nicolas, me and Em, forever. We'll find someone for Simon, don't worry."

Nicolas glanced over to his brother just clambering up onto the grass, then caught Emma's eye watching them. He waved to her, calling her into the water and as she waded in took her hand and pulled her in close. He kissed her cheek, then rolling her closer kissed her lips and then her whole mouth and she responded to him.

"Sarah said you both love me forever, but you're the first, Em. You're my first love and that's never going to change." He turned slightly to Sarah and kissed her too, with the same passion, not allowing her any escape. "I don't love you less, but Emma's the first, all right?"

She nodded, hugging them both, but by then Robbie and Laura were back in the water breaking it up. Nicolas pushed away, swimming backward until he was clear of them and turning stepped out onto the bank. Picking up his clothes he took Simon by the hand and led the way back up the hill toward the house.

Chapter Twenty Eight

Jennie was very angry with them, and so was Karl. Nicolas still had quite a lot of money in the bank from the festival; he had nothing to spend it on so they made him pay for the beer. It was a good lesson for him anyway. That agreed, Emma took her mother aside and told her about Simon and how he'd been feeling, and about Nicolas being entirely oblivious until now, and when she'd finished called them both in. Emma was told to wait outside while Jennie spent some time with the two brothers, talking quietly with them awhile before asking Karl to come in as well.

In the event they decided that he should move into Simon's room in the big house while they made Nicolas responsible for the old place. He needed focus, and something to occupy his mind aside from working with Wally on the farm, instead of dreaming all day. He could move into Karl's bigger room with Simon and leave the sleepout for Robbie when he came to stay. They made no arrangements at all for Laura, she being with her own parents with whom they'd had no contact; taking it on faith that Liz had her under her wing.

Done with that, Ted called them all together to review his pencil sketches taking Nicolas' objections into account. He'd retained the long deep stretch of bush over on the other side as a refuge, suggesting designated walk trails to protect it further from visitors wandering about. And the long slope leading down to the swimming pool he terraced in the same manner as the other side of that same ridge forming the bowl of the amphitheatre, planting strips of native trees along the contours to protect it as well. His problem was to avoid building houses along the main road out front, but leave those paddocks for Nicolas's community gardens, including fruit and nut orchards for cash crops as the trees matured.

So, he explained, what that meant was to demolish the old house and the nearest shed, and build two housing clusters here on this side of the property. The big shed could be converted into a studio with two smaller classrooms at one end, with the actual performing stage still presenting to the amphitheatre at the end of the building. If we are going to build a studio, he said, we can include a music and dance school.

"What about the other shed?" Nicolas wanted to know.

"Just leave it as a shed. We still need a shed for our farming operations, and I guess you'll still want to be growing your spuds and vegetables there at that end, where the ground is wet."

Robbie had been watching and listening intently. He leaned over and taking a blank sheet of paper started laying out house plans, different from his father's and arranged in two rows along the contour, facing each other instead of clustered in groups but using the same service grid. He fit two more houses in that way, without changing the overall footprint or distance between them, but adding a greater sense of space and privacy.

Nicolas leaned against him, watching closely, until finally he murmured almost in his ear, "Hey, you're pretty good."

"You're pretty good yourself," Robbie said, smiling. "It'll work, eh?"

They both looked up at Ted and nodded in unison. He took Robbie's drawing and started packing up.

"You're not going, are you?"

"Yep, sorry, we have to be getting back."

"No, they can stay another night can't they, Robbie and Laura? They can go back with Liz tomorrow. It'll still only be Sunday. They don't have to be anywhere."

Ted glanced across at his wife but she only shrugged, ignoring him, intrigued by the way the boys had bonded.

Marcus suggested he could bring them back in the morning if Ted really wanted to leave tonight. He wasn't planning to go until Monday, but tomorrow was no big deal. He winked at Nicolas who turned away slightly; a shy smile brightening his face, and then without replying went to the big fridge and took out some parcels of meat before taking a basket and filling it with vegetables and fresh bread.

Nicolas smiled again at Marcus on the way out, and grabbing Robbie by the arm gave him the basket to carry and shoved him toward the door. He then took Simon by the hand and led him out as well, with a last glance back at the girls to get their sweet little pussies into gear.

"We might need a bit of that hair of that dog," he called back finally, "all right? Not too much."

But he was gone before anyone had a chance to rebuke him.

Karl rose to follow. He was definitely not moving out just yet, but then suggested maybe they all bring their instruments across later and make a night of it, in the old house, at which Ted and Liz gave up and decided to stay as well.

That night as it turned out was one of the best Nicolas had experienced in his life, for the first time feeling really at home; the effect of the previous night's hangover dulling his mind and its unending adventures, and Simon staying so close and trusting making him feel really very good about himself. On occasion he glanced across at Emma, and Sarah sitting there with her; the two of them together, and he marveled at them. Finally Robbie when came over and asked him if he'd like a game of rummy he said he would if he taught him how to play, but when the girls saw them rise from the table they came and joined in as well.

Wally kept the music going. It was truly amazing the energy he had, taking a break to bring them over a fresh bottle of beer every now and then, advising them to drink slowly and enjoy it, and eat something, not like last night, eh? No good mate, wiping yerself out like that.

But then about midnight Simon crashed so he picked him up and tucked him into bed. He was almost going back to the party, but then decided to crash himself and when Emma came in to see where he'd got to she saw them both there in the bed completely dead to the world. She called Sarah over to look, and smiling turned out the light.

Chapter Twenty Nine

About ten days later Graeme Little was out again with his new surveying brief. Karl sent them all out to work with him after deciding it was a good exercise for the class, and Nicolas once he'd studied Ted's revised plans nodded in agreement. The new survey was a lot more difficult than the original because landform on this side of the farm denied them clear lines of sight. As he thought about it he realized what Ted had been trying to avoid, but at the same he time thought he and Robbie were right. It would be interesting.

He studied and studied the drawings, his mind racing ahead until Graeme came up and asked him what the matter was. He looked up.

"Is that another boundary marker peg there," he wanted to know, pointing at a spot on the drawing where the back fence turned back at an angle toward the house, then to the next, "the same as that bottom peg near the road, and that one there too?"

"Yes, you're right. Why do you want to know that?"

"Well, if we work up from here, every little mistake will have to be fixed won't it, before we're too far out on that side. I mean, if this is right, and that's right, and that's right, we can work back and make the adjustment as we go along."

"Ha!" Graeme slapped him on the shoulder. "You're a smart boy. Yes, we'll triangulate back once we get our line of sight, and we'll be right. Don't worry about it. If you want to, when we get there you can take Sarah with you across the gully, and we'll check both pegs. Let's see how far out we are, eh?"

Nicolas grinned, eyes bright, and gearing himself up with his axe and kit bag got Simon set up as well, with the heavier axe since while he was much younger his growing body was solid with good muscle belying his age, while Sarah got herself ready.

The work sped by as they learned quickly to interpret Graeme's little hand signals. After only the first half hour on the job Nicolas sent Sarah striding across by herself to work the second housing alignment along the next contour, while Graeme and Emma at the theodolite kept pace with them both.

It was while they were up there on the slope running down into the gully through which the stream flowed finally into the swimming pool, that Nicolas decided here was the place for their own house. The view across the farm was breathtaking, and he could keep an eye from this height on everything that happened. They could cut native timber up here for the stumps and bearers, and if need be fall some of the taller trees in the bush over the other side and have them milled for the house frame and roofing timbers. He became distracted by the idea, head to head with Simon talking about his plans and building another room for him along the back veranda, when Sarah called across telling them to pay attention.

Simon looked over at her curiously. He turned back to Nicolas and said quietly, "She thinks I'm being brainwashed. She wants to "un-brainwash" me; that's what she said."

He reddened, embarrassed, giggling slightly before glancing back up again.

Nicolas studied him a moment, then looked back at Sarah standing there with the pole in her hand, head cocked to one side and a slight Mona Lisa smile on her face. She flicked an eyebrow at him. He leaned over to Simon and shoved him gently by the shoulder toward her before waving back up the slope to Graeme that he was ready.

Once he was free they got the job finished by lunchtime, Sarah and Simon distracting one another and slowing down because of it. He went across and finished their line for them, and with Graeme checked their work against the two boundary pegs along the back fence. They were out on one line by less than four inches, and on the other by two, so once Emma made the corrections in her field book they packed up and walked back down to the house.

Graeme didn't stop for lunch but drove straight back into town, although by then Sarah and Simon had disappeared, probably down to the swimming pool after the dirty work in the bush, leaving him and Emma at loose ends. Back at the old house they went in to shower together, Nicolas talking quietly with her about Simon, and what Sarah had said. She held her fingers up to his lips, and kissed him, and when they finished showering took a towel and dried him before turning around while he dried her back and legs. She wrapped her long wet hair up in the towel while they went to their rooms to dress. Karl was in the kitchen and looked up as they passed naked through the house, but they simply held his gaze at they went by.

When Simon came in later he was smiling broadly, though Sarah was nowhere to be seen. He went and showered, then came in to lie on the bed in his underpants while Nicolas sat at his desk reading. Finally he put his book down and started to say something, but Simon had dozed off so he sat on the bed next to him, shaking him gently awake.

"Simon," he said, "if Jack's living by himself in Mum's house and we're not getting rent, maybe we should just sell it and split the money up, between the four of us I mean. Then you and I can use our share to build a new house up here."

Simon simply nodded, half dreamily.

"Do you want to sleep with Emma tonight," he said rather, "and let me sleep with Sarah?"

Nicolas sighed. "Is she being good to you?"

Simon nodded again, eyes distant, and then looked directly at his brother.

"You're not jealous, are you?"

"Me? No. I've never seen you happy like this, so of course I don't mind. You look like you won the lottery. It's a lot better than you wanting to sleep with me because you're so scared all the time. You snore like Wally, and talk to yourself like he does, keeping me awake." He paused, thoughtfully, "Just make sure you don't get arrested, that's all."

"You won't say anything to anybody, will you?"

"Not me, no, I don't care really. It's not that important. I don't know why everyone gets so twisted about it; rooting girls. It's nice, but it's not everything." He paused, watching Simon's face. "I didn't think you were queer either, I never thought that, so I think Sarah's right. She helped me a lot too you know, to come out of myself, and Emma's good. Yeah, sure, all right. You go and tell Em."

Simon rose from the bed, but Nicolas grabbed his arm holding him back. "But what I still want to know is what about Mum's house?"

"Yeah, sell it. Grant's not here anymore and Eric doesn't give a stuff about anything. If he gets any money he'll only spend it, or Sean and those other kids will spend it for him. Or Mrs. O'Reilly will. Jack can go back and live with Nanna, if he doesn't want to come out here with us."

"What if we ask Wally to look after the money, or his lawyer maybe?"

Simon nodded, "Yeah, that's all right. I don't care, Nicolas." With that he broke away and pulling on his shorts and t-shirt went looking for Sarah, adjusting his crotch on the way out.

They did nothing about the house that week, and on Friday afternoon Robbie arrived for the long weekend with Laura. Liz drove them out intending to spend her own weekend with Jennie, leaving them to their own devices. When they discovered Simon sleeping in the same room with Sarah and Emma in with Nicolas, Laura promptly stowed her bag in the sleepout with Robbie. Nothing else was said beyond the boys sharing the bathroom when it was their turn.

Later when Nicolas asked Emma what was happening with Jennie; why she and Liz were spending so much time together, she explained she was pregnant again. They thought maybe she had another set of twins. He shrugged, scratching his head.

Chapter Thirty

Marcus arrived on Saturday with a letter for Nicolas. It was from Mensa, telling him he'd qualified for membership. When Liz found out she gazed at him with an odd expression, up and down, appraising him like an abstract painting with the comment that she'd thought as much, but he could very much better than Mensa. She used to be a member of Mensa and became quite bored with it, with their endless social events and puzzle competitions. No, he should be doing a lot more with his intelligence than simply joining Mensa, to stand around wanking with the rest of them about having a high IQ.

Nicolas was bemused by the comment. He'd thought the test was too easy and came home wondering what the fuss was about, though Liz held back from further comment until Robbie leaned over and said he was in Mensa too, but his Mum had joined Intertel and the ISPE as well. They all pricked their ears up as Liz dismissed the whole thing with that merry tinkling laugh she had, explaining that while Mensa measured in the top two percent of the population, Intertel and ISPE measured in the top two percent of Mensa. Unlike Mensa, one joined ISPE at the level of Associate and worked one's way up through the ranks by their achievements.

That would be much, much better for Nicolas, she added, though since Robbie was in Mensa anyway it wouldn't hurt for him to join also since he'd qualified. They still had quite a few members their age and a little older, and they could socialise from time to time away from the adults and their peculiarities.

They all turned to Marcus for his opinion, but he sat there quietly taking it all in, nodding to himself until finally he leaned over to ask Liz whether she could arrange for Nicolas to be tested. She replied that the test was self-administered, it was so difficult, but they could do it under supervision if they were all comfortable with the procedure, and then sent Robbie out to the car to bring in her briefcase. Nicolas found himself astonished that Liz always carted so very much with her, everywhere she went it seemed, though he didn't want to do it there and then anyway. He hadn't been thinking about it, or even Mensa, but everyone was watching and waiting on him. Frustrated with them and shaking his head, to get out of the house he called Wally and they went out for a long walk around the farm. He really wanted to get all this other stuff sorted out with his mother's house; that was the thing, so they talked about that until he had an idea in his head about what to do.

Then he stopped suddenly, staring sharply back across to their lines of survey pegs along the ridge opposite with their little iridescent flags fluttering gaily in the breeze, and ran back to the house. In the kitchen he asked Liz for a copy of the test, then taking a pencil started down the first page quickly becoming lost in it. A bit over two hours later he stopped and handed the sheets over to her, but still not quite back down to earth stood and in a daze wandered over to the old house where absently removing his shoes and socks he collapsed onto the bed.

Emma came in a little later to see how he was, Sarah on her heels and Simon right behind her, but he was sound asleep so they left him there. It was dark when Robbie came in to find him sitting reading, and making him put his book down dragged him out into the kitchen and poured him a cold beer from the fridge. It was good for him, he said, made his brain slow down allowing him to relax; that's what Liz said anyway, but after a glass or two sitting there by themselves they went back to the big house where the music was already in full swing.

It wasn't until Tuesday that they got into town finally. Wally had made a late appointment for Nicolas to see Mr.. Lynch and discuss his plans, so they dropped Simon off at Jack's first and came back down the main street. The lawyer took him through all the legal documents associated with their housing project, assuring him that everything was in order and all they had to do now was wait for the system to make its slow grinding way through the approvals process, and finally get it through Council.

"How long is all that going to take?" he wanted to know.

"Maybe two or three years, if we're lucky; five if we're not."

"Five years? Hell, I'll be grown up by then!"

"Timed just about right, I'd say," the old lawyer parried; wryly, but a twinkle in his eye nonetheless.

Nicolas pulled up abruptly, unable to answer; another idea entering his head. "What chance do we have then, of getting approved, do you think? Good?"

"Well yes, excellent I'd say. The new zoning guidelines have come through and this is a model project, in my opinion. It's exemplary, everything they say they're anticipating for all those old market gardens out that way. Your emphasis on the environment, education and the arts is a stroke of genius; it centres your place within the whole complex. If they knocked it back they'd have a lot of explaining to do."

He nodded. "All right, do you think we should sell Mum's house?"

The lawyer studied his face a moment. "There is no reason to hang onto it. Land values aren't so good right now, with all these subdivisions going in and a lot of new blocks on the market. The house is a bit dated as well. Maybe you could renovate it; redo the old kitchen and perhaps knock down a wall or two to open it up a bit."

"Can we do that, Wally?"

"Yeah, fink we might manage it, eh."

Nicolas turned and nodded, indicating his business finished and the lawyer showed them out. On the street he turned to Wally smiling, but the old bloke just clapped him gently on the shoulder and said nothing, nodding quietly to himself. He drove him over to Jack's.

They wanted to stay the night and spend a bit of time with Jack, who Nicolas liked quite a lot; he'd always been good to him and had worked hard doing all the scenery for his big play, though he was more inquisitive about him than resentful now that he'd been awakened to his private life.

Jack could bring them back out tomorrow in his old ute so Wally simply dropped him off at the gate. Getting out of the truck however recalled the first time he'd given him a lift home; that first day at high school when he was in shock after being introduced to the headmaster's methods. It wasn't long ago though it seemed a lifetime, and a shiver went up his spine. He stayed there at the front gate, frozen, gazing absently down the street as Wally drove off.

As he stood there the memories came flooding back; dead baby mice; his mother yelling, and yelling and yelling, and coming around the table to belt him; Jack bringing him all the way back home from Berriwal, and Grant. Grant. He found himself unable to turn and face the house, until Simon noticed him there and came down the path to get him.

Chapter Thirty One

"Nicolas, are you all right?" Simon asked softly as he came close, but Nicolas stood there watching.

"Where's Jack?" he wanted to know.

"He went out somewhere, said he'd be back later and we can go out for dinner."

He was uneasy. There was something wrong. He stared up and down the street, but there was nothing remiss that he could think. The old dog three houses down barked its old slow bark at everything that moved. There was a tom cat the same as always, yowling on the shed roof straight across, and the lounge room light was on next door meaning nobody was home, they'd gone out; just to scare any burglars. He walked slowly back up the path to the house, stopping thoughtfully at the door before going inside.

"Simon, there's something the matter," he said quietly. "Jack should be home by now. Ring your Nanna and see if he's there, will you?"

Simon did as he was asked, but after only a brief exchange turned and said no, she hadn't seen him all day. He stood holding the handset, but then spoke briefly into it before hanging up.

That decided Nicolas. "Come on," he said, and taking Simon by the hand went out through the gate and along the street toward town.

Three blocks down they turned right onto the street, and headed up toward the café where they thought Jack might have taken them for dinner. There was only a small crowd there but he was nowhere to be seen. Coming out again they saw Eric across the road and called out to him but he ducked suddenly down a narrow alley between the two buildings. They crossed over and followed him, to come out into an enclosed yard behind one of the garages.

Jack was lying on the hard ground, groaning. He'd been badly beaten. Nicolas crossed the yard to kneel beside him, lifting his head into his lap.

"Don't bloody touch him, Nicolas," Eric said.

For the first time they noticed the ring of adolescents there, standing back in the shadows.

"What have you done, Eric? He's your Dad!"

"Bloody poofter, he is. Get away from him."

"I will not. Bugger you, mate, that's wrong. You can't do that."

One of the older boys shoved his way forward. "He's got to learn a lesson, doesn't he?"

"What lesson? What lesson does he have to learn? Hell!"

"What, are you a poofter too? Pretty boy, aren't you. Yeah, I remember you, from school. They kicked you out, didn't they? Think yer fuckin' shit doesn't stink, eh." He turned around to his mates, grinning. "We can have a bit if fun, eh. Whole family of bloody poofters, aren't ya."

"Not me," Eric cried. "I'm not; I'm your mate, aren't I?"

"Yeah, you're all right. Just a queer family yer got, that's all; poor silly bastard."

Nicolas started to edge back toward the alley but found his way blocked. Simon came in close, shivering, and the two stood back to back waiting to see what would happen. They didn't have to wait long because they all came in a rush, and before he knew it Nicolas was on the bottom of the heap with his arms and legs pinned. They pushed Simon off but he came back again fighting until he was shoved bodily back into a pile of oil drums. Nicolas saw him hit his head on the rim of the top drum and go down stone cold. He didn't move after that, but Nicolas was distracted by then having his belt and fly undone and his jeans pulled down. His underpants came off next, and he was lifted bodily over and onto his hands and knees.

He felt some spit or something slippery at his backside, and a hand rubbing him up and down amid guffaws and giggling. Another hand grabbed at his dick, and squeezed his cods until he gasped in pain, then a finger went in and he arched his back but at that moment he was belted on the side of the head and went down again. They lifted him back up. Now he felt something much larger being inserted and he moaned as it seemed to fill his whole body. He lost focus, and when he opened his eyes again all he could see was Simon lying there on his side beneath the drums, his cheek and neck red as blood welled from his left ear, and he tried to crawl forward reaching out to him.

By then each slow rhythmic thrust held him captive and he slipped away again, his breath coming and going with the mass of movement holding him down, rocking him back and forth, on and on, with only slight pause in between that he simply couldn't fathom, until eventually things went quiet and he fell sideways onto the concrete. He rolled slowly onto his back and looked up but all he could see was the sky. There was nothing but the sky, until he began to hear his own breath rasp in his chest and a shaking hand reaching under his head lifted it off the hard ground.

"Oh, Nicolas, I'm sorry. I'm so sorry. It had nothing to do with you. God help us."

But all he could murmur was Simon's name. He called softly to him, as if there was no use calling him out loud, when he could no longer hear anyway. He knew he was no longer there with them, but he couldn't quite put it into words until Jack cried out and began to wail in anguish.

Chapter Thirty Two

When Nicolas woke next morning he was in a white room smelling of antiseptic, in a huge bed with starched sheets surrounded by curtains and some sort of frame over his abdomen to keep the bed cover up off his body. His backside throbbed, but he was not in any pain merely disoriented.

Some of the people from the north reserve heard the noise, he found out when Sergeant Lewis came in to see him, and had wandered over to investigate. He was the only one living, lying there with his pants down around his ankles and semen leaking from his bottom. Simon was dead from some sort of wound to the side of his head and ear bleeding, and Jack had slashed his wrists and forearms with broken glass. There was blood everywhere, great gouts of it, though he wasn't told of any such detail beyond his scant recall of the scene, only that Simon and Jack were gone and he was still here.

As he lay there on the bed he fell in and out of sleep; not noticing the policeman leave, shaking his head. He couldn't tell at times whether he was making love with Emma or Sarah, or whether something else was happening behind him that he couldn't quite see, or both at once, except that every now and then his entire abdomen came alive with a great thrusting and orgasmic pain and ecstasy, and a sort of numbness between him and that part of his body that disconnected him from the experience. It was as if his lower parts were pulsing with ecstatic earthen life rhythm while his brain looked on impassively, observing from a great distance, with nothing in between.

He was woken by somebody gently shaking his shoulder and speaking to him. It was the nurse saying he had visitors, would he like to see them, and he nodded slightly. Movement at the door made him turn his head to see Sarah and Emma coming in with Jennie, with Wally quietly behind them.

Nobody said anything.

The girls simply came over and sat at the bed, their heads on the cover sobbing. They caught at something inside him and his own tears started, then Jennie starting crying as well so Wally went across to the window to look out across the river and leave them to it. Sarah started to say something, but Nicolas held his fingers to her lips not allowing any sound to emerge. They stayed like that for an hour or more until he drifted off to sleep again and they left without saying goodbye.

After that he seemed to start reconnecting. His pelvic floor subsided and later when he got up to use the toilet he had a chance to inspect his bottom in the mirror, and check the bruising on his backside, and his arms and legs, and his cods, deciding there was nothing really badly amiss. He shrugged, and calling out to the nurse told her he wanted to go home.

They wanted him to stay overnight, however, under observation, though he suspected there might be another reason that after thinking about he decided he really didn't want to know. He was all right. He wasn't worried about himself. The moment she disappeared he dressed and slipped out the back door.

Outside he went straight up along the main street to the café where he went in to see some of the boys there at the counter. The whole place fell deathly silent as he went in calmly to buy fish and chips with a chocolate milkshake, and sat by himself at one of the tables with his meal. He was hungry since he hadn't eaten since yesterday morning, but that was beside the point. He simply refused to allow them any leeway.

They stared sullenly while he ignored them as if nothing had happened, and when he finished stood and paying his bill went out again without a word.

He walked up to Jack's house, where apart from two broken windows at the front nothing had been touched. They hadn't the guts to come inside and cause any damage, he decided, so he rang Wally asking him to come in and pick him up.

When he arrived they packed Simon's things and his own, not needing to speak just yet, and with that job done went through Jack's belongings and packed them all carefully into two suitcases, and placed them in the truck with their own bags.

They went down the back yard to collect the eggs and feed the chooks. For the first time Nicolas looked up at Wally suggesting they come back again in the morning and catch them all. Maybe Auntie Elsie could use some of them; we can take some over to her place, but we should take some home too for ourselves he added, nodding absently.

Wally offered nothing apart from the occasional nod in reply; his old eyes watching him before flickering back over the chook yard. Finally he reached sideways and pulled Nicolas bodily into his arms, bending his head to kiss him on both cheeks, tears glistening. Nicolas had never thought of Wally as having any real emotions like that, but then at that moment it occurred to him of course he would have, he must have; his whole family were testimony to his kindness.

Wally was the turnaround in his own life.

He looked up at him, and touched his face gently to wipe the tears from his cheeks saying, "Don't worry about me, Wal. I'm all right, except I'm going to miss Simon a lot. He didn't deserve going like that, but he didn't die hopeless. He's in Heaven. He was in Heaven already. I know. Don't be unhappy, all right?"

He looked away, thinking of Sarah, and Robbie, and looked up. "But we'd better be getting home, eh, and see how everybody is."

Wally held on to him, his hand gripping his shoulder. "Good lad," he murmured softly. "Good stout lad, that's what we want, eh? Fine young colt you are, lad. I was right the first time, when Jack read yer letter out to me, the one in the newspaper. Don't give those bastards a mongrel fuckin' inch, eh," until smiling at nobody in particular Nicolas slowly extricated himself.

Chapter Thirty Three

At the front gate as they were about to get into the truck a police car pulled up. The big sergeant got out and ambled across the verge to speak with them. Nicolas turned and looked up at him in askance.

"Wally," he nodded, unsmiling, before turning to the boy. "Care to tell me what's going on, Nicolas?"

"No. There was a fight, that's all. Me and Simon thought Eric had something to do with it, and went to look."

"You're sure? I have two dead bodies on my hands that say different."

"No," Nicolas replied, standing his ground. "I got knocked over, and Simon was banged up against the drums and hit his head. I don't remember anything after that."

"What were you doing with your pants down like that?"

"What? I didn't have my pants down, did I? No I didn't. I don't remember anything like that. I got knocked out. I didn't see anything, until I woke up in hospital and you came to see me."

The policeman made him turn around. "What's that on your backside, then?"

Nicolas looked, twisting on his heels and pulling at the cloth trying to see what he meant, but then he shrugged and said maybe it's dried egg yolk or something.

The sergeant glanced away into the distance, then back again nodding quietly to himself. "I understand, Nicolas, all right. Don't worry about it. Any time you want to come in for a quiet chat I'll be at the station."

"Well, yes I will then," he looked away and back again, "if something comes up. I can't think of anything, but I will if I do."

"I'm sure you will; there's a good lad. Except you talk too much. Right now you'd better come back into town and discharge yourself from the hospital. You can't just walk out like that, you know."

Nicolas glanced over at Wally and cocking his head nodded slightly.

At the hospital he went in and apologised that he'd run away, but he was all right, really, if a doctor wanted to check him. They looked at him oddly, but then he asked if he could see the nurse who'd looked after him and they called her. She came out, and he apologised, but then she took him in her arms and kissed his forehead before pushing him away, crying.

He stood there momentarily bewildered, until she turned on him. "Off you go then."

Chapter Thirty Four

Liz and Robbie were there when they got home. They'd heard some sort of news and drove straight back out, so it was a much stranger night for Nicolas than usual. He told Jennie and Liz both to leave him alone, and when Karl came up to the old house with Marcus in tow he stood and said they'd both better fuck off, loudly, before sitting hesitantly back down with his eye still on the door.

He missed Simon so terribly it filled him, absent from the table, yet once they settled all he could do was try and reconnect with where they'd been in days just past.

Between he and Emma, and Robbie and Sarah, they knocked back six bottles of beer from the fridge before Nicolas suddenly rose and stripped off his soiled jeans, with the egg yolk, and looking at it started crying. He stood, wiping his eyes with the back of his hand, not wanting to sit down. Instead he unbuttoned his dirty shirt and took it off, then pulled up his singlet and lifted it over his head, finally dropping his stained underpants.

"Plan of action. Time for truth, that's what I think."

Emma took his cue first. She stood and stripped then Robbie, and finally Sarah though Nicolas thought she'd be first being so hot. She looked him in the eye and taking her clothes off slowly walked around the table distracting them, kicking their things aside as she went.

"I'm with you Nicolas, don't think I'm not," she said. "You and Robbie are so nice. And so was Simon; such nice boys. And lovely Emma, whose body is so beautiful I'd die for it. But you boys are too; I don't care. I'm a dyke and a bike and a slut, whatever they want to call me. I had to put up with Karl for so long, looking after him all the time I was a little girl like I was his mother, after Mummy died. She hurt so bad, it was so painful for her I thought I was going to die myself, and he didn't even care. Poor Karl, everyone said, he's lost his loving wife, so sad, but not one person asked me how I felt. I never dreamed I'd end up meeting anybody like you. Now every day I dread the thought of losing you, and going back to being so lonely like that."

But she couldn't look at them after that, and turning her head away went back to the fridge and taking another bottle of beer filled their glasses. Nicolas turned and tipped them all down the sink, and taking the bottle from her emptied it too; something there in the back of his mind making him think of something Simon had done, or said.

"How old were you, Sair?" he wanted to know.

"Eight."

"Who was it, not Karl or one of his friends, anything like that, was it?"

"Oh, no, they're not like that! It was a boy. His father was a muso, played trombone and sax in Karl's band. They were always out, leaving us home alone." She stared off a little then came back catching his eye. "He was so nice, you know. When he left I missed him so much."

"How old was he, eleven or twelve, something?"

"Yes, how did you know that?"

"Simon, he said something once but I wasn't paying much attention. He reminded you of someone, didn't he?"

"Yes, Nicolas. But it wasn't what you think, not with him. I loved Simon for himself, you have to believe that. He was very very special to me, like I could repay Greg maybe by loving Simon, and thank him."

"Was that his name, Greg?"

He turned to her curiously, and taking her into his arms held her to him. "It's all right; you made Simon so happy you know. I'm really glad he died so quickly like that, and didn't hurt, if it was going to happen I mean. I hope we all go like that, someday, like, just being here one minute and gone the next."

He went to his room and lay down on the bed, leaving the door open.

Robbie came in first and sat on the chair at his desk, but then got up and lay with him, hand on his arm. Nicolas ignored him so he got out again and going back in the kitchen looked both girls in the eyes, and taking them by the hand led them back into Nicolas' room to sit on the bed gazing at him.

Nicolas was crying, face to the wall, no longer knowing from the effect of the beer or what else, as if it mattered.

When he felt the bed move he turned over and looked at Robbie. He ran his fingers lightly down his arm and took his hand, holding it up in front of his face as he traced the lines on his palm, and minutely examined each fingernail. He then slid Robbie's hand down his chest and belly and placed it over his cods, adjusting himself comfortably while he had Robbie cup him and hold him before reaching over to caress his thigh. Looking him in the eye he fondled him, fingering his tight blond pubes before moving up his belly to his navel, then his pectorals and nipples.

"God," he said finally, "it is true, you're like one of those Greek bloody statues, and you girls are Goddesses, but ordinary, like things should be, except we're on this different planet and it's all become some sort of relativity question."

They stared at him.

"And Simon got killed because of it."

"Nicolas," Emma faced him. "What? Shut up, will you."

She took his hand off Robbie's chest, and Robbie's hand off him, and started looking over his bruised legs. She spread them, holding them up while she inspected his bottom; lifting his scrotum out of the way while she worked. Nicolas leaned back on the pillow with his legs up but she pushed Robbie away finally and standing him up off the bed knelt down to check his back and legs, bending him over again to look at his backside then his buttocks and the rest of him. She touched his anus, tenderly, then went and got some lotion from the bathroom and worked it in.

He trusted her a lot more than he did Sarah, or Robbie, and let her have her way.

"Does it hurt?"

"No."

"What about when you poo?"

"I don't know yet. I didn't eat anything much yesterday, not after breakfast, when I went last. Probably a good thing, else I would have shit on them, wouldn't I?"

"What did they do to you?" Robbie wanted to know.

"You can see. They fucked me, didn't they? Up the bum, like they were dogs."

"Yeah, well, that's pretty obvious. But that's not what I meant."

He turned on them, loudly this time. "What they fucking did to me was kill Simon. If they just fucked him like they did to me then left him it wouldn't be so bad, but they just pushed him away like he was nothing and he was dead, like he wasn't even there; just something in the way. And Eric was there and didn't do a thing about it. He was the one who set it up, which is worse. And Jack didn't do a bloody thing to help either. Gutless cunt!"

He looked as if he was going to be really upset until Sarah rose from the bed, and taking him by the hand pulled him down with her, holding him close until he settled again. She got up again leaving him there and went over to the door to turn off the light. On the way back she brushed Robbie's left thigh lightly with her fingers, and Emma's right breast, and kissed them both.

"Is this bed big enough for us," she wanted to know, "or do we have to change rooms, or maybe swap houses, or something?"

"Sarah," Nicolas said, quietly, almost to himself. "You shut up too, eh? And you too, Em, sorry, I don't feel like it. Go sleep in your own bed if you want to."

He turned over on his side to face the wall again; ignoring them, until Robbie whispered that Sarah's bed was bigger anyway and went into the other room. Emma went to the kitchen and came back with another bottle of beer, with two glasses, but he ignored that too so she left them there on his desk.

Ordinarily, he thought to himself, Robbie had a really nice body, and a nice neat dick, but so had Simon. And they were both really funny about it, like it was all just one big joke, once Simon got it. He could understand that now, what other people might be thinking, and taking it far too seriously when they thought it was all so humorous. The girls were really nice too, so beautiful, maybe other people were jealous, but that was no reason for fucking someone up the bum like that. No, it's not us it's them, he decided.

He got up again and taking Emma by the hand went into the bathroom, standing her in front of the mirror.

"What do you want, Nicolas?"

"What is it about us, do you think? I mean, what's your opinion?"

"Nothing! Bloody nothing, all right! I don't have any fucking opinion." She turned on him. "I'm just not smart like you, Nicolas, nobody is."

"What?"

"I mean, anybody else in the world would've been completely traumatised, having that happening to them, but you're just analysing it. You fucking analyse every little bloody thing, you know that!" She turned away, withdrawing back into herself.

"Except for Simon," she added gently. "That hurts, doesn't it?"

He said nothing, but ran his hand up her body. In reply she ran her hand up his, gently touching his bruises as if her very caress would heal them, and he stood there with his eyes closed. She leaned in close and wiped his tears away again, though he wasn't sobbing at that moment simply letting them run.

"Well, it was quick, Em, he wouldn't have known. And he was so happy until then, like in the last few days he'd lived out his whole life. So it's not that, really. It's just that I'm going to miss him SO much; I can't begin to think yet. All right?"

She looked at him and nodded, but her tears started again and he held her, crying out loud himself now, letting it go.

Finally taking his hand she led him into her room where Robbie and Sarah on the big bed were at it as if the world was about to end. Emma tucked him into her own bed then turned off the light before lying beside him, but he was already dead asleep. He'd gone out like the light.

She sat there in the half dark from the moonlight, reaching over to stroke his bruised cheek, flicking a curly lock from his forehead, until there was a discernable quiet and from the corner of her eye she noticed Sarah and Robbie had stopped and were gazing across at her, still joined. Sarah had her legs wrapped around him, so the shape looked odd with the light behind them.

She observed them quizzically but they both smiled, like two children under the Christmas tree just opening their presents. She rose and in two steps sat beside them as she had Nicolas, leaning over to kiss Robbie's shoulder and back. She whispered softly into his ear and moving Sarah's legs aside ran her fingertips down his spine until she reached his coccyx where she began to scratch lightly with her fingernails. He gasped out loud, trembling, and started loving Sarah again; slowly and from a great depth, until she moaned deep in her throat and Emma lay down beside them.

Chapter Thirty Five

When Nicolas got his ISPE results back, the accompanying certificate declared that he'd achieved a score exceeding 99.9993 percentile and was thus eligible to become an Associate of the Society. He rang Liz to give her the news and Robbie answered the phone, saying she was at work and maybe he could ring her there. He did so.

"You're smarter than I am, Nicolas," she declared when he read out the score, "that's better than one in ten thousand." Then she asked whether he wanted to join.

"I'm not sure, really. I don't even know what ISPE means."

"It's the International Society for Philosophical Enquiry, although they call themselves The Thousand because to qualify for entry you must exceed one in a thousand."

"That means, if there's two million people here there'll be two thousand members."

"Well, potentially," she chuckled, "But not that many people are interested."

"How many are there?"

"About 15, I think, here in Australia. Globally there are a few hundred, mostly academics and business executives; professional people. They're an interesting bunch, and you never know who you might run into one day."

"All right, I'll think about it."

"Yes, think about it, but not too much. I'd better go, Nicolas, my boss is looking at me. Thanks for ringing. Congratulations."

He hung up, before calling Marcus to give him the news.

"Are you all right about it, Nicolas?" he wanted to know.

"Yeah, I'm fine. It's a bit weird but, don't you think?"

"Well, some people think it's a dangerous practice letting people know their IQ score."

"Dangerous? God, life's dangerous. How much more dangerous can it get?" He paused. "I didn't mean that, but. What I meant was it's just sort of weird."

Marcus sighed. Nicolas heard him through the handset.

"What was that about?"

"You'll be going places I can't even dream of going. You think in ways I can't even begin to imagine. I don't know if I can go anywhere near to doing justice to your question. Maybe one day you'll be a famous philosopher, and I'll be learning from you." He paused, adding; "already, Nicolas."

Undeterred Nicolas replied, "But you'll still help me, won't you?"

"Yes, sure, of course I will. You're a nice kid and I'm sorry about what's happened to you."

"I'm not, sorry I mean. Stop worrying about it. I don't want people to be sorry; it gets too much for me sometimes, when people are like that. It's boring, anyway. What I want to know is can you help me get into the university, or something?"

"Just wait, Nicolas. You'll become eligible in due course. You are far better off right now to focus on your reading. If you want something else to do in the meantime write me a couple of your wonderful plays, and we'll see about getting some theatre happening."

"Do you think we should have another festival, next year?"

There was a pause on the line, until Marcus said finally, "Look, I'll be out again on the weekend. See you then, perhaps."

"All right, see you."

He hung up and went back over to the old house. Karl glanced up from showing Owen his sums but Nicolas simply stood there in the doorway, leaning against the jamb, until finally he announced that he'd got his ISPE score back and it was, sort of, off the scale.

Sarah and Emma stared at him, then turned and started whispering to one another. Karl pulled them up saying he wanted their assignments finished by lunch. He gazed back across at Nicolas still there in the doorway, suggesting he'd better come in and sit down, or go find something useful to do; if he wanted he could help Kennie with his arithmetic.

"Can you help me get into University?" he wanted to know.

"You'll get there anyway, Nicolas. But you're not helping yourself by not doing any work right now. You should at least have something to show, so when the time comes we can do a proper assessment and place you better in what you want to be doing later. How old are you now? Fourteen?"

"A couple of months yet; end of October."

"Well, that means it will be three years at least before you get into Uni. Even then, you'll be around for another sixty years after that. There's no rush, take your time, eh?"

"Marcus said maybe I should start working on a couple of plays, but I think I'll write a book instead. Or some short stories, about kids, like us."

"Yes, all right, do that then." Karl replied dismissively. "But right now come and help me with the boys."

He went in and sat down with Kennie, who moved in close and taking his arm wrapped it around his shoulders. Nicolas smiled down at him, but then Owen got up from his desk and moving his chair across came over to sit with him as well.

Chapter Thirty Six

The sale of Margaret's house went through. Nicolas had lost interest in renovating the place but the price was good nonetheless and he really only wanted to put it behind him. The money went into a trust account on the insistence that it be split four ways, not three, because Simon had already stated what he wanted to do with his share, with the remainder of Jack's estate going entirely to Eric.

Their solicitor would not allow him to have the money and appointed Chas and Elsie as his trustees until he came of age. Grant didn't complain. Frank had already made him a silent partner in the garage until he came of age, and once he had his trade papers he'd make him foreman in the workshop.

Nicolas decided that he wanted to start building his new house. He still had a good sum in his account, quite enough to get some timber milled, but Wally wouldn't have a bar of it and had one of his mates come over and fall some trees for him, and mill them there on the spot.

They spent almost a week sawing up bearers and joists, and strapping them up there in the bush to season for a year or so, then another few days cutting floor boards which they carted down to the shed on the long trailer and stacked them along one wall before strapping them too.

Not allowed to spend his money on timber, Nicolas finally purchased a great big old slow combustion stove for his kitchen and had Wally bring it out on the back of the truck. He got a couple of pot-bellied stoves from the hardware when they were in town and brought them out as well. The broad saddle along the ridge back away from the swimming hole was exposed to the cold southerly wind in winter, but he wanted the view. He decided this time of year would be best to work out his solar passive design to maximise internal warmth and stability, leaving a broad overhung veranda for summer where they could sit and enjoy the cool breeze.

That was about as far as he was allowed, however. Once the girls got wind of his plot he was sharply rebuked, and from that point they refused him any say whatsoever on the internal layout. He wasn't at all unhappy with their design; it was a big house and made a lot of sense, except when Robbie Ashcroft came out again with his parents, bringing Laura with him this time, he made them take their plans over to show him, and accept his advice. Robbie showed them to his father, who nodded quietly to himself before reaching over to place a big tick in the top corner, and promptly went back to his own work on the final plans for the property.

That was all there was to it.

The weekends they spent labouring up there, pegging the site out with a long tape, and soon began digging post holes and excavating back into the ridge slightly where the kitchen stove was going to be. They wanted a long brick wall there with a cement floor taking into account all the wet areas, with the big double bathroom on one side and laundry on the other, with a big toilet at the back with a bookshelf along the wall.

A walk-in pantry went between the laundry and kitchen, behind the alcove where the big stove was to sit. Emma insisted they leave enough space for drying racks in there, and water pipes and a whole lot of useful hooks and gadgets, before they went any further. Wally came to the rescue with a few of his brickie mates once the slab was down, who built a nice chimney for them over the alcove, precisely the way Emma wanted it. When she saw it she sat and wept.

Next week when they were in town she took Sarah with her to choose tiles, and when they arrived they went up there every afternoon after school and worked until almost dark tiling the alcove and the length of brick wall within the kitchen, leaving the bathroom and laundry until the rest of the house was built. All she said when Nicolas asked her, was that they needed to cart the big stove up and set it in properly place before the walls went up, else they'd have to demolish a whole section to get it in.

Chas arrived back a week later with another mob of cattle and horses, planning to stay longer this time, at least until the end of summer or later if necessary. He spoke of giving up droving and transporting cattle once the babies were born, and stay here farming. He and Wally spent quite a few days with their heads together, occasionally inviting Nicolas in on their plans.

They decided to go ahead anyway with purchasing the new farm, a little way further out beyond Council's plans for rezoning where they thought they'd be safe from speculators, but still not too far to have to travel in and out every day. Jennie wanted to stay there in the big house where she'd grown up, and Chas didn't complain. That would be a good base for their operations anyway, and they could put a farm manager on the new place if need be, or simply rent the house.

"Tell you what, Nicolas," he turned and said one day, "what about we do a swap for all that nice timber you've already cut, and I'll shout you the building costs for your new house. We can take it off the farm account. That way you'll be able to move in by Christmas and we can get someone in with Karl. In the meantime he can go back into the old house.

"Well, we're not even supposed to be building yet."

"Ah, you'll be right. They can't see you from the road, and what they don't bloody know won't hurt them. Better this way. When the new bubs arrive we're going to need the room."

"Yes, all right, good," he beamed after a long thoughtful pause, and ran back down to the old house to tell the girls.

Chas watched him run off before shaking his head, and turned to Wally, "What's he going to do about those hooligans in town, do you reckon?"

"Nuffin'. Leave 'im alone, eh? 'E did the best thing anyone coulda done, and that took a heck of a lot of guts, for a young fella, more than they've got among the lot of 'em. They'll get what for, in their own time. Evwyone knows who they are. We'll just wait a bit, eh."

The other nodded before striding off a few paces to look across the farm at the lovely tiled wall with the huge combustion stove right in the middle, standing out on the ridge opposite. "Emma did a lovely job on that wall, eh?" he said finally. "Thought I might help 'em with it, least I could do. Just don't tell them, Dad, all right."

He turned back to face the old man. "I have a couple of nice stock horses for them as well, sort of wedding present," he winked. "We'll send those rough brumbies they've been riding to the knackers, and teach them to ride properly. If that lad isn't doing too well at school he can come work for me on the farm."

"Yeah, that'll do 'im the world of good. Good worker, you know. 'E's never let me down once. You listen to 'im, Chas. Fuckin' good brain 'e's got, picks things up real quick, so teach 'im everything you can, eh? Best time to learn, while they're young and fresh like that."

Chapter Thirty Seven

A few days later Nicolas was working at the side of the shed helping Wally plant trees, when Jennie called from the house saying there was a phone call for him. He dropped his shovel and went across. It was Robbie. He was in town and wanted Wally or Chas to come in and pick him up.

"What are you doing there?" Nicolas wanted to know.

"I had a big bust up with Laura. She thinks I've become degenerate, and she's ashamed about what happened to you, and then Ted started on me too so I pissed off. I told Mum. I rang her at work and told her, so there's no problem, not really. She said I'm better off with you anyway, than moping around home by myself."

"All right, yeah, OK. Wait at the Post Office and we'll come and get you."

He hung up thoughtfully, then walking across to the old house went in and taking the girls by the hand, without a sideways glance at Karl took them out to the fig tree.

"Robbie ran away," he said quietly. "He wants Wally to go into town and pick him up."

The girls looked at one another. "Why are you telling us? Why didn't you just go and get him?" Emma wanted to know, frowning.

Nicolas looked away, across to the new house going up. "Well, you remember once you said to me there's going to be more than you two, but I thought then you meant more girls, like me with more wives. But I wasn't thinking about Robbie, I didn't even know him then."

Sarah glanced up at him, incredulous. "You want Robbie to be another wife?"

"What? No, get off it. I meant another husband, for you. I haven't got the hots for him, not at all, we just sort of click. When you're not around we don't think about sex, he's more like Groucho Marx when you get him going, not Sabrina; not to me, anyway."

"But you were touching him," Emma replied, "and he was touching you."

"Not like that. We weren't randy. You were there." He looked away, thinking, trying to put his words in order. "I just sort of needed to connect you know, after what happened; get back to normal. You taught me that, except he's a boy like me and I wanted to be, sort of, I don't know, relaxed about it. Boys are never allowed to be happy having a dick, like it's some sort of weapon, or a deformity or something, but I don't need approval. I like my body the way it is, why shouldn't I? I bet he loves his too, that's why we click. Me and him, and Simon."

He looked away, off into the distance, shaking the spectre off.

"But you made him randy, Sarah, not me. He spent the night fucking with you and Em, not me. I didn't mind, I was glad for him. He was really very happy, you know, he told me. I bet Laura never loved him like you did, so that's why I wasn't surprised when he rang just now. But I thought I'd better ask you first, before we went into town."

"Anyway," he added seriously, "girls don't own boy's bodies. You'd better get that out of your head as well. We can touch one another if we want."

"How do you think we're going to live together then, the way things are?"

"Good. It'll be good. It'll work, like a group marriage. I was reading about it. Some people do that, you know, and it looked really interesting. We all know each other. We've got nothing to hide from one another, and maybe that's the answer for us. The house is going to be huge, anyway, by time we finish building it, so long as we don't have any children, not yet. You'll have to talk to him about that too, won't you?"

Chas drove past in the truck just then, and noticing them there pulled over. Nicolas held his hand up, and walking across asked him if he could go and pick up Robbie, he was at the Post Office waiting for him. Chas glanced across at Wally who seemed to be reading their minds, but he just nodded in his wise old way and went on with his tree planting.

Nicolas turned back to Chas. "You go in by yourself, please. Is that all right? He ran away, and maybe you can talk to him a bit on the way out, and see what's going on."

He needn't have bothered. Robbie was smart, when he saw Chas in the truck by himself, and when asked simply told him he was bored with school, and lonely at home with nothing to do, but it was all right with Liz she'd be coming out on the weekend with his things, and they could talk about it then.

"Can you ride?" Chas wanted to know.

"Of course I can, better than Nicolas. My uncle Alex has a farm down in the south-west he's converting into a vineyard, and we used to spend our holidays there. That's where Dad made all his money as an architect."

"Don't do drugs; do you, any of that shit?"

"What? No I don't. Do I look like I do drugs?"

"All right, don't panic," Chas retorted. "I don't have any trouble with you kids; good luck to you, I say. You can be doing a hell of a lot worse than you are right now. Just wanted to know what sort of worker you are; whether you can handle a farm. I'll give you a job if you want it, you and Nicolas, once we get the new place sorted out."

Robbie turned at that, astonished, and started to protest, but Chas simply reached over and tousled his blond curly hair before shoving at him, not ungently. "Just don't go getting my daughter pregnant, or Sarah, not for a good while yet, eh? Or there'll be hell to pay."

He turned sharply to him, unsmiling. "You get my drift?"

"Yes, sir."

Nothing else was said all the way, and by the time they arrived Robbie was subdued. He got out of the truck and politely thanking Chas for the lift went across to the old house and knocked on the door.

Nicolas rose from his seat next to Kennie and went over to let him in.

"Looks like you've got another pupil, Karl," he said. "We'll have to get that new classroom built, won't we?"

"Um, I'm not starting school here," Robbie interrupted. "We're going to work for Chas, on the farm."

He turned to Karl. "I'm already fourteen, so you can't stop me, and Nicolas will be soon so it won't matter that much, will it?"

"Well yes it will," Karl replied, disconsolate, frustrated. "Don't push it, all right? If you're any good at science or maths, anything, you can help me here for a while, at least until Chas gets organised. Then we'll see about the new school and the farm."

He turned on them. "Get people onside, boys; do yourselves a favour, that's leadership. If you keep it up, the way you're going you'll have the world against you instead of working for you. Do you hear me?"

He sat wearily at his desk thinking, before chin in hand he finally glanced across to the two littlies. "You two boys can have an early mark. I want to have a talk to the big kids, is that all right?"

"They can stay if they want," Nicolas butted in.

Karl rose and walking gently across tidied the two desks, helping the boys put away their pencils and placing their books back on the shelves. He then took them both by the hand and showed them the door. "Tell Mummy I'll be over later, will you?"

Kennie nodded, and taking hold of Owen hopped down the steps and ran over to the house. Karl stood there seeing them off before gazing around the farm collecting his thoughts. Back inside he sat at his desk again. He looked up at Sarah, holding her gaze.

"Sarah, I'm sorry I haven't been such a good Dad. I only ever wanted to be a musician, and live a beautiful life, so I thought. My family had no money and turned to teaching so I'd have a steady income, so don't tell me what it is to be hurt, or going without. Maybe we grown-ups have trouble getting over what happened to us, we forget that every new child is a new start, that we hadn't dreamed about."

He turned to Nicolas. "You've taught me a lot about that," he said quietly. "I'm not saying anything about you, all right, I know what happened, better than you perhaps realise. So long as you don't think we don't care. We care deeply, but you have to let us into your life."

"But we'll get into trouble," Sarah began. He held his hand up not to be interrupted.

He sat back in his chair, and sighed. "If you were going to get into trouble, believe me you'd already be in such deep trouble you'd probably be institutionalised by now. But you're not in trouble, are you? We've been protecting you, only because we believe in you, do you understand that?"

They sat, dumbfounded.

"Are you going to get off the drugs, and the grog?" Nicolas wanted to know.

Karl glanced away, eyes down, then looked up steadily. "Probably not, I'll admit."

"All right, then let us get on with what we're doing."

He turned to Sarah. "We won't get into trouble. They just make you think that, so then they can say they're looking after you. I worked that out already. Sorry Karl, but anyway, thanks, I heard what you said. Don't feel bad, eh?"

He turned and left, and the girls rose to follow him with Robbie coming along behind, heading for the bush reserve up on top of the ridge.

After a moment he caught up. "Hey," he said hurriedly, "I found out something. You know that bloke Gronault who's a big-shot with all those dead shits in town, he wasn't a commando, it's all bullshit. He was an armourer, officially, but it's only a fancy title for a storeman. He's not a gunsmith, he doesn't make guns or rifles, like old Angus Nixon did, he just used to clean them and check them out when the soldiers needed them. If he needed any gun parts he just bought them in, he didn't make them. I know, he failed the commando course because he had no idea of teamwork and nobody could trust him to back them up, so they never sent him out anywhere to fight. They used to call him Crow, that was his nickname in the regiment."

They all stopped, listening carefully.

"How did you find that out?"

"Ted's got a big client who owns a string of those estate agencies down south. He was over for dinner last weekend and I heard them talking about him, about his famous war record, but none of it's true. That's why he's selling insurance on commission, instead of being a manager; sells a lot of it apparently, got a real gab for putting fear in people and making lots of money out of them."

Nicolas gazed off into the distance, then shrugged and continued his walk.

Chapter Thirty Eight

"Wally", he asked quietly one day while they were weeding the spuds, "can you show me how you make home brew; that good beer you drink?"

"Ah, yer not gettin' on the grog are yer, young fella your age?"

"What? No. What I mean is it's a hell of a lot better than that bought stuff, and I thought why would that be? I was looking at the worms and the way they work the soil, around the spuds. I thought maybe there must be some little animal, or something that does the same sort of job, when you make bread, or beer; things like that. Like something was making the soil, that's all, like it doesn't just happen by itself; something does it."

Wally stood up, easing his back. "What made you say that, lad?"

He looked away, then bent down to pick up a handful and held it up to his nose. He passed it across, holding it up in front of Wally's face, inviting him. "Smell it. The way it smells. Isn't that something?"

"Like pussy, ain't it?" the old bloke chuckled. "Yeast, eh? Pussy's got yeast in it. Best little friend we've got, eh?" He looked up. "Not the bad stuff, not that; keep 'em fed and happy, son and you'll be right. Nature takes its own course. Only don't let 'em get run down, or worrying about anything, and keep the good tucker up to 'em, that's your job."

The old bloke came over, looking him in the eye. "And when you do it right their titty milk's so sweet, eh, good strong sweet stuff. Look at their babies, you'll see, growin' like Topsy."

Nicolas stood, surprising himself. "Not their babies, Wally, ours; they're our babies. They don't own them. And I have to keep my sperm good to make babies like that don't I; my nuts right, and my body, and my brain, not just bits? I have to have a good heart too. It doesn't all start or end with fucking, or drugs or grog or any sort of shit, or wars; else we're dogs with no history or philosophy, or art or any sort of lovely thing. I mean, that's necessary maybe but it doesn't have to be ugly, or functional; it can be beautiful can't it?"

Wally put down his shovel, looking as if he was going to say something, but then he bent over to pick it up again and walked across to put it in the shed. He called Nicolas up and watched him place his tools back neatly before turning to walk away. He put his arm around his shoulders as they walked off, without saying anything until they were up through the bush on top of the high ridge right across from Emma's tiled wall, there with that great big stove in the middle, in its alcove with the tarpaulin to keep it out of the weather until the roof went on.

He sat back on a log, patting the place beside him, and Nicolas sat down.

"What do ya want to do wiv the new farm?"

"What? The farm? I don't know. Maybe you should ask Chas, don't you think?"

Wally glanced down, momentarily, then back across the valley.

"No, it's for you. We weren't gonna tell yer for a bit, but what the heck. What do ya fink yerself? What else would we be doin'? All this is for you, and yours. Now it is any rate."

"What do you mean?"

"I left it to ya, eh? Didn't I. Changed me fuckin' will. Told 'em all what I fought; bunch a fuckers. Cunts they are. Nah, Chas is good, and so's Jen, and Em's me childhood sweetheart. Glad it's you, son. They'll be right. Anyway," he looked at him finally, "yer didn't answer me question."

Nicolas sat dazed, no longer listening; finding himself watching the birds flitting from tree to tree, and the ants scurrying, and his mind wandering. He knew then why the old bloke had been such a good farmer all his life. He was in love with the earth itself; like it was a beautiful woman he made love to every single day. He stood finally, and touching Wally lightly on the shoulder walked off down the slope. He knew the old bloke was smiling after him and didn't need to turn back to him and check.

Down past the sheds he went across to the old house and in the back door through the conservatory, into the kitchen. Chas and Jennie were at the table, with the two boys having their lunch. They looked up as he came in.

He paused for breath before glancing across. "You'll have to teach me an awful lot, Chas. I'm not sure if I'm ready for all this just yet," he said shyly, almost to himself.

"You'll be right, son," Chas said. "Wally told you, did he?"

He looked at Jennie and she cocked her head.

"We'll come up and see you tomorrow, maybe after lunch, all right?"

Nicolas nodded and left. Up past the fig tree toward the old house he stopped to watch Wally go back into the shed; about his own business without looking up, though he must have watched him striding back out through the conservatory from talking to Jennie and Chas.

Robbie caught his mood too; when he arrived finally back at the old house. He looked him in the eye.

"Nothing, it's all right," Nicolas said.

He looked down at himself. He was filthy, with dirt under his fingernails. He went out to the laundry and left his boots and soiled clothing there before returning through the house to his room, and taking a towel crossed to the bathroom leaving the door open. He stood filling the big tub until Emma came in and leaned against the door jamb.

He looked up. "Shut the door, Em, and have a bath with me; just you and me, eh? I want to talk to you a bit."

"No, Nicolas."

"Why not?"

"You forgot your promise, so quick."

"What?"

"We're all married now, you said so. If you want to say anything to me you can say it to Robbie and Sarah too."

"I didn't know about Wally then, and what he'd been doing, without telling me."

She spun around and slammed the door on him. He stood there, stunned, and suddenly the door flew open again. She reached in and took his hand, but he held her to him for a moment until she settled and they went out together.

"Sorry everyone," he said, "but we've just inherited the whole place, everything, the new farm as well. Wally told me, and Chas. Chas is still going to be the boss, 'til we come of age, but it looks like it's up to us now."

He paused, looking from one to the other and back again. "Can we do it, do you think?"

They all stared at him, speechless, and he glanced away, nodding to himself.

"Yes, all right," he murmured, "dumb question. Sorry. Um, what we'll do first is get rid of Karl's beer out of the fridge. We're not drinking that any more. Wally's going to show us how to make the real stuff. Then we'd better get started on the house, properly, and get that under way so we can move in fairly quickly. Anything else?"

Sarah gazed about her before glancing petulantly at Nicolas. "Yes, I agree with Emma. You said we're all married, but that house has got a main bedroom and a second bedroom. What's that all about?"

"What are you saying? I don't know anything about that, you designed it. Do what you want."

"She wants to leave that wall out and make, like, one big dormitory, but with two double beds, or four single beds, or whatever," Robbie said quietly. "Then we can sleep where we want."

Nicolas looked at them, and felt himself stir at the thought, forgetting he was standing there ready for his bath until Sarah smiled and nodded.

"Ah, you agree then," she giggled. "You can't fool us."

He looked at her. "Well, maybe it's your turn for a bath then. Maybe we can build one big bath up there as well, with one of those saunas or something. Do it properly, why not?"

He stepped over to her and taking her hand stood her up facing him. Unbuttoning her dress he stripped her leaving her things there on the floor, and without looking back led her into the bathroom.

Robbie watched them go past. Turning to Emma he stood and stripped too, then went into the bathroom and stepped into the middle of the bath. He sat straight down, smiling, without saying anything.

Emma wasn't watching, but nodding to herself turned away muttering, "Plan of action."

She wasn't going to put up with any bullshit. "Fuck off, Robbie," she said, reaching down and pulling him up out of the bathwater, and with one deft movement shoved him back behind Sarah and made him sit there. She stood back; hands on hips, looking down at them, then slowly started to dance and as she did so began to remove her clothing. She undressed slowly, thoughtfully, not looking at them but glancing occasionally into the mirror, until fully naked she stepped into the bath, between Sarah and Nicolas, and in the same movement reached behind her to take Robbie's hand and draw him in close.

"Sorry, there's not enough room," she said. "I don't mean to be awkward. Maybe we do need a big bath; if this is the way we're going to have our board meetings."

Robbie looked at her over Sarah's shoulder. He stood and stepping over them all turned and sat behind Nicolas. "Better turn the tap off first," he said. "Cut back on spending."

Nobody challenged him. He nodded, turning Nicolas around to face him as well, taking his place.

He looked him directly in the eye ignoring the girls, and reached down slowly to caress his belly and cup his cods, holding them in his hand as they had before, connecting; making sure he had his full attention. "You're the brains, don't argue with me Nicolas."

Then with his other hand he leaned forward slightly, running his hand up Sarah's silken thigh, fingering her, "And you're the balls, Sarah," he chuckled. "I mean, you make things happen, wake people up. I don't think you're a slut, or a bike; you're beautiful. You have the nicest pussy. What you do with it is amazing, what you do for us, and you've got more balls than any of us."

But then he simply caressed Emma's cheek before running his hand down her slim neck to her breast, gently thumbing her nipple. "Emma, you're the magic, you're our Fairy Princess. Without you none of this would have happened; Wally and you."

Nicolas looked up, across Sarah's bare shoulder, smiling. "He said you're his childhood sweetheart."

She looked at them, earnestly, one after the other. "Poppy never doubted you, that's all. He knows things."

They looked at one another before turning back at her in recognition.

Nicolas half turned again and shoved at Robbie with his elbow. "All right, so what are you then?"

"I'm the Chairman."

"What does the chairman do?"

"I'm the facilitator, keeping you lot in some sort of direction. I'm the director, right?"

Chapter Thirty Nine

As they walked around the house pad facing away from the back wall and kitchen alcove the faults in the original diagram became obvious, now that the bedroom dividing wall was no longer required and there was going to be a large collective sleeping space, not bedrooms. It had lost its sense of balance, and synchrony.

"If we're going to do things that way," Robbie explained, "here in the middle we have our living area, but we also need our work spaces as well."

"I don't need anything." Nicolas said.

"No, your office is central. Everything swings around that."

"No it bloody doesn't. I'm not anybody in particular, just another dead shit. We're a team, aren't we?"

Sarah took his hand trying to hold his attention, but he stepped out onto the southern edge of the big concrete slab looking over the swimming hole and the bush beyond. He gazed about, and exasperated stepped off and walked down the slope a little before turning back up to face them.

"We can excavate here, can't we?" he said pointing straight forward. "I can work here if you want, if that's what you need. The children can play here too; we can make space for them here, and if you build a deck out over here," he looked up waving his arms, "you can have your studio over there, on that side; you and Sair, Robbie."

"Why, Nicolas? Why do you want to do it like that?"

"Because, I don't know; I don't even know why you want walls up there at all. Why not just leave it open, with pillars and buttresses holding the roof up like a big sort of medieval hall; sideways not lengthways, then anyone can live the way they want. And I can just do things; we all can, really."

He turned away. "Maybe we can build a shed for me over there next to your studio; let me have my space."

"The thermal mass won't work like that, Nicolas."

"Yes it will. Bullshit. Your roof's wrong, and the overhangs. I know, I read about it. If you adjust your winter angles for a passive exposure, at this latitude you'll be all right. In summer we have the breeze. The aspect works, facing this way, that's why I first thought this'd be a good spot for a house, up here in the crook of this ridge with that sort of close nook to build into, when we were up here surveying; me and Simon. Do it like that."

"We've got the big stove, haven't we, for our living space," he added finally, "If it's not exact? Doesn't matter, we can rug up and have hot stew if it turns out wrong, in winter. Or if it's too hot in the summer," he went on, "we can all go skinny dipping in the creek, like we usually do."

He turned down the slope at that, wanting to end the conversation and go and meet Chas.

"I haven't finished yet, Nicolas."

"What?"

"We won't have any electricity either."

"Good. We'll make do then, won't we? We can all get up early, and go to bed early, like everybody in history, and be human beings again instead of robots. We'll get some bees and make candles if we have to. Who cares?"

"What are we going to call it then?" Sarah called out, excited, "Rivendell? That'd be nice."

He turned away before looking up again. "No. What about Edoras?" he called back. "You be Éowyn. We can build stables there just down the ridge, and live like human beings, with horses. That'll balance your design as well. But we're not elves, are we? It can't be Rivendell. We can name the farm Riddermark, don't you think, or maybe Rohan? Not Gondor, that's right next to bloody Mordor where the troglodytes and subhumans live."

He looked up again. "Think about it like that," he continued, "then it's easier to imagine how the whole thing fits together; like it's just another play we're putting on, isn't it?"

But they were paying him no further attention. He was out of earshot. He turned muttering absently to himself and continued downslope, disappearing among the trees. It was only a little after lunch, he wasn't late. He slowed down, taking his time to watch the birds flitting about in their lovely mating plumage. Early spring made his pulse quicken.

Chapter Forty

Wally and Chas went into town together and arranged for Nicolas's building account to be credited back to their main farming account, and with that done they drove out to pick up Elsie. Dropping by Mr.. Lynch's office they withdrew enough from the trust account to cover the house costs. When they returned home and gave everyone the go-ahead to start building Robbie complained that he didn't want to be paying the extra cost of carpenters doing work they could do themselves. To make his point he promptly resigned from the farm to work for Wally's contractor.

Sarah and Emma went with him, though Nicolas said he wanted to spend more time with Chas, and start getting the horses and stables organised. Going through the old maps one day he'd discovered a track along their south boundary stretching for about ten miles east before deviating along an easement through state forest right onto the new farm. For the time being they could stable the horses in the first shed near the old house, he insisted, and ride back and forth every day. Nobody on the main road would know who was coming and going.

Wally was beside himself. "Told ya!" he cried, dancing about like a leprechaun. "Fine lad, 'e is, got it all sorted! 'E knows! Didn't 'ave ta tell 'im a bloody thing!"

Chas was up at first light, and after the first few mornings found him there at the back door, or in the kitchen already, table set and starting on breakfast. That out of the way, once they started work they found little to say to one another; Nicolas staying with him like a shadow, moving as he moved, never quite watching or looking but ever attentive, learning almost by osmosis, until when it came to the horses he was out there by himself.

At night Chas sat talking quietly to Jennie, and when in town went to the library to borrow books on mental disorders, until one night during a session he was picking his guitar and sat back chuckling to himself. He put his guitar up.

"Jen, that autism Nicolas has, what do they call it? Asperger's Syndrome, is it? You know what I think? Those old doctors were protecting kids like that, not diagnosing them. They made themselves a business of it. He's not silly, though, we are. He's like the old blackfellas, you know; we've been treating him like we treat them, just the same, but what's happening is he's teaching us."

"He keeps repeating, Chas. He has the same narrow focus all the time, and we have to keep attracting his attention to get him to do anything."

"Maybe he's saying something, woman, but we're not listening so he thinks he has to say it over and over again. Maybe we're too scattered, unfocussed, or not deep enough." He leaned forward. "I've spent too much time in the bush with those fellas, Jen, nearly all my life, and with Nicolas it's the same. Working with him's exactly the same, I tell you."

"What are you saying, husband?"

"I'm not sure yet, you know." He sat back thinking.

"I should say," he continued after a long moment, "I've seen a lot of ruined horses like that too. Maybe he's just sad, after everything that's happened. Maybe he has chronic depression or something, and can't really trust people anymore. Maybe he's simply drawn into himself, since he was little, and that's the way he's grown up so he can't tell any different. I mean, you couldn't blame the poor tyke, could you?"

He glanced aside, picking up his guitar to resume playing. "Come over to the shed in the morning and I'll show you something, then you tell me."

After Jennie had the boys fed next morning and delivered them to Karl she walked across to the shed where Chas was showing Nicolas how to mend a bridle, cutting leather strips and skiving them back to uniform thickness with his pocket knife before cutting grooves along the edge and making holes with an awl, then using two needles and waxed thread stitching them together.

She sat and watched as they finished the job, until Chas almost absently asked Nicolas to go bring that mare over so they could try it out. He stood, and as he turned away Chas cocked his head. They both watched him walk across the shed. The mare shied, skittish, but instead of putting his hand up to quieten her Nicolas stood slightly aside, his head down not looking at her, but skirting her until close enough he spoke quietly and leaning in almost kissed her, caressing her shoulder with his fingertips. With his other hand he touched her cheek lightly, still talking softly to her, and reaching under her jaw pulled her head to him and started walking away. She pricked her ears and came with him. As she did so his face lit up, beaming with happiness.

Back in front of Chas he bent down to pick up the repaired bridle, and turning placed it straight over her ears with his other hand at her mouth placing the bit straight between her teeth. He adjusted the cheek straps, and running his finger under the throat turned and nodded.

"Who taught you that, Nicolas?"

"What?"

"Who taught you to handle horses like that?"

He looked from one to the other, confused. "How else would you do it?"

Then he glanced back suddenly; face reddening, and leaned into the mare with his cheek against her neck.

"Emma," he said, almost inaudibly. He turned to them abruptly, nodding, defiant, "and Sarah. That's why we're married."

Chas looked him in the eye, but he didn't flinch.

"All right, go and bring that big yearling colt in for me."

"Which one? There are three there, we haven't joined them up yet."

"Anyone you want."

He handed the reins over for Jennie to hold, and ducking under the mare's neck went out through the back of the shed. The horses they'd brought across were scattered up along the terraced amphitheatre, nibbling the grass, but he walked straight up whistling softly and they came in toward him. The two younger colts came with the others while the third hung back, eyeing him, so he ignored the rest and stepping up onto the next terrace ran along and shooed it straight down the side fence before going back to the others. He watched it from the corner of his eye, and deciding it was only fooling stepped in separating the mares and fillies until back down near the shed he had the three colts together, and with a wave of his hand and a single cough from his throat sent them in. He followed right behind and pushing them across to the wall ran his left hand up the big colt's flank and along his back until past his withers he reached down to cup his jaw in his right, turning it to him. He turned around smiling, radiant, talking to it in his soft voice, and the colt quietly followed as the mare had done.

Chas was sitting back by then without looking up, tobacco pouch out, rolling himself a cigarette.

"What do you reckon we should do with the farm, son?" he asked suddenly.

Nicolas sat next to him, thoughtfully, taking his question on face value and mulling it over before framing a reply.

"Well, I was reading about cattle markets, and long term trends, and I really do think we should put everything into Black Angus," he said finally. "If we run these good stock horses and maybe a few sheep with them and cut back on all this other stuff, I mean, we might have to stick together for a while, but in the long run it's the best course."

"What other stuff?"

"Oh well, Robbie was complaining about having no electricity, up at the house, but really it'll cost us over $1,000 per pole to run wires up there, and it's still going to cost us, forever you know, when we can get by without it. We're a lot better off spending that money on some really good stud bulls, and some nice heifers, and improving the place, while we're getting investors here anyway; for the housing. We can wire them up to their own grids later, maybe underground, and still save all that money."

Chas glanced over his head at Jennie, and she smiled, and without saying anything stood to hand him the reins she'd been holding and went back over to the house.

Chapter Forty One

One evening when they rode in along the ridge with their horses Nicolas stopped off at the hall; Edoras as he began to think of it, leaving Chas to take the mob down by himself. He walked among the bare timbers of his new study, scanning the cut joists and beams; fingering the adzed joints and pushing hard against the posts with his body while looking up to see what happened. He saw Robbie's work, so very much more meticulously detailed than the builder's, wondering that the bloke must have been really frustrated with the extra time it took. Then he climbed the ladder up to the kitchen and living area, examining the new parquetry, chuckling to himself as he eyed Sarah's mistakes and the corrections Emma made for her, going back over the work, not angrily but patiently explaining how she wanted it done.

He remounted and took the horse at a canter down to the shed where he took his saddle and bridle off and giving him a feed brushed him down. He walked over to the old house when he finished, coming in smelling of cattle and horses, and without a word went into both their bedrooms and pulling the mattresses off the beds dragged them out into the main lounge, tossing the bedsteads into the smaller room. He got Robbie to help him move Karl's desk into the main bedroom, and Kennie's and Owen's, and moving the kitchen table out of the way joined the two double mattresses there on the floor. Standing back scratching his head, he went in and taking their sheets and blankets and pillows made them up.

"Might as well get started," he said.

Nobody said anything and he glanced at one after the other, and said finally, "Swap, Sair, give Chas a hand with the horses, eh? Your turn now, then next week we'll swap back again, all right. We all have to learn from each other, and from them; we're still young yet. But I also want to spend a bit more time with Wally."

"What are you doing with the mattresses?" Emma stared across from the stove where she'd been cooking.

"I just said, might as well get started. If we're going to live together like that up at Edoras when it's finished, we can start getting used to it."

"It's a bit cramped here though, isn't it?"

"Doesn't matter, good; more cosy, don't you think? Robbie," he turned slightly, "can you make us a big long sort of table where we can eat our meals, like a medieval thing?"

Robbie stared at him, shaking his head. "No. If you want something like that I'll make us a round table. Like King Arthur, that'd be better." But then he paused, thoughtfully. "That won't fit though. Oval, what about oval; an oval table, with plain chairs not benches?"

"Yeah, all right." He turned back to Emma. "How long before dinner?"

"Ten minutes, at least."

He went out to the laundry and taking off his boots starting removing his work clothes, and she yelled after him. "We've got another new rule too, by the way; boots off at the front door. All right?"

"All right, sorry." Naked he carried them back through the house and deposited them on the front porch, and taking Sarah by the hand went in and started running the bath. Robbie came in to join them, soaping his back once the bath was ready, while Sarah scrubbed his fingernails.

"Do you really think it'll work?" he said after a while, after he and Robbie swapped and Sarah started on him next.

"Course it will, silly. It's going to be the best thing, ever."

"Emma came and have your bath, when you're ready," he called out to the kitchen.

"Is there a board meeting, for some reason?" she called back.

Nicolas glanced at the other two but they shook their heads.

"Not really, no. We might start a custom, what do you think? When we come in dirty every day we have our bath first, and get dressed in nice clean clothes for dinner."

"Why?"

"Well, it's nice. But if we're going to be living together in a medieval hall, at least nobody can say we're uncivilised, or barbarians."

Robbie looked at him curiously. "You'll have to start shaving then, Nicolas, if you want to be civilised. You've got bum fluff on your top lip."

He stood and glanced into the mirror, then sat down again. He looked closely at Robbie's face. "So have you, except it's blond."

By the time Emma came in Sarah had rummaged through the bathroom cupboard to find one of Karl's old razors and some fresh blades, and was shaving them both. She felt Nicolas' top lip with her fingertips, tenderly, and kissed him, then Robbie the moment Sarah finished working on him. She took the cloth to start washing herself but Nicolas took it from her, and the three washed her and standing her up dried her body before they all stepped out and taking their towels dried each other and went to get dressed for dinner.

Nicolas took a clean table cloth and set the table, making things nice, and lighting some candles went over and turned off the light before taking his place. There was nobody at the head; they simply faced one another from each side.

Sarah glanced from him to Robbie and back again.

"Can I ask you boys a question?"

"Anything you want," Robbie replied. "We're married aren't we? No secrets."

She took a breath, then asked, "What would happen if Emma and I are pregnant, both at the same time, and you boys needed to be with one of us, but you couldn't? I mean, could you make each other happy, like we do now?"

They glanced at one another.

"Well I was already wondering myself what'd happen if Robbie and I were away, working maybe; would you and Emma?" Nicolas countered with his own question, his voice quiet.

"I would," she said, "but I already told you that. I didn't ask her yet, though. Do you think it would be gay?"

"I don't need it, Sair," Robbie butted in. "I just like it, that's all. I like it a lot, but Nicolas doesn't turn me on, like Simon didn't either. I don't think I do anything for him; he never said anything to me, and we muck around

161

together without any trouble. He trusts me like I never thought anyone would, like I'm his real twin brother, and I feel privileged when we're close like that. But that's not sex, is it; more like we're looking in a mirror together, at some part of ourselves that we can't see otherwise. It's not sexual, so no, probably not."

"People are going to be wondering," Emma said thoughtfully.

"Let them!" Nicolas burst out. "They can go to hell."

He turned on them, hurt. "If I was going to get it off with Robbie I'd put on a big show of it, and give 'em something to gossip about until the cows came home. That'd sort them out, wouldn't it? Fucking hypocrites."

"Not with me, you won't, Nicolas."

"Well, you know what I mean." He turned to Sarah, "Does that answer your question?"

"What about you, Em? Would you do it with me, if the boys were away; keep me from being lonely."

Emma simply reached over taking her hand in hers, looking her in the eye. "You won't ever be lonely, Sair. We already sleep together when we want, so do the boys, so it's not an issue is it? Is there a reason you wanted to talk about it?"

"No, well, yes and no. Nicolas putting the mattresses out there together made me start thinking about it, and I just wondered."

Nicolas looked oddly at her. "Me making you go work with Chas as well, is that true?"

She nodded to herself then looked up.

"Don't be shy. He's terrific." Nicolas reassured her. "He won't treat you bad, just like the rest of us. But I wasn't thinking about that either, really, I wanted him to see how you handle the horses. You'll be good. He'll be impressed, I bet. You'll see."

Robbie looked down at his hands.

"Anyway," he murmured, "if we broke this up now I don't know what I'd do either. I'd be ripped apart, you know that. We all would."

He looked up, glancing from one to the other. "Stop talking about it."

162

Chapter Forty Two

As it turned out Chas still wanted Nicolas working with him, and wouldn't allow him to swap. When he said Sarah should come too he simply nodded. They were up at first light and seeing her awake and already dressed in his own work pants waiting for him, together they crept down in the semi-darkness of false dawn to the big house where Jennie, now six months pregnant, had a good hearty breakfast ready for them, and lunches packed in their saddle bags.

In the shed Chas watched closely as Sarah saddled up, talking quietly to her horse as she did so, and swung herself easily up without asking for a hand. The ride down along the back ridge was lovely in the early morning, with their mounts at a good steady trot that ate up the miles until they came down off the final slope onto the flatter country, and when they got to the back gate Nicolas reached down to undo the chain and let them through. There was good spring grass all about and the place was a picture.

Chas's stores were there grazing; mixed Shorthorns mainly with some *Bos Indicus* in with them. He stayed back until Nicolas caught up, explaining to Sarah their plans to have them all on the market by Christmas when they'd start bringing in some good stud bulls for their new enterprise. Nicolas complained that he wanted to set up a real stud farm, but Chas talked him out of it arguing there was more money for the time being in stores down from the north-west. Over time they could build up their own commercial herd for the premium beef market, not snags and hamburgers as he called these animals.

What they had to do first was restore their pasture. The farm they'd bought was badly run down, let go with the old bloke who'd owned it previously no longer able to keep up, and his sons married and working in town, but it was still a good purchase for them.

They rode down to the house and dismounting went into the kitchen with their gear. Chas lit the stove and made them a cup of tea, and put his feet up after the ride while Sarah looked around the house. It was a nice brick place; she was surprised even though it echoed bare of furniture and floor coverings, but the gardens had been well kept and only needed a little bit of tidying to make them presentable.

Chas didn't want her distracted by it. "Come and have your cuppa, sweetheart," he called, "Don't worry about the place, all right. We'll advertise for a tenant if you want, but we need to get on with our own work."

He watched her as she came back into the kitchen, and grinned. "We'd better get you some togs of your own, eh? Bit tight around the fanny, aren't they?"

She looked down. "They're all right." She slipped her hand in under the waist and jacked them up a little. "There, see?"

"You still need your own work clothes, Sair," Nicolas argued. "We'll still have to get you something, and some good boots; maybe we'll go into town later."

"Well, what do we have to do then?"

"Fencing mainly, after we muck out the stables," Chas said. "We'll get the horses sorted first and take the tractor. Nicolas will show you what we've been doing, or if you want we need some super and trace elements spread up on those top paddocks with a bit of mixed pasture seed. They're a bit bare. What do you reckon?"

"Can I work with you, Chas? Nicolas can drive the tractor."

"All right, drink up. The day'll be gone." He turned to Nicolas. "You'll be right, will you?"

"Show me what you want mixed in the hopper, that's all."

They finished their tea and went back out, leading the horses across to the shed where Chas explained how many bags from each stack to mix in the super spreader, then taking his horse sent him out to get started straight away. He and Sarah cleaned the stables and get the horses settled before taking the other smaller tractor with the fencing gear on it.

She was shy with Chas at first, worrying what he might be thinking of her, but as the day progressed warmed to him as he made it clear how he appreciated their honesty and integrity, and the way the four of them did everything together. He hadn't known Simon very well, and didn't know Grant or Eric at all apart from the day at the festival, and meeting Frank at the funeral, so he had nothing much to say about them. Emma was his daughter after all; he had to reckon that in. There was a lot of him in her, not just her mother, or old Wally. He didn't have the chance to be here with her when he should have been, perhaps, but that was water under the bridge. He still had time to make amends.

By time they went back down for lunch they were on loose chattering terms, and Nicolas sat back smiling as he watched them with their banter.

Over that week he watched Sarah come into herself finally as a young woman, attracting the courtesy and attention of a grown man who treated her with respect; letting the last of her girlhood slip away. He watched Chas with her, understanding in the transaction what it meant to be a real bush gentleman.

But then Emma complained that she needed her back at the building site, and with Robbie hinting that he needed her there as well the week came to an abrupt end.

Chapter Forty Three

Over the next two months the work on the farm went on apace, and Edoras drew near to completion. Nicolas never did get back to working with Wally, and before he knew it the new house was done. Without telling him a combined house-warming and party to celebrate his fourteenth birthday was organised.

Karl and Marcus showed up first, as usual, though not long after Chas and Jennie arrived with the boys, with Wally not far behind fidgeting and worrying about the weather. A while later Ted and Liz knocked on the door and were invited in, then finally Robbie came up from the shed with Nicolas blindfolded, having watched for Sarah's signal that everyone was ready. He'd been kept away for two days, sleeping over at the farm with Chas who'd been bought in on the plot the week before, while Jennie went up each day to supervise the cooking and show the girls how to master the big combustion stove, and Robbie went around giving the place a final spit and polish.

The whole house smelled of new wax and varnish, and candles shone from wall brackets and candlesticks down the centre of the big table. The moment Robbie removed his blindfold they all stood and clapped, and like a little boy at his first theatre performance he crossed one foot over the other and bowed. He went around touching everything, eyes bright, until Emma took his hand and led him to the head of the table saying just this once, all right, because it's your birthday.

Everybody seated Jennie started serving dinner, making the girls sit there on either side of Nicolas with Robbie next chair down on his right, and Wally to his left. Throughout the meal he sat there smiling to himself, glancing occasionally from one to the other without saying anything, until after sweets and the table was cleared he started peering down at the table top, fingering the fine wood grain and polished wax surface. By the time Jennie came across with his birthday cake he was no longer paying any attention.

"This is so lovely," he said to nobody in particular, then pushed his chair back to inspect Emma's parquetry, and getting down on his hands and knees starting tracing the wood grain pattern from one tile to the next, following her design with his fingers. He sat up suddenly, gazing about. He stood and went over to one of the great timber posts they had holding the roof up, touching with his fingertips then rubbing it absently with his palm feeling the knots and roughness beneath the varnish. Turning, he went across to the bench near the stove, and tracing that too with his hand starting walking around the whole place examining every nook and cranny.

While they all watched he went back across to his dresser next to the big bed and started undressing, until naked he went around the whole place again, rolling his body against the polished timbers, caressing the fine wood grain with his fingers, until back in the middle once more he lay down on his back and gazed up at the roof timbers. Then he sat up, as if waking suddenly, on his bare backside on the floor, legs bent and apart like a baby sitting there. He fingered the parquetry again, almost as if to check it was still there, and looked up.

"What you can do, Chas," he said, "is lease the farm from us, all right? I think that'll be a lot better, and you can run your own business from there. Jennie and you can move into that nice house we have over there. The boys will have a lot more room to run around, and when the twins arrive it will be better for them too."

"Nicolas," Emma interjected, "you have to blow your candles out. It's your birthday."

He held his hand up and turned to Liz. "You and Ted move into the big house, and Marcus and Karl can have the old house. You can pay for your shares when you're ready; when you move in if you like. Once we get that money in we'll start on the new school and the theatre, and build the new houses later if we ever get approval."

Then he nodded and sat back, satisfied, but then glanced back up the table to Wally, who was no longer there.

"What happened to Wally?"

"He said there's a storm coming," Chas said, "He wanted to go down and get something in out of the weather."

"Really? Well I want to see him. It's important. We need his agreement."

Nicolas looked toward the door, worried now, and standing suddenly rushed out to jump off the porch and race down the slope looking for the old fellow. He was nowhere to be seen so he went down to the big house and checked his room and the kitchen before racing back out through the conservatory.

At that moment the storm hit and the first great gobs of rain started kicking up the dust. The wind lashed at him and he momentarily lost sight of where he was until a huge bolt of lightning lit up the entire area. His hair stood on end with the charged air and he heard Wally calling to him. He couldn't see where he was and felt his way out past the gate, when another great lightning bolt and crashing thunder knocked him onto his backside, and head ringing slowly turned onto his hands and knees to see the giant fig tree down and flames licking at the split trunk.

He called out distractedly, but there was silence. He stood away, shaking his head trying to clear it, as much as he could without hurting too much. Still dazed he wandered slowly across to where he thought Wally's voice had come from earlier, in that general direction, skirting the big tree and across to the shed. Nothing. It was fully dark now so he took a lantern down from the shelf and lit it.

Back outside, from this side of the tree he noticed the rear end of the trailer sticking out from under the leaves. One side was down, as if the spring on that side had collapsed. Or it could have simply been tipped half over by the weight. He stood wondering for a moment before it occurred to him that the trailer had been hooked up to the tractor, and shouldn't have been out there anyway. Why wasn't it parked in the shed, as it was supposed to be? Where was the tractor?

Wandering around disoriented and confused, he eventually clambered up onto the back of the trailer and over the branches. About 10 feet into the centre of the mess he bumped his head on the exhaust pipe sticking up through the leaves. He sat gazing stupidly at it for a moment wondering what it was doing here, until with a shock he realized what had happened. Backing carefully from branch to branch he held the lantern up away from his eyes, peering down through the tangle until something caught his eye and he looked down to see that the big main branch had landed just forward of the driver's seat, right in Wally's lap. The old man had drawn his hands up as if to push the thing off, but looking down it appeared as if he was holding the steering wheel, still driving the tractor.

Nicolas called softly to him, then when no answer came reached down and touched his hat. Wally didn't move. He sank back onto his haunches on another branch and leaned forward so he could reach him better. He pulled his hat off and saw that he was dead. For the next ten minutes or so he squatted there while the wind buffeted him and rain pelted down, gently stroking his fine grey hair, not knowing even as he thought about it later whether he cried or not.

Next thing he felt somebody lifting him bodily out of the branches and Chas's voice calmly in his ear. He was wet through and shivering with cold. Emma took his hand and with Robbie hurried him over to the old house and poured him a warm bath, then undressed with him and getting in started rubbing his body with the cloth.

From outside he could dimly hear the chainsaw working at clearing away the fallen tree.

Chapter Forty Four

Sarah came running in to see them there in the bath, and Emma turned asking her to run back up to the house and bring Nicolas's clothes. She disappeared, reappearing five minutes later out of breath, and together they stood him up and dried him, then dressed him while he stood there dumbly allowing them whatever it was they were doing. As they finished red and blue lights flashed through the window, and Liz came up to see how he was.

They went out to the kitchen and sat at the table, Emma busying herself making a pot of tea, still sitting there at the stove when Sergeant Lewis and one of his constables came to the door and knocked politely. Robbie got up and let them in.

The sergeant looked steadily at Nicolas, shivering slightly and holding his warm cup in his hands.

"You all right, mate?"

He nodded.

"Mind if we sit down?"

Nicolas glanced up at him curiously but said nothing, so Sarah pulled out two chairs for them and asked if they'd like a cup of tea.

"No thanks, love. We'll be quick," he said quietly, eyes still on Nicolas. "Care to tell us what happened?"

"Lightning hit the tree and knocked me over, that's all."

"Do you know what happened to Wally? Did you see what happened?"

"No. I didn't see anything. I couldn't find him. I had to look for him, but he wasn't there anymore. Wally's not here now is he, like Simon's not here, somewhere else."

He furrowed his brow, trying to think where they might be, and then turned to Emma. He started crying softly to himself, shaking his head slowly from side to side as his lip trembled and he lost his words. He sat there without saying anything, gazing into the distance as if trying to think.

Finally he glanced at the policemen sitting there. "You didn't come to my party, did you? I don't remember you at my party."

They all looked at him. Robbie leaned forward slightly. "It's his birthday today; we were having a party for him and Wally went outside worrying about the storm coming. Nicolas went to look for him, because we were just about to cut the cake, blow the candles out, you know, he didn't want to start without Wally. That's what happened. We were all waiting for them to come back so we could light the candles, but they'd disappeared so we went looking for them. That's where we found them, and we brought Nicolas inside and got him some dry clothes. He was drenched to the skin, and Wally was there under the tree, the big branch must have come down on him."

"Is that it; nothing else?"

"No sir, nothing, that's all there is."

"We can have our cake now." Nicolas said suddenly, looking up.

The sergeant watched his face a moment before glancing out the window and back again. "Give us ten minutes or so will you son, while we clean up. Will that be all right?"

Nicolas nodded, unsmiling, and the two police went out escorted by Liz who turned back briefly at the door motioning them to stay where they were. Robbie went to the door and stood watching a stretcher being slid into the back of the ambulance, and the police going over to the shed, out of the rain, and start talking to Chas. Eventually they finished and back in the police car drove out following the ambulance.

Soon after Liz returned with Jennie and Chas, but Emma intervened suggesting they go on up to the house and they'd be along in a minute. Jennie sent the others off before turning to her daughter asking her to go up herself now and take Robbie and Sarah with her, meeting her gaze directly and holding steady, then absorbing Emma's challenge sent them all packing. The moment they left she went across and sat with Nicolas.

She reached over and took his hand while he stared into the distance, not saying anything merely caressing the back of his hand with her thumb, then his bare forearm with her other hand until he looked down curiously to see what she was doing. He followed her arm up and level with her shoulder glanced across suddenly and caught her eye. He stood and stepping sideways took her head in his arms, murmuring to her as if she were a child, then taking her hand led her across to one of the mattresses still there on the floor and lay down with her.

"Nicolas," she asked him softly, "it's not Emma, or Sarah. Do you know who I am?"

"Yes, you're Jennie, Emma's Mum. Of course I know. How are you feeling? Wally's gone, your Poppy's gone. He's not here anymore you know. You must know, poor thing. Are you all right?"

She took his head in his hands, looking him in the eye, and smiled. She put his hand on her round belly.

"Do you want to feel the babies kicking?"

He did so, and pressed his ear to her and listened, smiling, eyes wide with wonder, until eventually he looked up and said, "They'll be waiting for us. We haven't had our cake yet."

He stood and going to his old room took a coat from the cupboard. He brought it in and helping her up from the floor took her out onto the porch, and covering them both took her hand and stepped out into the rain. They were only slightly wet when they arrived back at Edoras, and removing their shoes went in and sat at the table. Everyone had been standing around talking, not in their places, so Nicolas rose again and leaving Wally's empty chair went around the table to move Chas down one place, leaving an empty chair next to Sarah, and asked them all to please be seated.

Marcus stood to light the candles on the cake, but then once lit instead of blowing them out Nicolas rose and taking the knife began cutting the cake.

"You're supposed to blow the candles out first, Nicolas," Karl said.

"No, not yet." He shook his head, frowning. Carefully he cut two slices and placed them in front of the two empty chairs, and abruptly turning blew out all the candles on the cake in one breath, leaving only those two burning there before the empty chairs.

"There, that's right," he said "We're all back together now, the way it should've been."

He glanced from one to the other and went and sat in his seat waiting for a slice of the cake to be passed along to him.

After a moment he looked up from eating.

"Um, Chas, yes, you lease the farm, all right. It'll work better that way. I still want to work for you, I'll help, but you can pay me wages so I can buy my own clothes, and my own food and things while we get the theatre built. And you can teach me things, like I'm sort of your apprentice, while we get the place set up properly. Then when I've done that Marcus can help me go to University. By then we should be able to pay for it all right, and have some money if Kennie wants to go later. He's really clever you know, I've been teaching him."

He smiled happily at that, then pausing a moment looked back down the table again until Emma glanced at Jennie before reaching across to take his hand said, "Talk about it tomorrow, Nicolas. Or leave it for a few days, and we'll have a meeting, all of us."

He watched her face, thoughtfully. "I still want to talk about planting walnuts or pecans in the two front paddocks along the road, where Wally had his cabbages, or maybe almonds. Liz can help us with that, I'm sure."

Robbie came in from his other side. "Put it on the agenda. It's all right, we'll discuss it. I'm the chairman, we agreed, and I'll make sure we do, all right?"

"Do you think we should?" he asked, distracted from his idea.

"That'd be a good thing to do finally," he nodded, "yes, well, that's what we'll do then."

But before Robbie was able to answer he dropped his head and started sobbing to himself.

Chapter Forty Five

Nicolas didn't want to go to the funeral. They said it would do him good to see Wally off but he looked away without saying anything. Later in the day he went down to the big house and caught Jennie in the kitchen. Taking her hand he told her about all the strange people at his mother's funeral who drove away in their big cars saying they'd catch up with them some time, but still haven't, and Grant and Frank at Simon's funeral yelling at him. He didn't want to go to any more of those sorts of things, but he didn't want anyone to think he didn't care about Wally either.

He lost his words after that, and stood gazing out the window before turning back looking her in the eye, bottom lip quivering and tears running down his cheeks. She took up her apron and dried his eyes soothing him, and kissed him, telling him not to worry about it; it was all right. Later she had a quiet word with Robbie and Sarah.

They went out riding instead, Nicolas as usual clumsy in the saddle and no dressage rider but holding his own nonetheless because of his way with animals, while Sarah admonished Robbie saying he had no excuse. He said he was the better houseman, but she broke away and with a whoop spurred her mount into a cross-country event to prove him wrong. When they got back they rode down to the shed and unsaddling their horses fed them, and brushed them down, then walked up the hill to Edoras and sat breathless.

Nicolas looked around the place, thoughtfully, and leaned over touching Robbie's arm.

"What we should do, rightly, is go down and get the tractor and take it across to the old house, and load the trailer up with Wally's stash of home brew he's got down there, in the cellar. I know about it, he told me. We'll have time to bring it up here before they get back."

"The trailer's busted, Nicolas."

"No, only the spring on that side, and a few boards; I had a look at it. And the seat's a bit wonky but you can still drive it. It'll be good, he'd like the idea. When they get back you can be at the gate telling them to get their fannies up here, and bring their instruments, and we'll have a real cracking wing-ding. Wally'd have liked that, I know. Best thing we can do."

Sarah stood, eyes sparkling. "Yes, lets. That's the best idea I've heard in days. Come on, Nicolas, if the chairman doesn't want to shift his arse we'll head a spill on this committee and negotiate a new merger."

She looked at Robbie, frowning. "You're acting just like Karl, Robbie. We'll have to do something about that you know. First you tell me I've got balls, but you're the chairman, and next thing you reckon you're a better rider but I pissed on you and you won't admit it. Now you think the trailer's busted, I mean, too much to bring up the beer so we can hold a wake for Wally."

Nicolas lifted himself onto his elbow, and cupping his head in his hand said, "See, you're not so clever, Robbie. We might have to review your prerogative if you don't learn to behave yourself. I'm fourteen too now; I can leave school as well, so you can take a jump."

At that moment Kennie burst in the door and seeing them there stopped suddenly, staring. Emma came in right behind him, and taking the situation in with a glance turned him around and whispered in his ear. He ran back outside.

"What is this, a palace revolt?" Emma wanted to know. "Not now, I won't stand for it. Anyway, everyone's back. They're all at the big house."

"Oh, bugger!" Nicolas sat up suddenly, pushing Sarah off. "We wanted everyone up here, so we could have a wake. We were just about to bring up a load of Wally's brew."

"Well, shows what happens when you disobey me, doesn't it, smart arse," Robbie laughed.

"Shut up you." Sarah slapped him. "It's all right; we can have it down there. Tell them we'll be down in a minute, Em. Say we've just got back from riding and need to clean up."

"Yes, all right," she said quietly, "but hurry up, will you."

On the way past she bent down to kiss Nicolas. "It was all right," she said quietly, "a bit too churchy though; boring really, so you didn't miss anything much. We'll see him off properly ourselves."

Chapter Forty Six

Sitting there at the kitchen table after a few of Wally's brews, with his body replete and mind slowed, Nicolas's normally tight focus blurred and wandered. They worked around him, bustling, cooking and putting plates out followed by great platters of food. Absently he picked at *canapés* and *hor d'oeuvres*, and sipping the good beer thought about how good things came about, loving everybody; loving life. He hadn't really been thinking before this moment how well these people were so settled on the land, with their talent and self-sufficiency and saving and frugality, or what they saw in him, or how they knew things.

When Emma and Sarah came up asking how he was he stared at them absently, but when Kennie came he sat him in his lap, and Owen, until after a while he got chairs for them and sat them on either side. Robbie came to sit with him and he made room, until by time the music started the four of them had become something of a centrepiece.

Chas watched from the side, while Jack's mother who was there served them even more food, smiling in her quiet way until Nicolas looked at her suddenly, frowning.

"Aunty Elsie, what are you going to do with yourself now?" he wanted to know. "Why don't you sell your place and come live here with us?"

She glanced at him a moment, then taking off her apron left Jennie and the girls with the catering and sat down opposite.

"I won't sell the farm," she said, leaning forward. "No, we'll keep the place. Chas can use the farm if he wants, when he's ready. I think you have a good plan, Nicolas, but I have a sharefarmer on there at the moment."

"But you can still come and live here with us, can't you?"

"If I'm way out here, who's going to keep an eye on that wayward brother of yours?"

"Who? Eric? What's he been up to?"

"He's a hooligan, on the street hanging around with a bad lot. You know that yourself."

"What? Sorry, I forgot about him. I thought he was staying with you. Didn't he even go to the funeral? Shit, that's no good."

He glanced up at Chas, and getting up from his seat went across to the telephone where he dialed a number and waited. Before long someone answered and after a brief conversation he hung up. He came and sat down again without saying anything.

Karl picked up his guitar and cigarette characteristically out the corner of his mouth began playing, then Chas joined in, and Marcus with his bass. Emma turned to her mother; hand on her arm to stop her fussing around with the food until she too doffed her apron and taking up her violin joined the band. Nicolas caught Emma's eye, to stop mucking around too and start playing, which she did, then Elsie turned around in her chair and spoke to Sarah.

All seated finally, Robbie got up and opening another bottle of beer went and topped up the musician's glasses before sitting back down and filling their own, though by this time Nicolas had become distracted by the music. Karl's a really very good musician, he thought, watching him with new eyes. Marcus set aside his bass and picked up a clarinet to join Emma's flute, and that's when Jennie's violin took over and Chas accompanied her with his guitar. Karl put his down and sat listening, sipping his beer.

When they finished the set Chas rose and went down to Wally's old room, returning with his banjo and gave it to Karl who sat tuning it a moment before nodding, but then Liz stood suddenly and went out to her car rummaging around in the boot. She brought in a long thin case and sitting next to Emma took out her own flute, looking up to indicate she was ready, then Chas led off with his guitar. Marcus took up the big bass again, and once they had the piece running Jennie came in again with her violin, and then Liz and Emma with flutes.

There was a knock on the back door so Nicolas got up to answer it. It was Sergeant Lewis as he'd expected with Eric, and he showed them both in.

Eric was filthy and unkempt. He looked as if he'd been in a fight, or hadn't bathed for a week, so once the music stopped and he poured the big sergeant a beer, he had Robbie come with him while they took Eric for a bath. He turned back momentarily at the door.

"Do you mind staying?" he asked the policeman. "We're having a wake for old Wally, and you'd be very welcome."

"Well, I'm off duty. Just knocking off when you rang, in fact. It'll be a pleasure," he said. "But the name's Mick when I'm out of uniform, all right, son?"

Nicolas nodded slightly and disappeared, shoving Eric ahead. They went over to the old house and made him go into the bathroom and strip while they poured him a bath. He didn't say a thing, looking more relieved than upset, though he did look up plaintively when they made him get in the bath and start washing himself.

Robbie sat on the side of the tub while Nicolas went rummaging through his old cupboard to find some clean clothes for him; old clothes that no longer fit him and would suit Eric, and came back with them.

"All right Eric, you're not going back into town. You'll live here with us from now on, and cut out all the bullshit. Stay with Chas and Jennie for the time being. When Karl and Marcus move back in here, you live in the big house with Ted and Liz and we'll get Aunty Elsie, your Nanna, to come and live there too. You can go to school here, with Kennie and Owen."

Eric looked up as if to say something but Nicolas interrupted him. "If you fucking argue with me Eric I'll bloody well kill you. I'll rip your nuts off and kick your cock so far up your fanny you'll have to open your mouth to piss, and that's only for starters. I tell you, I've had enough bullshit to last me the rest of my life, we all have."

Robbie glanced sharply at him then stared down at Eric. "Right, did you hear that? Before he kills you I'll get the pigs to fuck you up the arse like your mates did to your own brother, while you stood there watching; maybe piss on you first. Then I'll give you back to him."

"All right? Get out now and dry yourself. And you can get dressed."

Eric stood, covering himself, but Nicolas moved his hand aside, holding it away, then the other one. "See, Robbie, he looks nice too, don't you think? Pretty face, nice body; runs in the family. He's no hooligan, is he, not a shape of it. If Sair was here now she'd be going berserk. We'd have to beat her off or she'd swallow him in one gulp."

He paused, looking him up and down. "A bit undernourished though, like an orphan, and it's a pity about the attitude."

"Bloody poofter you are, Nicolas!" Eric cried, but the two stood back laughing.

"Get over it, Eric," Robbie said. "You're a loser and we're going to fix that. You don't even know yet, but wait 'til we find you a nice tight piece of pussy, a real hot chickie babe, and get you a life; you'll never want to go back hanging around town with those dead-shit mates of yours, because you'll know what life's about. They're not your mates, just fuck-heads. "

Leaving him there alone the other two went out chuckling and waited for him to cool off, and dress and comb his hair. When he was ready they walked back across to the other house, Nicolas putting his arm around him.

"Family, all right. Nothing else matters. Forget everything else, do you hear me? I'm the big boss now. Any time you go back into town and have anything more to do with that lot, the sergeant will pick you up and bring you back here; if he doesn't lock you in a cell and give you a good hiding first. And don't worry about Robbie, he's really only a comedian. He thinks God stuck a dick on us boys because of this weird cosmic sense of humour, and he can't get over it."

Back inside however they almost forgot him, leaving him seated in the corner by himself while everyone simply worked around him; the girls especially avoiding him. Nicolas soon became absorbed by the music and sitting there with the sergeant sipped his beer, quietly, without saying anything much except when Chas took a break from playing and sat down next to him, and he leaned over talking to him about Eric doing some farm work after school, and learning to ride.

The sergeant sat listening, smiling stoically, nodding occasionally and glancing at Nicolas. Eventually he stood and excused himself. Reaching across he scruffed his hair, saying he'd better be off. He then thanked everybody for their hospitality, and with a final glance down at Eric quietly let himself out.

Chas watched at the window as the big police car drove out, before turning to Nicolas.

"You rang the police just in time, Nicolas," he said quietly. "The sergeant told me there'd been complaints about your brother, and he was going to be picked up anyway."

"Who?"

"That Mrs. O'Reilly, and Mrs Bannon, and Vicky Kulinski; you know, that child protection activist setting herself up as a social worker, and a few others."

"What? That woman?" Nicolas burst out. "That's her son who fucked me up the arse. It was him. Those other women, Eric was living with them, with their kids, and now they complain. They're the worst of the lot. That Mrs. Kulinski is the one going on about sex and drugs all the time, and child abuse, nobody else. But they're the abusers. They're the perverts, voyeurs; that's the word, isn't it, I read it in a book. What would they know about protecting children?"

They all turned to stare at him, but he glanced around at Eric. "It was, wasn't it, Eric. You were there, you saw them. They set you up. They're the ones who gave Jack a hiding, and killed Simon. Gutless bastards they are! They listen to their stupid parents, and set up their own street gangs like they do at school."

Eric gazed dumbly at him, and nodded slightly.

"What are you telling us, Nicolas?" Marcus broke in. "She's President of the High School P & C. Her husband is a teacher, at the primary school."

"They're sub-human species, *untermenschen*, bloody Neanderthals, I read about them too," Nicolas replied coldly. "That's why that bloody school is the way it is. She got stuck into me on the street, that women, when that headmaster died, said it was me who killed him."

He glared defiantly around the room, but then seemed to withdraw into himself, shrink in size.

"Nothing," he stammered finally. "I didn't say anything. I don't know anything. They don't exist, those people."

"They can cause us a lot of trouble, Nicolas," Marcus replied. "They can make a big case against us if they choose. They have all the connections and control the town. If we have Eric here they'll argue that we're harbouring delinquents and undesirables."

"Well you better fix it, Marcus! Because I'm going to see those Aboriginal people, and ask them if they'd like to live here too. All the misfits. It was their country anyway, Wally told me."

Turning, he took Robbie and Eric in hand and started angrily for the door, but stopped suddenly and said, "No, this is Wally's wake. They even come in here, into our space, to ruin things for us. Chas, you shouldn't have said anything. Shut up about it, talk about it tomorrow, or later sometime, or never again would be better. They don't exist. Here we exist, and this is our party, for old Wally."

Liz gazed curiously at him. Gently she reached over and touched her finger to his lips. She held it there for a moment before picking up her flute and started to play.

Chapter Forty Seven

Straight away next morning they were back to normal; there was far too much work about the farm, and without Wally being there to know what needed to be done day by day they had to stop and consult one another.

Jennie took Nicolas aside first to discuss his housing plans, and suggested if he really did want them over on the new farm they'd move next year some time, perhaps after their Easter folk festival and things quietened down over winter, and the babies were strong enough. She welcomed Elsie with a sigh of relief, however, and as Nicolas looked on with the girls' help quickly had Wally's room cleaned right out and repainted for her.

Liz decided to quit her job and move as well, much to Ted's annoyance, but he was away all the time she argued, and Robbie was here already. Anyway, she wanted to be here for the birth, so that was that. Nicolas watched them thinking their marriage had probably broken up already, but he wanted her here to help with the nut orchard so he was happy with what she was saying. Robbie said to him once that they argued a lot and Ted was just plain grumpy all the time, especially after he ran away and news of his apparently precocious sex life leaked back to him, when he'd naïvely thought all these exceptionally intelligent Mensa children were developing their fine minds ready for early University, while Liz stood by her son all the way.

Marcus would be finished semester by mid-November and had already started installing bookshelves and a study for himself in the old house, since Karl had moved his classroom back out into the open living area next to the kitchen and dining room. Neither was at all unhappy with the arrangements, having the whole place to themselves finally without anyone getting under their feet, and in the balmy late spring evenings sat on the front porch playing their music.

Chas took Eric under his wing and wouldn't let him out of his sight. Having him there in the big house he could drag him out of bed at first light and have him fed before they rode their horses down to the farm, not listening to his complaints, until he finally shut up. He quickly started treating him as he had Nicolas, showering with him after work and as the boys came in for their bath of an evening; leaving him no privacy or room for any of his crap, as he called it.

Within weeks Eric started putting on weight, walking upright with his head up as he went about his chores, and even started coming out in clean clothes after Chas bought him a nice pair of riding boots and a cowboy hat. After the first month, after Liz and he had reconnected the old sprinklers and started laying out the front paddocks for tree planting, Nicolas came down and invited him up to Edoras for dinner.

When he arrived they failed to notice him hesitantly at the door, but then he knocked almost imperceptibly and Nicolas went to let him in. Both girls got up and went to the stove to get dinner ready, and when he was seated at the table Nicolas went over and taking Sarah by the hand brought her back and introduced them, making them shake hands at least. With Emma it was far more difficult. She held up a carving knife and grimaced, but he made her put it down and at least be civil.

Instead when she stood before him she said, "Are you proud of yourself, Eric?"

He looked up at her. "No. I'm really sorry. Will you let me say something?"

She scanned his face, and then nodded.

"I never had anything to do with Nicolas," Eric said quietly. "He was always just sort of weird, and Grant hated him. Nobody liked him, all the time at school, and I never got to know him that's all. Simon never said anything, but he never said much anyway. I didn't think he was such a good kid either but not really odd like Nicolas, just not with us sometimes. It was so embarrassing for me all the time. I never meant for him to be dead, they all just wanted to muck around with Jack for being a homo and I had the shits with him about it. How do you think I felt? How do you think I still feel?"

"All right, stop there. It's all right. If that's really the way you feel we'll just drop it. You need to know that Nicolas has autism. He suffers from Asperger's Syndrome, but nobody ever told you that did they? He's a registered genius, but nobody told you that yet either. He can't follow people's body language, or their emotions, or their facial expressions. He's not cold or hard-hearted; he simply can't see people's ugliness. When you get to know him and get his attention he's the warmest, kindest, and funniest, most direct and interesting person you ever met. You have to give him a chance, Eric."

"Shut up now, Em," Nicolas broke in. "Just shut up, all right. People are weird, not horses or dogs or children or any of the little birds and animals. It's not us it's them. People are hard to read because they're full of bullshit. People aren't in God's image like the birds and animals, they're just bullshit, I don't know how or why yet, that's all. So just shut up about it. I'm sorry I can't figure it out, if I could I would, wouldn't I?"

She turned to him. Tears started down his cheeks and she leaned in close to wipe them away while Sarah passed her handkerchief and she took it and dried his eyes. Eric looked up at him, and away again into the distance before he started sobbing too.

"Oh well, fuck, there goes dinner," Robbie broke in. "Why don't we just get pissed and be done with it?"

"No," Emma said. "Come on, I've spent all afternoon cooking. I really wanted this to be special, and it is, really."

"Yes, Robbie, what's got into you?" Sarah interrupted. "Eric's lost both his parents, and his twin brother, and his Uncle Wally, and he's barely twelve. Shit, that's not fair. It's about time he had a good cry. If Nicolas hadn't rung Sergeant Lewis at the police station when he did, in another couple of years he'd be in jail, or worse, wouldn't he? Your family's rich, and there's only you isn't there, so how would you know?"

"He knows," Nicolas said quietly. "You still don't know how lonely he's been all his life; as bad as you Sair, or worse. He just covers it up by being a comedian, but I know him a lot better than you ever will. I wanted him in on this. It was me who asked you, not him. And you're right it was me who brought Eric back. I only spoke to him the way I did to shock him back to reality, and it worked, didn't it? I'm not worried about Grant, he'll be all right; I don't care. He always hurt me so much; he can't see anything at all."

He stopped there, thoughtfully, before continuing.

"I'm sorry I hit him when Mum died. I think about that a lot, and feel really bad about it. I promised myself I'd never hit anybody again, not ever. Everyone's got something wrong with them, haven't they? If it's not one thing it's always something else. I never thought there was anything wrong with me, I live on my own beautiful planet and I'm glad I do. But you're all slowly coming into my space to live with me, aren't you, not the other way around. That says something, doesn't it? Anyway, I don't want to listen to any of this anymore."

"So you'd better get some cold beer, Rob, and you can line them up Eric, and we will get pissed I think, after we've had dinner. One more thing, Sair; Eric's not in the marriage. Forget it, don't even think about it. We'll find him someone else."

"What?" Eric looked up.

"Nothing; mind your own business, and keep away from Em and Sair or there will be big trouble."

"But I didn't even look at them!"

"Good then, that's it. And you can get over your dick problem while you're at it, if you're going to be living out here." He shoved at him with his hand. "Go outside with Robbie, there are still a couple of crates of Wally's beer in the toilet out the back and you can put some in the fridge. After that's gone we'll have to make some more. He showed me his secret."

Chapter Forty Eight

Emma looked up sharply and turned on Eric. "Eric, sorry, but you're not getting pissed with them tonight. Come back on Saturday, all right. Party's cancelled."

There was silence throughout the meal but Emma held her ground, until cleaning up the table afterward she turned abruptly and escorted Eric to the door.

"Nothing personal, I'm glad you came up, really. Come back on the weekend and we can go riding, maybe, and have a swim. It'll be good."

She returned to the table and looking up at Nicolas said quietly, "This is between us, all right? It's not you either, Nicolas. It's not your world we're in now, its Poppy's. He did all this. All his life he was searching for someone like you, who could see things the way he did and not be bothered by it, and smart enough to figure it out. I told you about his family, but he never thought the way everyone was telling him to do things was right. None of us ever saw him so happy until you came to live with us; he used to get so drunk and rave on about things, you know, but as soon as you arrived he shut up suddenly."

Nicolas stared at her, struck by a thought. "You know too, don't you Em?" he said, "and your Mum? That's why you came onto me like you did, and brought Sarah in."

"We had to reach you Nicolas," she burst out, "and I'm glad we did. I'm so glad finally!"

"But that's not what I mean. I thought like that before, like you just said, about this being Wally's, not mine. But I don't think like that anymore. Something happened."

"God took him," Emma said, leaning forward earnestly, "God's lightning took him, and at the same time it knocked you out, and that's when everything shifted. We felt it up here, all of us, like something was happening. Now you know what he knew, everything, that's why you can't think it's not him anymore, because it's you now. When I listen to you I can hear him talking, except with your lovely soft voice not his funny mouth."

"Anything else you've noticed?"

"Yes, it wasn't you who rang the police station to go and pick up Eric. It was Wally. That was him, exactly. You wouldn't have done that before, but we were all there watching. And it was Wally who told him he'd kick his cock up his cunt if he didn't behave." She stopped and giggled. "Robbie told us! I nearly wet myself laughing when I heard what you said. You never talk like that at all; you're so polite all the time."

Nicolas turned to Robbie, who just sat their laughing before finally he got up and started helping clear the table, and do the washing up. Emma stood to follow him, and taking Sarah by the hand told them both to leave the dishes. Together they went over to the big bed and taking off their clothes turned to face the boys.

It was after midnight when Robbie woke from a short sleep to see the others still tangled together. He started chuckling to himself, and Sarah looked oddly at him.

"What's so funny, Rob? You're really weird, you know."

"No, he's right," he said quietly, "it's all bullshit. Wally was right too, he could see. All we get is fucking deadshit crap all the time, but how do you get around it? The answer is, only by being your own true self, having your own clear mind, like that old Descartes said. He didn't say passively "I think, therefore I am," for someone to appropriate the idea and bind everyone else with it like they were nothing more than machines, he said in the active voice, "I am thinking, therefore I exist! That's it, isn't it!"

He looked away a moment playing with the idea, but as he turned back to add something Nicolas hit him with a pillow.

Chapter Forty Nine

Happy with the preparation of the front orchard paddocks Nicolas sowed white clover for summer that he could assist with the sprinklers if it got too dry, and moved into the old shed to begin planting out almond seeds in trays. Intrigued, Jennie came over with Liz and Elsie every morning to help; sitting there cracking the nut shells gently with pliers and half burying them in damp soil ready for someone to transplant once they'd sprouted.

Karl insisted that the girls stay in school, allowing Emma long periods to practice on her flute though he'd long ago given up on the idea of Sarah learning music. Instead he had her take Nicolas' place tutoring the two boys in spelling and composition, and with nothing much else to do Robbie started coming back to take them through their sums. Chas and Eric went off on their horses every morning just as the sun came up; their regular clip-clop waking him by their steady rhythm and for the first time Nicolas began to have a sense of order and calm about the place. That's what his festival play had been about, he thought; not the silly bit with Marcus at the end, but this abiding sense of calm he felt once the world was put back right. As he worked potting out seedlings and doing his rounds of the farm he marveled at how things came to be. It was late spring.

Mid-morning one day he was sitting with the women having their cup of tea, and frowning a little leaned forward and asked, "Jennie, what do you know about Lilith?"

She glanced up sharply, but hesitated, shyly, looking for words. "Who told you about Lilith, Nicolas?"

He sat back trying to think, then shook his head while Elsie sipped her tea, gazing at him over the rim of her cup, and Liz looked on carefully.

"I don't know. I must have read it in a book somewhere; I've been trying to think where."

"Was Poppy talking to you about her?"

"No, I don't think so. Sometimes he'd say things that sort of reminded me of something, but it didn't really connect until now and I wondered if you knew something."

Jennie leaned forward. "Lilith was Adam's first wife, Nicolas, before Eve. History blames her for the fall from Grace, but Poppy never believed it. He always said, no it's wrong, it was Eve who broke up their marriage because she was so jealous; a silly spoiled slip of a girl who destroyed everything because she couldn't get what she wanted, calling Lilith a slut and trying to make out Eve as pure and virginal, but had been led astray."

"So who was Lilith?"

"She was the original Earth Mother. In ancient times she was the Goddess of Fertility, and that's why Poppy worshipped her so." She blushed slightly. "He always said that to be a good farmer you must love the soil like it was a woman, and when you do it will produce all good things for you."

He looked away through the open door of the shed, across the amphitheatre. "Do you think it's true," he asked absently, almost to himself.

Elsie put her cup down and said curiously, "We have high hopes for you, Nicolas. Wally was right to have chosen you to carry things on, but none of us could see it at the time, until your mother passed away and it all started coming together as he said it would."

He sat there silently, lost for a while, not even looking at her until Liz said suddenly, "A penny for your thoughts."

He glanced at her, brow furrowing. "I was thinking maybe we should put on a play, but maybe one of the old plays not one of mine. There must be a lot of them that we could adapt, or rewrite or something; about all this. Why don't we do that, for next Easter I mean?"

"Euripides," Liz said. "Go and see Marcus about it, and tell him what's on your mind." She watched his face. "He won't be up for another few weeks, but as you wish I'll take you back up on Friday and we can spend the weekend with him, and discuss it perhaps."

Nicolas thought about it a moment and nodded, but as he did so something else came into his mind and he looked at her, head cocked to one side making her blush.

"Don't do that, Nicolas," she said quietly.

"Do what?"

"Look at people like that. I'm sorry; you're simply far too intelligent and nobody can keep anything from you. But you bare their souls when you do that, and it's not fair." She gazed at him, seriously, and then turned to the others.

"Yes, Marcus and I are getting together," she sighed. "That's the reason Ted and I have separated; it has nothing to do with Robbie, not directly, but we weren't ready to announce it quite yet."

Then she stood and with a backward glance at Nicolas took their cups over to the water trough. She washed them and left them to drain before coming back over to take a tray of seedlings and resume potting them out.

Chapter Fifty

Once they arrived in the city Liz drove straight through and along the river to pick up Marcus, who'd finished his lectures for the day and when he knew Nicolas was with her wanted to take them both out to dinner. It was a little early so they went for a walk along the foreshore, and when they held hands Nicolas simply smiled.

Strolling along Liz explained Nicolas's idea of performing a classical play at the festival while he listened absently to what she was saying. He didn't spark up until Marcus leaned forward to gain his attention, suggesting they perform *The Baccantes* by Euripides as Liz had been suggesting; he had copies in his office if they wanted to go back and get them.

"We can have our walk first, it's all right," he replied, "but we'll do it. If it's what you say it is we'll do it; sounds good."

"Ah, we wanted to have a bit of time together, Liz and I. That's what we were discussing; you weren't listening. I thought maybe we could leave you with the play, to study."

He glanced up, puzzled. "It's all right; I won't look if you don't want me too. I know what people do when they love one another. What do you think?"

Liz burst out laughing, covering her mouth with her fingers and squeezing Marcus's hand. "Isn't he sweet!" she cried.

"Well, I thought you and Ted were just arguing all the time and it made me sad." He said seriously. "If you'd told me what was happening I would have put you both in the old house, with Karl maybe for the time being, and make that the new music school. It's a good house, really, quite solid, and I was going to change my mind about knocking it down to build a new one. Ted just didn't get it, did he, do you think?"

Marcus stopped, gazing off into the distance across the river and shaking his head. He let Liz's hand go and taking Nicolas in his arms hugged him for a long moment before holding him slightly away to study his face; stroking his cheek gently with his thumb. Finally he shrugged, turning around to take them both in hand, and walked back along the path.

Nicolas didn't start reading the play until they'd sat down for dinner, while Marcus and Liz scanned the menu and ordered wine. When his meal arrived Marcus reached across to take it from him, making him concentrate on the food though he ate mechanically, eyes distant, while they spoke quietly with their heads together.

Back at Marcus's apartment Liz went in to shower, and without thinking he put the script down on the desk and followed her in, undressing and running a bath for himself while she showered. He looked up momentarily.

"You're very pretty, Liz," he said. "I can see why Robbie's so handsome. Do you want to play Agave for me, in the play? You'd be ideal. We'll do the whole thing nude; only Pentheus in his royal robes and the Baccantes and everybody else naked. That'd be hell truthful, and really radical, don't you think?"

Marcus came in, raising an eyebrow, but Liz held her finger to her lips to shush him and let Nicolas continue. But with the bath full he'd stopped there, and stepping into the warm water began soaping himself.

When Marcus disrobed and stepped into the shower with Liz, Nicolas merely added, "You can play Pentheus, Marcus, and get ripped apart. That'll be fun; get you back for taking over my Dowager Duchess. Robbie can play Dionysos." Then he pulled the plug and stepped out of the bath chuckling to himself. Taking a towel he went out, and only partly drying his body draped it over the chair and sat down again to continue reading.

Next morning, not unexpectedly they found him there asleep, his notes stacked neatly to one side and the original script covered in jottings and diagrams in order next to them. Liz tried to wake him for breakfast but Marcus brushed her gently aside and picking him bodily up carried him into their bedroom and put him to bed. Over toast and coffee he went through the play, page after page shaking his head in wonder.

"We'll never get away with it," he said quietly, and handed the sheets over to Liz.

"Not like this, we certainly will not," she said, skimming the pages, "but if we allow for body stockings or flesh coloured briefs perhaps, we just might. Let me talk to him, Marcus; we'll work something out if I write him a music score and help him understand something of impressionism in place of this direct realism. He'll come around on a good argument, you know, and if he sees the beauty of what we want to achieve. I doubt you'll get him to agree on purely censorship grounds; he won't know what the word means."

She nodded thoughtfully to herself.

Chapter Fifty One

When they got back to the farm on Sunday Liz went up to Edoras to see Emma, talking quietly to her while Nicolas unpacked his things. They came over to him, saying they wanted to read his script and start work on the music, but he simply nodded. Changing into his work clothes he turned away and went out down the hill to the potting shed. He went over the work Jennie and Elsie had been doing the past two days; counting pots and seedlings, and nuts, and happy with the result walked across to the big house. They were at the kitchen table shelling peas.

"Um, Aunty Elsie, I think that's enough almond trees," he said. "We can leave it now; just water them sometimes if they look like drying out too much. We can do the pecans later, in autumn, or walnuts if we go that way. What we might do next is get some sheep onto the new white clover, maybe after Christmas when it's up more than it is. Is that all right do you think?"

Elsie stared up at him, and picking up a tea towel threw it at him.

"Come in here telling your grandmother how to suck eggs, young whipper-snapper! Be off with yer."

He looked at her a long moment then smiled at the old lady sitting there at the table, eyes sparkling. Back out through the conservatory he ran into Liz and Emma who'd followed him down.

"Sorry," he said, turning briefly to them before disappearing. "Yes, come and tell me what you want to do, once you've played around with it a bit."

He went to find Robbie.

"Come for a swim," he said when he found him.

Together they disappeared behind the big lightning-riven fig tree and behind the sheds. Out of sight Nicolas took him by the hand, leading him fingers entwined while they skirted the amphitheatre and ascended the long opposite slope to cross the ridge and down the other side. Nicolas glanced up briefly to see if anyone followed before turning to undress. He indicated for Robbie to do the same.

Standing there facing one another Nicolas asked him, "Can you play Dionysos, properly, I mean, really?"

"What do you mean; Dionysos? That's Bacchus, the god of wine and getting really drunk, and fooling around. All you have to do is get pissed, don't you?"

"No, not if you do it right; that's what they all think, but I don't."

Robbie stood back, watching him. "What do you think?"

"Your nice body is what I think, and the way you look at me sometimes; beautiful, sensual, making things happen; that's the real Dionysos. Of course, he's a God. You know, but you're hiding something and I want to know what it is."

"No, I'm not," Robbie said, "it's not me. I'm only a comedian. Sometimes you can't see things, until later, or what you want to see; I don't know. We're married, you said so yourself, and I had to, sort of, adjust. So did the girls, except you can't take even the most blatant hint. I never met anyone like you before. It took me a long time to figure you out."

Nicolas glanced at him then away again. "What's happening?" he asked himself, absently, before glancing sharply back.

Robbie came close and took his hand, "Nothing's happening, Nic. You just want to know everything but you can't, you don't have the right. You want power to change the world, but you can't have it. I've read that play, of course I have; it's one of Liz's favourites and I grew up on it, so I do know something about it. I never took it seriously, that's all; Pentheus isn't the only one who's stupid."

He walked with him across the dam wall to sit him in the grass on the other side, under the trees. Then he sat on a tussock and spread his legs, and started his puppet show while Nicolas looked on, with no-one to turn to.

"Can you play Dionysos yourself, the way you want?" Robbie looked up suddenly.

When he didn't reply he asked him again, "If you can't, how do you expect me to? I mean, that's the question, isn't it?"

He watched him closely.

"After Wally was killed you've been treating me like shit, do you know that?"

"No, no I haven't."

"Yes you have. I'm your husband; you married me just the same as the girls did."

Nicolas looked at him curiously. "But you said you weren't gay, not interested, and I really wanted the girls to be happy. They said I was too much for them, but I can't think quite right about things like that so I didn't really know what they were talking about, and then you came along, Rob. I've never regretted it, what we did; what we do together. What's the matter now, I don't understand."

"Shit, you are a dumb arse; you can't read people, can you, even in front of everyone, no matter how many there are. Now there's just you and me. Come on, concentrate; show me how you want Dionysos played, how you think he really is, like you said. Do it to me, I'll be Pentheus. Then we can swap around; muck around with it a bit."

Nicolas looked at him, then away again. He turned his back on him, and taking a big deep breath swung around to face him. "All right," he said quietly.

Radiating aura suddenly, he came at Robbie projecting Dionysos with full force. He was completely taken aback, goose bumps breaking out over his body, and he stopped playing with himself and blushed. Nicolas stopped, frowning.

"You're supposed to resist, Rob," he said. "You're not supposed to be affected. Pentheus is a real cold bastard and has to learn the hard way. That's what the play's about, isn't it? That's why he got torn apart, for being a pervert, you know, and he was supposed to be a king. If you played him like that there'd be no argument, he'd be away with the Baccantes before you could blink."

He looked at him thoughtfully, head cocked to one side as he changed his mind. "No, you try Dionysos first. I need to show you how Pentheus is played, and then we'll do it again."

"No, Nic, I don't want to. You scared the shit out of me, throwing everything back in my face that I just said to you, and I don't know if I could handle that in front of everyone. I'm a comedian, I told you. Comedians hide their true feelings, else they wouldn't be funny; they'd be tragic."

"But you wanted to a minute ago. You asked me to show you, and I did."

"No, you'll have to get Marcus to do it." Robbie turned to walk away, back into the bush a little under the shade, leaning against a tree with his back to him.

Nicolas came up behind him. "What, Rob? I thought you weren't coming out properly, now you say comedians hide their true feelings. Tell me."

Robbie half turned to him. "I'm not homosexual, I never thought I was. I never looked at boys, even at school, after swimming. I never looked at your body like that either, until now; I always chased girls. But what you do to people, Nicolas, is change them somehow. We're all falling in love with you, everyone is."

"Don't say that. What? I can't help it; everything just comes into my head, like I'm thinking something. I don't know, until after, when everyone's saying things and I try to think about what happened."

"But you're doing it now, and you knew."

"It's a fucking play, Rob! It's acting; make believe, but saying something. And you asked me, so I did. What the hell do you want me to do about it? Anyway, you're not in love with me, only an idea of me, like those other people hate it. But it's only an idea, it's not real; I'm not real, I'm not even here sometimes, I'm off somewhere else, like, on a different planet."

Robbie turned to him and took both hands in his own. "First, I can't act like that; I'm not that good, really. Don't put me in any of your plays," he said shyly.

Nicolas nodded, hesitating, looking him in the eye. "What's second?" he asked, almost in a whisper.

Robbie didn't answer. He simply leaned in and kissed him, tenderly at first then letting go his hands began to caress his hips and buttocks, drawing him in close. He licked his ear and kissed his neck, then his shoulder, and Nicolas closed his eyes and let him.

Later as they walked home they followed the creek up along the south face of the ridge, swimming across to bathe and pick up their clothes from the grass on the other side as they went, approaching Edoras unusually from that side. They entered without saying anything, through when Liz looked up from her sheets of music she stopped playing, causing Emma to stop too and Sarah to turn around. The boys tossed their clothes casually on the bed and went over to the stove to see what was cooking.

"I think we've about finished for the day, Em," Liz said a little too loudly, "we can do some more tomorrow."

She tidied her music and placing it neatly in her briefcase rose and left, with only a quick backward glance at Robbie.

When she'd gone Sarah said, "We're a foursome now, are we?"

Nicolas gazed steadily at her a moment before answering, "Yes, it seems that way. Is it that obvious?"

She glanced down and smiled. "You're not Dionysos," she giggled; "more like Alexander the Great, if you want to be Greek about it. You'd better be careful walking around like that."

"Sarah!" Emma complained.

"What? It's all right, Em. Don't get uptight suddenly."

"No, it's not that."

She looked across at them. "I'm glad, finally. I've been waiting and waiting for you silly boys to come to your senses. We couldn't have kept going with two threesomes; that's what it was, you two never connecting properly, only pretending, trying to be men. That's what boys do, isn't it, making us responsible for loving because you can't grow up and face yourselves; because you've got a dick and you think it's something important. But now our marriage is complete; it's all consummated finally, and I'm glad."

Robbie looked at her strangely, then skirting the end of the table stood beside her. He took her hand and ran it up inside his thigh, and had her stroke him until she giggled.

"All right?" he said. "Get over it, Em; sometimes you're as bad as Eric."

Chapter Fifty Two

Elsie without telling anyone went ahead and bought a small flock of Corriedale ewes in lamb to a black-faced Suffolk, and put them straight on the white clover in the front paddock. Nicolas complained that they wanted it for the horses for now but she said they'd get too fat if they're not getting enough work, and that was the end of the discussion. After a few days on the rich pasture she moved her sheep back onto the amphitheatre which was drying off now, and a week later moved them onto the other front paddock with the horses.

Nicolas stopped to talk with Chas about all this but he shrugged and grinned, and scruffing his hair suggested he'd better not argue with Elsie if he wanted to keep his foreskin intact; she'd stretch it right out and pull it over his head like a condom, if you got her dander up.

Grinning at the idea yet frustrated he went and got Robbie out of the school to help build a fence across the front of the amphitheatre, keeping sheep away from where he was working, and having done that decided to give him the job of building a permanent stage there on the embankment between the middle shed and the potatoes. He wanted his actors to walk from the shed straight across the path onto the stage, where they could create backdrops any time.

Robbie argued, telling him to stop worrying about Elsie's stupid fucking sheep and just build a good solid platform with tall posts back and centre front, and the rest would sort it itself out. They had some bush poles up there on the top of the ridge, and bearers and joists left over from building Edoras; it wasn't a problem.

Nicolas stared at him, then abruptly turned on his heel and walked away. Robbie watched as he disappeared into the bush past the end shed, and shaking his head went back to helping Karl with the boys.

When he wasn't back by lunch Marcus went up the hill to get him and after half an hour or so came back with him hand in hand. They walked in past the sheds but as Nicolas turned to go up to Edoras Marcus pulled him back toward the old house, saying they all wanted to sit and have a talk.

"Would you like to have lunch with us?" he asked quietly, looking thoughtfully down at him.

"Is Robbie there?"

"Yes, of course."

Nicolas let go his hand and stepping forward went in through the conservatorium. He sat next to Robbie, then thinking about it a moment stood and going around the table sat between Em and Sarah, across from him. Karl stayed at the other end, leaning back in his chair rolling a cigarette, while Liz sat at the head next to Marcus. When Jennie sat next to Robbie Nicolas got up again and going around the table made Robbie stand, offering his chair to Elsie, and taking his hand brought him around to sit next to Sarah.

He looked over at Marcus. "Are you chairing this meeting?" he wanted to know.

"Yes. Do you want to know what's on the agenda?"

"No, not really; just say what you want."

Marcus sat back, watching him, until Emma leaned forward and said, "Yes, Marcus, what do you want?"

She turned back to Nicolas, holding his hand. "What did he say to you?"

"Well, nothing really; I wasn't thinking about that. I only want to know why we can't stage the play the way I wrote it. I mean, it's not my play; it's ancient, but it's so beautiful and real, and I think we should do it. But it seems to be a problem and nobody will tell me why."

"Nicolas," Marcus leaned forward, "we've had this conversation before, you and I. Do you remember?"

Nicolas sat back a moment, then nodded.

"But it's not my fault," he said. "It's not my fault. I just, I don't know. I'm a good person, but this world we're in, sort of, hurts all the time and I'm trying to help. I don't know what else."

Emma took his hand in hers, leaning in close whispering in his ear. He listened to her, eyes distant before turning back to Marcus.

"They really think we are Gods, don't they . . . anything that's lovely. They can't cope with it; that's what you were saying to me, wasn't it."

He glanced past Sarah at Robbie who was staring at him, tears running down his cheeks. He looked down at his hands, then letting Emma go took Sarah's, then Robbie's, rubbing his fingers between his, and looked up again.

"All right, what do we need to do?"

Liz looked up sharply but Marcus held her back. "Do you agree with going around the table, Nic?" he asked.

Nicolas nodded, and Marcus looked toward Elsie.

She leaned forward. "You've got too much pasture coming on, son; should've been grazing it weeks ago. I was thinking about getting some goats too; cut back the rubbish, and with the horses we'd be right." She sat back, gazing out the window, nodding. "Yes, that'd be about right; lambs'll drop April, and we'll have some good pasture over winter, that'll pay our bills."

He looked across at her, thinking. "But if that's true Chas has too much pasture," he replied finally, "and your place as well. I did all the sums, but I thought Chas and Eric wanted to run their cattle over there, and you said you had a sharefarmer. If we want to play with that and spread things around, why not buy more sheep? If we had more lambs dropping in Spring that'd be better, wouldn't it? I only wanted to put the fence up so we could start building a stage."

"They're not going to worry you. Work away if you want," Elsie replied.

He nodded, and shrugged, glancing back at Marcus.

"Jen?"

"No, nothing; I have nothing to say."

"Liz?"

"Well, yes, yes I do." She leaned forward and opened her briefcase. "I really do need to go over these scores with you, Nicolas, if you don't mind. I find your interpretation rather bold. I think we might concentrate more on aesthetics and presentation."

He sat back in his chair, frowning, before glancing sideways at Robbie and Karl at the foot of the table, then back to Marcus. He stood to leave.

"You can be the producer, Liz, but you're not going to direct it. I'm the director; it's my play. I know I'll have to work with what you give me, but that's it. I'm going to see Chas, all right? I might work with him for a few weeks on the farm, until after Christmas. He's getting some bulls in, anyway, and I want him to teach me about them."

"Sit down, Nicolas," Marcus interrupted.

"No, you do it. Tell Robbie how you want the stage done and he'll build it. We can come and help him put the posts up. If you want to wear costumes that's all right too, but I'm not."

With that he turned and disappeared through the conservatory.

Chapter Fifty Three

Riding out of the bush reserve along the back fence of the farm Nicolas gazed across the top paddocks at their cattle grazing. Chas and Eric were nowhere to be seen so he unlatched the gate and rode through, turning his horse to close it before heading down to the house. He dismounted and went inside, but they weren't there either. Hungry, he made himself lunch from the pot of stew on the stove, with bread and a cup of tea, and had just sat at the table when Eric poked his head through the door.

"We're down at the yards, Nic. Come and look."

As he glanced up Eric disappeared; he barely glimpsed him so he sat eating. He was still thinking about the play, and Elsie's sheep, and getting the stage built and bringing the poles down from the ridge, and Liz, and bloody fucking Marcus, and Karl. Maybe they were part of it, an important part; they drew the crowds, but he struggled with their saying what the crowds can see, or not see. They were part of what was wrong, he thought, but how would they know unless they let people see, and saw what might happen? How can we fix things, otherwise?

Eric came back again, curious to see where he was. "What's the matter?"

"Oh, what, nothing. What, Eric?"

"They're inseminating the cows."

"What?"

"Come and look."

He stood and followed him out. Down the path beside the house they went out through the trees and crossed to the cattle yards where Chas and some other men were working. There was a fair bit of noise with animals crushed together, bawling and jostling restlessly, but the men were quiet and patient with them.

A man in a filthy white t-shirt and plastic apron had a cow in the crush, standing behind her while Chas held her tail up. He had his left arm up the cow's backside almost to his shoulder, while with his right hand he fed a long thin tube into her vagina, manipulating it into position until finally he pushed the plunger on the end and withdrew. He pulled his arm out and shook off the manure, then pulled off the long rubber glove as Chas let the cow go. Turning around he saw Nicolas standing there, apologising for not shaking hands as Chas introduced them.

"Are you the vet?"

"Nah, I'm just the AI man, Stan Lawrence, mate. Good to meet ya. Chas, he's the vet; bloody bush doctor." He looked up, "fuckin' bushwhacker."

"What's up, son?" Chas asked, watching him.

"They're giving me the shits, Chas. I thought I'd come over and work with you for a few weeks. Is that all right?"

"No worries, we're short of hands right now so we could use you. Tell your mate Robbie he'd be handy too. You three boys can do a bit of stock work for me. You happy to camp over here on swags for a while, instead of going home to sleep?"

"Yeah, sure, that'll be good. But I thought you were getting some bulls."

"Too dear right now, they can wait. You want to see what we're doing?"

"Yes, of course. How do you know they're ready?"

"Have a look, you tell me; bright young fella like you."

Nicolas stood back, watching the cows for a moment while they jostled and milled around.

"They're hot, aren't they? They're fannies are dripping, and swollen."

"What else?"

"They're mooing too much, and restless, sniffing around, looking for a bull." But then he grinned, embarrassed, and gave himself away. Chas stared at him a moment, and nodded to himself.

"All right, you get the picture. What's it called?

"Oestrus. What that means is, when the female is receptive to sperm; when her egg comes down every month, before her menses if she doesn't conceive."

"What happens if she does?"

"Well, the foetus will attach to the uterus through the umbilicus and placenta, and after that no more eggs will come down until after the calf is born and she's receptive again."

"All right, how long does that take?"

"Nine months. It's the same as us, humans I mean."

Chas smiled. "Good boy. You want try?"

"What, me; you're sure?"

"Give him a glove, Stan."

Nicolas removed his shirt and held up his right arm for Stan to roll on a new surgical glove while Eric sent the next cow into the crush and fastened her.

"Left arm, son," Stan said. "In cattle the uterus is displaced to the right by the rumen, so you'll be cack-handed if you go that way."

Nicolas changed hands. Standing behind the cow he listened carefully as the procedure was explained to him. He reached up and pushing his middle fingers into her rectum while Stan inserted the straw containing the semen into her vagina, then slowly shoved his hand and arm following the straw right up into her colon, feeling with his fingers along the floor of her colon until he found the cervix.

"You right, son?"

"Yes, I think so. I can feel it."

"OK, let Stan do it, all right," Chas interrupted. "It's a bit of a technique. We can't afford to waste the straw if it's not right."

Nicolas pulled his arm out and scraped off the manure, then rolled the glove down his arm and pulled it off, fascinated, to watch Stan at work. He finished fairly quickly and waved at Eric to let her go.

"We'll come and get you in the morning, Nicolas, be awake," Chas said. "I'll sort out what jobs I want you to do tonight, and give you a start tomorrow; all right?"

He looked up. "Do you want me to go now?"

"I haven't got much for you, unless you want to help Eric."

"Is it all right if I watch?"

"Yep, no worries; stand over there, mate, and if we need a hand I'll give you a call." Chas looked across at the house, and back down at him. "How did you get over here, ride?"

"Yes, the horse is still at the house."

"There's a job for you, isn't it? Go and look after your horse, will you, same as I showed you, then come back here."

They finished the afternoon and when the four returned early next morning Chas had the three boys toss their swags into the big main bedroom, and he threw his own into the old kids' room so he could have a bit of peace and quiet, so he said. It made little difference because by time they came in at night, showered and ate dinner they were exhausted, and rolling in their blankets went straight to sleep. He kept them working from sunup to sundown, while Elsie brought over cooked meals for them in Jack's car.

Eric turned out to be a very good rider, with a natural flair for staying in the saddle while Nicolas's clumsiness saw him tossed off more than once or twice as the stock horse wheeled suddenly to chase a beast breaking away from the herd. He learned the hard way not to let go the reins as he came to earth with a thump, and to ignore their chuckling at his expense, but once he got past that and learned to keep his seat Chas began sending the other two up into the back paddocks, keeping Nicolas there with him to pick up the finer points of judging cattle.

Only a few days later he started thinking seriously that maybe a small stud would work for them, assuming Elsie's farm was available and they could run a commercial herd within their overall operations. He'd stand watching Nicolas when he thought he wasn't looking, almost hearing his brain whirring away after he'd finished explaining something, eyes distant, before snapping back abruptly to turn to him explaining something he'd just worked out about which stud they might buy that sort of bull from, and why. When he looked through their catalogues with him over lunch he saw he was right; the consistent balance and proportion in his bulls' conformation was outstanding with good growth on their type of grass, and they all had good temperament.

They began to be distracted constantly by Robbie and Eric mucking around, laughing all the time and not focusing on their work, but Nicolas simply smiled and said let them have their fun; it was all right. He knew Eric was sprouting thick black pubic hair and that Robbie was taking the mickie out of him about it, except Chas lost his temper with them one morning and bawled them out. They quietened for a while but it made Nicolas start thinking about Simon and how he missed him so. After lunch he went for a long walk by himself until they rode up with a spare horse saddled for him, and the three took the rest of the afternoon off to go riding.

It wasn't that which interrupted their work, however, but Liz arriving on horseback the next day to tell Chas that Jennie needed to be driven into the hospital because her water had broken suddenly. He looked across asking whether Elsie was with her, and the two girls, and when she replied yes he went on to finish the job he was doing before packing up.

Nicolas watched him taking his time until he turned slightly to wink, and he glanced across at Liz.

"You go with Liz, Chas, we'll be right," he said softly, out of earshot. "We can tidy up here and we'll follow you over later. Tell the boys to come down, will you. They can help me clean up."

"Good lad."

Chapter Fifty Four

It was too late for Jennie to go to hospital; the new twins were born before Chas with Liz not far behind arrived back at the big house. They were still there when the boys came in an hour or so later, by which time the house was crowded with people making each other cups of tea and standing around waiting. Eventually Elsie came out giving them the all clear.

Trooping into the bedroom they found the babies being passed around for everyone to hold. Nicolas stayed shyly there in the doorway while Chas went first, then Robbie, and Eric, until Emma looked up to see where he was and noticing him standing back came to draw him in close. He sat on the bed next to Jennie while she held his hand, and then leaned over and handed him one of the babies.

He sat there mesmerised, unwrapping the towel he was swaddled in to look him up and down, at his tiny fingers and toes, his wizened monkey face and wooden clothes peg on his cut umbilicus, and his hugely disproportionate cods. The baby opened its eyes to look up at him, and as he did Nicolas gasped and smiled, then chuckled to himself.

"Wally," he said, "little Wally. He's got his eyes, look!"

They all leaned forward and Emma said, frowning, "Don't you think he looks like Chas?"

Nicolas thought a moment, studying the baby's face. "Yes, he does," he said finally, "but he has Wally's eyes, his mischief. He's an imp; it's a little Wally in there, not Chas."

"God help us, we're doomed," Elsie exclaimed. She leaned forward to take the baby but Nicolas held onto him. He laid him in his lap and folded the towel neatly around him, making him snug again before taking him back in his arms.

"What's his name," he wanted to know. "What are we going to call him?"

Jennie gazed at him. "You name him, Nicolas," she said quietly. "What do you think?"

"It has to be Walter, don't you think? Walter Charles, except he'll be a Walter Larkin the gentleman not another Wally Cavanaugh. He can behave himself, this one." He looked up at Chas who simply smiled and nodded, so he handed the baby over and Jennie gave him the other one which he unwrapped just the same. It was a girl.

"I thought there were two boys," he said, surprised; "twins."

"Don't you like it?" Sarah asked.

"No! No, I mean yes, I didn't mean to say I didn't like her. I didn't say that did I? No I didn't; it's wonderful. What's her name? What are we going to call her?"

"You say; you name her, Nicolas."

He looked at her. "Grace," he said suddenly. "We can't call her Elsie Jennifer Emma Sarah Larkin, can we? No, she's so sweet so maybe just Gracie. Then everyone'll love her."

"Why Gracie, where did you get that from?"

He shrugged and said nothing, preoccupied with wrapping her again before giving her up, but at that moment Kennie came across looking at her. Nicolas looked at him.

"This is your little sister, Kennie. Do you like her?"

Kennie looked up frowning. "They came out of mummy's bottom."

"No, that's a different part," he said, chucking him under the chin. "Do you love her?"

Kennie just look at up him until Elsie interrupted, "All right, everybody go now, out! Jen needs her sleep and so do the bubs, they're all exhausted. You can come back in after dinner, all of you, scoot!"

Nicolas stood and took Chas's hand on the way out. "Want to have a beer with us, Chas?" he wanted to know. "Not much use going back to work is there? We should celebrate, don't you think?"

He turned to the others and said, "Come up to Edoras, everybody, and we might get a bit pissed. Come on Em, Sair, you too; and Eric. We'll have a celebration."

Before anyone could answer he disappeared through the conservatory, so Karl shrugged and went to retrieve his guitar and banjo. Chas took his guitar while the others followed Nicolas.

Once they settled and had a beer Emma started serving up her smoked sausage and pickles, and cheese she'd been making with Sarah unbeknown to the boys while they were away at the farm working, apart from the herbs she had hanging in her alcove around the big stove. The place was starting to smell more like the big Italian café in town than a barn, Nicolas thought, except better; like the restaurant where Marcus took him to dinner when they were up in the city. His mind started wandering again as he gazed about, until Chas picked up his guitar and hesitating only a moment sang *Nature Boy.*

There was a boy
A very strange enchanted boy
They say he wandered very far, very far
Over land and sea
A little shy, and sad of eye
But very wise was he
And then one day
A magic day he passed my way
And while we spoke of many things
Fools and kings
This he said to me
"The greatest thing you'll ever learn
Is just to love and be loved in return"
"The greatest thing you'll ever learn
Is just to love and be loved in return"

Nicolas glanced up as he stopped playing to find everyone looking at him. He gazed about, confused, then across at Chas.

"No, we love you, Chas," he said quietly. "You're the man. I'm not anybody; just a dumb kid really, but you're a legend. None of us would be here doing this without you."

Looking up and around, with a wave. "You built this place for us."

Eric nodded, glancing across. He stood and unabashed went to stand behind Chas, and hugged him.

"Ah, get away with you," he chuckled. "Come on, pour the beer, eh, and let's get this show on the road." He glanced across at Karl and nodded, tapping his right foot, but just before he started playing caught Nicolas's eye and winked. He turned to Eric and told him to go and sit down, then head up began playing.

Eric walked around Robbie and sat next to his brother, who reached over to fill his glass and sat back. After a moment he leaned forward slightly but Nicolas stopped him.

"Don't, Eric," he said. "Don't say anything, all right." He turned to him, and standing took his hand and led him outside onto the front veranda and sat down again. Still holding his hand he looked up before pulled him down to sit next to him.

"Don't say anything," he repeated almost to himself, and paused thinking a moment, and taking a deep breath said, "Eric, I don't know, maybe, what's wrong with me is I just can't think what happens before or after, only now. But I don't really know what now is, and when people want me to explain I get confused. I'm really going to have to work on that, if we're to get anywhere. I don't want you to think I'm a bad person or anything like that because I'm not."

He looked away thinking to himself, *'Sometimes I have really bad memories, but I can't think what they are,'* yet without voicing his thoughts said, "Do you want to go for a swim? We've got a lovely little spot down there, I'll show you."

"Tomorrow, Nic," Eric said, glancing up at him. "You can show me tomorrow. We'll take another day off, all right, you and me and Rob. Chas'll be happy, don't worry about it."

He stood to go back inside but when Nicolas didn't move he sat down again. He put his hand on his shoulder.

After a moment he said, "What I've been thinking most about, Nic, is when you said to me family is everything. Nobody ever said anything like that to me before, the way you said it, and I never had a chance to say what it meant to me, all right? We are the same, aren't we, except I get angry when somebody's trying to embarrass me. I mean, your mate Robbie's a bit queer but he's not so bad, and he's a real funny bugger; that dick show he does breaks you right up, but Grant's not coming back is he. Out here is good, so there's us left, isn't there; you and me?"

Nicolas looked sharply at him. "You can't be in the marriage, Eric. It doesn't matter, we'll find you someone real nice; real hot, but from a nice family not that town lot. You don't need them."

He leaned in close and said, "They love it when it's up 'em, you know, when you both love one another like that. It's the best thing, there're no words for it."

Eric chuckled, "you didn't hear anything I said, did you."

"Yes I did," he looked him in the eye and took his hand. "Yes I did, but between you and me is a lot different from us and them, isn't it. That's what I meant. We don't understand one another so well, do we, but I'm glad we're trying, you know, because I miss Simon so much and I can't think of it, Eric; and our mother. Some things we're not to talk about, do you agree with me about that? We have to look ahead."

Eric nodded, quietly, looking away across the amphitheatre, then standing took Nicolas by the hand again and they went back inside.

Chapter Fifty Five

Back inside Eric let him go and went across to sit with Sarah and Robbie, while Nicolas sought out Marcus who was out on the back porch helping Emma salt onions in tubs of brine for her next batch of pickles. He stood watching them a while, until eventually he asked her if they could grow extra onions and make a business of it; the pickles were great.

She turned to him, smiling, wiping her hands on a towel. "Do you want to? Can you do some baby cucumbers for me as well, and olives?" She looked at him curiously. "Why are you planting all those almonds, anyway? If you plant more walnuts we can pickle them, and sell them like that."

"Can you pickle walnuts, really? I didn't know that; sure, why not? Why aren't we doing it already, does it have something to do with that quarantine or something?"

She glanced away and shrugged, and went back to her brine. Nicolas thought a moment, frowning, and went back inside.

"Chas, do you remember Wally said the place was quarantined, but he never said why. Do you know why?"

Chas flagged Karl and put down his guitar, and turned to him. "It's bullshit; Nic. Wally had funny ideas about organic farming and refused to follow Ag. Department policy. They wanted him to guarantee freedom from disease, but he said that wasn't good enough. Wally wanted to guarantee freedom from farm chemicals because he reckoned they created disease, so what was the point of their policy aside from making a business of protecting people from it? So he got offside with them and to get him back they placed the whole farm under quarantine."

"Can they do that?"

"They can do what they bloody well like, those pricks. The bastards don't have to be right or wrong, only hold you up in court for years on end. That's the way they work."

Nicolas sat back in his seat, astonished, and after a moment leaned forward again. "Do you mean, Chas, Wally never used farm chemicals; this farm hasn't had chemicals on it? Is that right? That's fantastic, bloody hell, I never thought."

Chas picked up his beer and took a sip, and putting it down again glanced back at him.

"What are you thinking about now, son?"

"Well, um, the quarantine is only for fresh vegetables, isn't it? It doesn't mean Emma can't be making pickles and selling them, does it?"

"Yes, that's right." Chas nodded and looked down at him. "All right, we'll do it. What we need to get is a commercial license for the kitchen, and we'll do it."

Nicolas sat back thinking only a moment, then glancing up said, "but if we are free of the chemicals we can be organic farmers, and sell certified organic pickles in the premium end of the market, at a good price. I read about it, and Wally was always talking about it. How can we do that?"

"Ha, Nicolas, no doubt about you, is there." He paused a moment, glancing sideways at him, and taking another sip of beer picked up his guitar. "Son," he said, "if you can get us certified organic we're in the race. You'll have a job ahead of you, I'll tell you that, but go for it, eh?"

Nicolas nodded. He stood and went out the back door.

"All right," he said to Emma, "we'll do it; we can. Do you think we can make a nice label, certified organic, and get some nice jars?"

She glanced sideways at him as her father had just done, with the same look on her face. She smiled and nodded, then turned back to her task. Marcus stood looking curiously at him, however.

"What, Marcus?" he wanted to know.

"Don't you think you're taking on too much?"

He frowned at that, gazing off into the bush behind the house, then back again. "No," he said, "we haven't started yet. If we're going to have people here they're going to need jobs, aren't they?"

"They'll be wanting to get away from all that, won't they, if they're dropping out."

"What? No, how will they live otherwise."

"On their investments, I should think."

Nicolas turned his back to go inside. "Silly idea," he muttered. "They'll miss out if they do that." But then from just inside the door he turned again. "Anyway, I still need to know how you're going with my play. What have you decided you want to do? Are you going to play Pentheus for me, or not?"

"No," Marcus shook his head. "Get Eric to do it, he'll be good. I bet he can act, nearly as good as you can, Nicolas."

"Why don't you want to do it?"

"No reason, I don't have to give a reason, do I?"

"So you won't help me?"

"I didn't say that. I'll help you, but I don't want to be an actor. The last one was fun but this one you're far too taking seriously, so what I might do is get some of our theatre students out to play the Baccantes, and sing the chorus for you. I'm not sure they'll play nude, but you can ask them yourself, all right."

Nicolas cocked his head, watching him thoughtfully. "All right, we'll do it that way," he said finally, and disappeared inside to find Eric.

He'd been stocking the fridge with beer and had turned back to the table with two cold bottles in hand, so Nicolas followed him across and sat down waiting for him to do the honours. When finished topping up everyone's glasses he sat down again.

"Eric, do you want to be in my play? I need someone to play the king, and you'll be just right."

Eric glanced at him. "So long as nobody tries to embarrass me, maybe I will. What's it about?"

Robbie started laughing. "They won't embarrass you, Eric, they'll rip you apart. Pentheus, he's the king, gets torn apart by angry ravaging women because he's a pervert hiding in a tree watching them while they're fucking, and they collect all his bits up in chaff bags."

"I'm not a bloody pervert," Eric answered indignantly. "No, Nicolas, you'll have to find somebody else."

Nicolas glared angrily at them. He rose and went outside by himself, but Robbie got up and followed him, grabbing his arm as he went through the door.

"Sorry, Nic, sorry; I was just having a joke."

"It wasn't bloody funny. Now who am I going to get? You're a real bastard sometimes, but you think it's a joke and everybody's just going to laugh at it. I'll make you do it, you know, that'll teach you, if I can't find anyone. You can get a hard-on in front of everyone, if that's what it takes."

He watched his face but Robbie's eyes went wide and he turned away. "You really are angry, aren't you," he murmured.

"Yes, of course I am. What did you think? You think you can treat me like I'm spastic or bloody autistic or something, and it doesn't make any difference. But it does. This is my play and I want to do it properly, but you're all being a bunch of shits about it."

He stormed back through the house, tears blurring his vision. "Marcus!" he called out. "Can you get me some decent actors, some of your theatre students? Or do I have to do all this by myself?"

Sarah stood and blocked his way. He tried to move around her but she stepped sideways and back again, capturing his attention.

"What, Sair?"

"It's nice and warm, isn't it? Come for a swim, just you and me," she said holding his gaze.

"I have to sort out this play, I mean; they're giving me the shits about it."

"No they're not, you're just not listening. Nicolas, come for a swim, all right?"

Chapter Fifty Six

When they finished their swim she sat him on his towel on the grass, and spreading her own right next to him. She ran her hand down his thigh. He reached down to stop her.

"You're seducing me, Sair."

"Yes, of course."

"Why? I mean, why right now, when I'm trying to say something? Why did you stop me from talking to Marcus, and saying what I thought?"

She looked at him curiously before answering, "Because we don't want you to say it, Nicolas."

"Why not?"

"Can't you guess? You're not putting on the play, that's why not. It's our privacy, and you want the whole world to know, but nobody can get through to you."

"But it's so beautiful, Sair. What if the world does now? What about that? Wouldn't it change everything?"

She lay back on her towel, watching him, but he leaned over her. She put her hand to his lips, stopping him from saying anything further. He tried to brush her aside but she grabbed his hand and put her fingers back to his lips.

He struggled with her until she cried, "Stop it, Nicolas; just stop it, all right. You've been outvoted."

She sat up, holding his face to stop him turning away. "Doesn't anything penetrate? Haven't you suffered enough? Don't you understand this world; all those stupid fucking people out there? They're not beautiful, they're arseholes. They're never going to understand your play; you'll get booed off the stage and we'll all be left looking like idiots, or worse. I know; I grew up there."

He was taken aback. "Well, what do you want me to do then? I have to have a play, for the festival, they'll be expecting something."

"If you really want to do *The Baccantes*, do it like they all do it, right the way through history, for a reason. If you don't want to, write us one of your lovely fairy tales. Liz and Marcus were only trying to help you, because you wanted to do one of the classics, but you can't do it like that. You have to give it to them the way they want it."

"What? What's the use of having a play then? What's the use of theatre?"

"Oh crap, Nic. Just get off it, will you. You're starting to give me the shits now. And you give me the shits about Eric too. It's not for you to decide who's in the marriage or not, and make him suffer like that; poor kid, missing out on everything." She lay back and pulled him down with her, whispering in his ear, "Just fuck me, that's what I want you to do. I've missed you boys so much the past few weeks, when you didn't come home, I really don't care about your stupid fucking play or any-fucking-thing-else, you hear me."

Nicolas looked at her, and then turned to lie on his own towel. "All right, Sair. If you want it so much do it to me first, the way you like it."

She rolled onto him, reaching down to him, and rubbed herself on him until she was wet, then inserted him just enough, and rippling her muscles made him close his eyes and moan out loud.

"God, Sair," he whispered, "what you can do with your pussy is amazing. That's just so fucking exquisite, you know."

"Do I do it better than Em?'

He opened his eyes. "Don't ask me that. No, you're both so different, not better."

"Do you want to tell me what it's like with her, and with Robbie?"

"Well," he gazed at her curiously, "she's like, more spiritual, if you know what I mean, and you're physical. And Robbie, he's just so funny, isn't he? Don't you think?"

"And you're so beautiful, Nicolas. It's the only time we can get past your brain, when your lovely body's so hot and it's like, your heart is singing. Nobody on earth can celebrate a good fuck like you can, and be so happy about it; Emma said the same thing to me, you know, and so did Robbie. We all love you the same, don't you know that?"

He looked at her oddly, and grinned. "All right then, agreed, but you'd better stop what it is you're doing down there else it'll be over too quick and we'll have to go home."

She lowered herself onto him all the way and he moaned again, and turning her over on her back rolled with her, still joined, and loved her with all his passion and frustration and weeks of working horses and cattle and his body hardening to solid muscle, and not thinking about anything else. He was home again.

That evening after they'd staggered Chas half-pissed down the hill with Karl and Marcus, they decided the three men had better sleep in the old house, and in the morning nurse their hangovers there than disturb Jennie and the babies.

When he got back up to Edoras Nicolas took Eric aside, who wasn't too far drunk simply happy, and looking as if he planned to stay the night anyway.

"Eric, sorry, but I've been told off. If you want to fuck with Sair, tonight, and Em, they've got the hell hots for your body. It's all right, we agreed, except you might have to take turns with Robbie because he won't be able to stand sitting back while you enjoy yourself. I want to write my new play."

Eric didn't say a thing but blushed a bright crimson, shifting from one foot to the other. Nicolas looked down at the front of his pants and grinned, then over his shoulder at the girls. He nodded slightly and turned him around to show them. Sarah put her hand to her mouth and stifled a laugh, and came over to take his hand.

"Oh, you poor boy, come with us." She reached down with the other, slipping it down the front of his trousers to take hold of him, but removed it fairly quickly and led him over to the bath where she stripped and stepping in started filling it with warm water.

She looked up to see him still standing there so she got out again and quickly undressing him stepped back with him into the big tub. Emma came in from seeing her Dad to bed and seeing them there strode across disrobing as she went, leaving a trail of shoes and skirts and blouse and bra and panties through the house. The two girls started on Eric while he giggled and cried out, but then Robbie joined them and Nicolas went across to the table and taking some pencils and sheaf of paper sat down to start writing.

Nobody got much sleep that night. When Marcus came up the next morning Nicolas was sound asleep at the table while the others were tangled up in the big bed, dead to the world. He had a quick glance through the new play and briefly scruffing Nicolas's hair shook his head in wonder, and went back down to the old house.

Chapter Fifty Seven

Following long debate at the big house it was decided that Nicolas should stay home and work on his play. He'd be more generally handy here anyway, and if he needed a break could tend the horses and help Elsie with the sheep. They wouldn't be able to grow onions until late winter but cucumbers could go in now if Emma wanted to start planting; he'd have plenty to occupy his time.

After further thought somebody suggested Robbie should stay here as well. The new stage still needed to be built, and anytime he needed a hand Chas wasn't too far away. Marcus and Karl could help out anywhere they could.

That left Eric and Sarah who could go and work for Chas. Sarah was the best horseman of the lot and was being wasted moping about the house, except when they slept over at the farm she could have the small room while Chas and Eric shared the main bedroom, and that would sort out the nonsense.

Elsie mentioned that her man would be moving back into town in the New Year sometime; once he had his wheat off. She and Chas got their heads together deciding to aerial sow the wheat stubble with pasture in early autumn instead of burning off, so it would be well up by mid-winter, and they'd shift the cows across to calve in the clean paddocks about June. Chas noticed Nicolas sitting there watching him intently, but he leaned over and said simply that late winter, after the calves had dropped, they go look for some good Angus bulls and maybe a few heifers if he wanted to get started on establishing his bloodlines.

He nodded and said nothing, and looking around the table with nothing more being said he rose and went out the back door. The others stood and followed him out, not laughing but not unhappy either. Eric hung back a little, until Sarah turned to ask what the matter was.

"Nothing much, um, thanks for last night it was good, but I want to get married the right way, all right? I don't want it to be like Mum, but you're going too far the other way, if you know what I mean."

Emma watched his face. "We thought you might," she said quietly, "but it's still no good you being a bloody virgin all your life; so bloody uptight, and resentful. It's just not human, and I don't think it's healthy anyway."

"You're probably right, I don't know. I feel a lot better now, so I can't complain; you're so nice you girls, and you really know how to make a man happy, but I know someone and now I might go and ask her out. She thought I was being a real deadshit before, and wouldn't talk to me."

"Well you were, weren't you, Eric. I wasn't talking to you either, nobody was."

Robbie turned to him. "Why don't you invite her over then? We'll have a Christmas party, maybe in the big house, and keep our thing here quiet. She can meet the family, and you can go on about jackerooing over on the new farm with Chas. I bet she'll want to jump into bed with you straight away."

"Ah, get fucked Robbie. If you're there embarrassing me you can go to buggery."

"Yes, shut up Rob," Nicolas said. "Leave him alone. Leave him be, all right."

"But it's a good idea isn't it, to have a Christmas party, and ask her over? We can invite a few more people. I know some of the people thinking about moving out here; Marcus's old friends from Uni, and a few others. Ted knows them all, and there's a few kids about our age we can get to know."

Sarah glanced sharply at him before turning away, smiling to herself. "Anyway, shut up now," she said, "we have to get our gear and meet Chas, Eric, else we'll be in the shit again."

Emma held him back a moment longer. "Who is she, Eric? Tell me. She's not a town girl, is she?"

"No, she's not. You know her anyway, from school, she's your friend; Sally Burgess."

"Really? Yes! I know, she was always looking at you, wondering if you were ever going to grow up; ooh, you lucky man." She jumped up and down on the spot, and turning abruptly on her heel went back to the house.

Chapter Fifty Eight

Once Robbie started on the theatre he decided to roof it. Impressed with his drawings, Chas set aside a whole day to bringing bush poles down off the ridge and cutting them to length; using the tractor to lift them into holes Robbie had dug. He then helped him measure the cut-outs for the bearers with a level off the top of the bank behind the shed, and cut them with the chainsaw before lifting the bearers and bolting them into place.

The deck finished, Marcus came down and showed him how he wanted the theatre lights hung under the roof, before they went too far, while Nicolas sallied back and forth, nervous with excitement, revising his script to account for the new staging layout.

The stage completed, however, Elsie decided she wanted some sheep yards as well, under the trees at the end of the track past the last shed where the bush started. She was adamant with Nicolas about cutting the corner out of his second paddock to make room, but there was good reason for it as she explained it to him, and the truck could back right up to the loading ramp. They needed to graze under the trees so sheep would be in those paddocks anyway, and they had to manage them from there; it was the best spot on the farm.

The idea clear in his head Nicolas went to see Robbie about doing the job, but he said he'd do it after Christmas if Chas brought some more posts down and cut them to length, and they brought the saw back to mill some rails rather than waste the studs and bearers still strapped up there on the ridge; meant for their new house. Right now he wanted to start organising the Christmas party as Emma had sent out their invitations weeks before and a lot of people were coming.

He went back up to Edoras to work on the play, but frustrated went over to the stove and started annoying Emma. She gave him some onions to peel and he spent an hour doing that until she glanced over at him.

"What's the matter, love?" she wanted to know.

"I don't really know, Em," he said quietly, not looking at her; "Everything's the matter, but nothing's the matter."

She sighed, and taking the peeling knife from his hand led him over to the sink to wash his hands, then came back and emptied the bucket of onions into a tub of brine. She took the bin of onion peel out to the back porch and came back to take him by the hand.

"Do you want to go down for a swim with me, Nic, or just both of us have a bath? A nice cool bath would be lovely."

She went over and closed the front door, and came back through the house to the big bath and undressing gazed back at him. He came over and sat on the edge of the bath to remove his shoes and socks, then pulled his shirt over his head and standing dropped his trousers and finally his underpants. She watched him as he stepped into the bath.

He looked down at himself, and looked up. "Sarah can hold my knob just inside her pussy, did you know that, and ripple her little muscles and just about make me come without moving any other part of her body. Don't you think that's amazing, to be able to do that?"

"She told me," Emma said. "She told me what you said about me as well."

"What did I say about you?"

"That I was more spiritual."

He looked at her directly now. "You and Wally, and your Mum, and now little Wally, and I bet Gracie more than any of you; there's something about you all, your family or something, something."

She nodded slightly, glancing away and back again. "Why did you come up here, Nicolas, just before?"

"Why did you introduce me to Sarah?"

For a long moment she sat there, looking away, until finally she said quietly, "Because I doubted you, Nicolas. I wasn't sure, after what we've been through. Poppy was so convinced, you know, and he kept talking about going to get you out of there, until that day you arrived on your bike and," she giggled, "you went crook at him because you thought you were going to earn some pocket money driving the tractor, dwivin' the twacta!"

"And what then?"

"I fell in love with you, and you kept ignoring me."

"You were too impatient, Em, and wouldn't let me get my thoughts together."

"Bloody hell! That's what you're doing to us now, all of us, isn't it? Isn't it, Nicolas?"

He sat back at that, and looked at her, thinking. He leaned forward. "Em, can we try an experiment, something I've been thinking about?"

"What experiment?"

"No," he said, "nothing. I don't mean nothing; I mean I don't mean anything by it. I was just thinking about what would happen if two people did join spiritually."

"What?"

He reached across the bath and drew her to him, and sat her next to him, holding her hand. He gazed into her eyes.

"What would happen if we loved each other, kissed each other all over maybe; something like that, as close as two people could possibly get; spiritual, without being sexual."

"No, we can't."

"Why not?"

"Bloody Nicolas, shit, all your questions all the time!"

"Why not?"

She pushed him away, and sat back on her own side of the bath looking away.

He watched her. "Why not, Em?"

"Because I'd get pregnant, that's why. I'd be letting my guard down, forgetting myself, and you'd get me pregnant. Then where would we be? We're far too young."

"How could touching you and joining with your spiritually possibly get you pregnant, Em? You need sperm to join with the ovum . . ."

"Just shut the fuck up!"

"No, I won't." He looked at her. "Did you read my play yet, the new one?"

"Yes, we all have."

"What did you think of it?"

She took a deep breath, engaging him. "I don't think of it, husband. I love you too dearly and I can't stand it when you're away from me. But we have to wait; we're too young, and I'm glad for Sair and Robbie because they help so much, except now I think sometimes Eric is right and they should be married, and you and me married, and stop this nonsense."

Emma glanced away, then back again. "They're not farming people anyway, they don't really know what it means to be organic, and they play games with it all the time. I think that's what Sair means about me being spiritual, and you so beautiful and loving, while they're both very physical. If Eric and Sally got together too, that would be ideal. They can move into that nice brick house on the farm."

"Do you really think that? How would we do it, us four; get another bed maybe? There's plenty of room, but I don't want them too far away."

"Nicolas, I'm not sure yet. We'll talk about it, all right?"

"You can if you want, I don't care. Say you were already talking to me about it and I'm easy. But what about you and me then, do you want to cuddle for a while? That's what I came up here for."

"No, love me please. I have a few days; it'll be all right."

Chapter Fifty Nine

Neither Robbie nor Sarah was happy with Emma's idea about two separate marriages so they decided to let it slide for the time being. In the end Robbie was right; they'd grown so comfortable with one another, tangled at night on the one huge bed. He had no real objection when the time came to be formally married to Sarah while Nicolas and Emma tied the knot, if that's what it meant to keep things on an even keel, but he refused to discuss it beyond that. Sarah simply went cold on Emma for a few days but as Christmas approached and she'd become so vibrant and full of life riding and working the cattle with Eric day after day, she quickly forgot about it.

What did happen to change things was a phone call early one morning from their builder, wanting to know if Robbie was willing to take an apprenticeship with him. Karl came up the hill with the message.

He came in and sat at the table while they were having breakfast, and Nicolas got up to make him a cup of tea.

"Robbie," he said, "do you remember Artie Millington, who built this house? He rang just now looking for an apprentice. He's very impressed with your work. Do you want the job?"

"Artie? He's got an apprentice, hasn't he?"

"He's finished his papers and wants to go work up in the city for a while; get some money behind him."

Robbie looked away. "I want to go to university," he said quietly.

"You can do that later, Rob," Nicolas interrupted. "Why not do this now and we can go to Uni together in a few years' time, when we're old enough?"

He glanced around the table at everyone sitting there watching him. "All right, what's the deal?"

"He wants you in town, Robbie, that's the thing; boarding with his family so he doesn't have to drive in and out every day. It'll be the same as working for Chas; you'll be able to come back here on the weekends unless he has work on, but we can sort that out later."

"You're not in on this, Karl, are you?"

228

"No, not at all; what makes you think that? Sarah's working for Chas so I really don't give a shit one way or the other about this job. You're no skin off my nose, mate, do you want it or not?"

"It's a good chance, Rob," Emma said, "Mr.. Millington's a good builder and he'll teach you the trade properly, and you can be making money. You can still do carpentry if you want."

He cocked his head thoughtfully and nodded. "Does he want me to ring him back and let him know, or what?"

"Sure. If you ring now he'll know you're keen, or you can leave it until later if that's what you prefer."

"No, it's all right. I've got everything done here; I'll start tomorrow if he wants me."

"Good lad, we'll go and tell him then."

Karl rose from the table and Robbie followed him out.

"Karl, tell Kennie and Owen to come up," Emma called after him. "They can spend the day up here and stay out of Mum's hair, all right?"

"What are we going to do with them?" Nicolas wanted to know, frowning.

"Well, they can help me bottle that last batch of pickles and then we can go riding over to the farm and back, or maybe through the bush. Then we might go for a swim. You can help me too, Nicolas, and get away from your stupid play for a while."

"It's not stupid."

"No," she giggled, "it's brilliant; we love it, but you do need to get out of the house. Leave it for a while, it doesn't matter, we're not putting it on until Easter."

Ten minutes later Robbie was back with the two boys in tow, smiling, saying he'd got the job. After the breakfast table was cleared and the washing up done Emma unpacked her clean pickle jars, and draining the brine from the tub filled it with clean water to rinse the onions before starting the others to work filling jars, while she warmed the vinegar and added spice and herbs.

She had to push Nicolas out of the way when he became engrossed in the patterns of rings in the onions, and started picking up whole onions from the box in the pantry to peel them and cut them in half lengthways to see how the bulb was formed. Finally she took them from him and sent him back to his desk to sort out his costumes and scenery, while Robbie looked on chuckling to himself.

When they went out riding later the two little boys rode bareback so Robbie and Nicolas walked their horses all the way, and at the swimming pool stayed close to Robbie talking to him; leaving Nicolas and Emma their own space.

He's so funny, Kennie said afterward.

Chapter Sixty

As Christmas approached Jennie started taking Nicolas aside to explain to him Wally's ideas about yuletide, and the summer solstice; upside down here in the southern hemisphere so they had to adapt their ways. She'd been talking to Emma and together they'd decided he was a lot better off for the time being to spend his days in the big house with her, looking after the babies and talking with her about their family and the way they thought about things.

Liz by this time had taken charge of the old house and had Karl as well as Marcus under her wing while Elsie tended her growing flocks of chickens and sheep. At the last moment she decided to get some turkeys and ducks as well. Jennie complained that it was too late to be getting them ready for Christmas, but Elsie fobbed her off and went about her own business.

Nicolas said to Jennie one morning don't worry about Else, she's a bit potty but she's good and she knows what's what; everything she'd said to him was right, about farming anyway, it was a pity they never learned to read and write, those old people.

He sat chuckling absently, and looked up. "They used to call it larnin', did you know that Jen? Book larnin', and figurin', they'd say, when they wanted to do their sums."

He cocked his head thoughtfully. "Did you know, in those days when they learned English they weren't taught spelling; they wrote any new word they'd heard someone speak on a slate, with chalk? When somebody else rode past on a horse they'd show them the slate and ask if they knew the word. They called that word a spell, did you know that, like magic; a magical thing. That's what children did, back then."

"What are you talking about, Nicolas?"

"Well, what happened was, instead of understanding the children's curiosity and explaining things they'd beat them and make them do things in a way that's just not natural. People like Wally and Elsie got away somehow, I don't know how, and did things naturally, and that's what they've both been trying to say except they don't have the right words

231

because nobody ever taught them to read properly. That's what my new play's about, when you think about it."

"How do you know all that, Nicolas?" she turned on him. "How can you know everything about us like that? How can I possibly teach you anything?"

"What? I don't know. I don't know everything, or anything, how would I know? Liz said that too, do you remember? What are you talking about?"

They looked at one another, then distracted glanced up to see Emma at the door staring at them. She watched Nicolas for a moment, and tears glistening flashed across at her mother.

"I don't mean for you two to argue, Mummy. What Poppy said, about him; you remember don't you?"

Emma came across the kitchen to hold her mother's arm, looking into her face, making Nicolas gaze in askance. "Jennie, how did you meet Chas?"

Jennie looked up, then away, while Emma followed her face around before turning back to Nicolas.

"Poppy introduced them," she said, almost in a whisper. "He's a sort of cousin, but a long way off, not like me and Eric, or Simon; through Jack, you know. His family hold a lot of land up north, running cattle."

"Does Chas know all this?"

"Yes, of course; of course he does, what do you think?"

He sighed, distracted for a moment by a big blowfly butting against the window pane, and shrugged, "I don't know what to think most of the time. It all just comes to me, without me actually doing anything, and I don't know why I get into trouble for it, or why Wally even wanted me out here with you. Do you know why?"

"You were just talking about it, Nicolas, only a moment ago, before Emma came." Jennie said. "You said it yourself; you write spells, and weave stories, and enchant people with your lovely words and your voice, and your beautiful body, and the way you hold yourself. Dad thought you might be a *shenechie*, or a Druid or something, reincarnated from the old times, but you got mixed up with the beautiful youth Angus somehow and startled everybody. They don't know how to deal with somebody like you."

He stared at them. "I don't want to be listening to this all the time. I don't like it. When I was little I thought I was on the wrong planet, but I'm not. This is the right planet and I do belong here, except something else has taken over in the meantime, that's ugly and hateful. Why is everyone so worried about beauty and nobody to say anything about that sort of ugly hatred all the time, or do anything about it?"

"Because they'll kill you, Nicolas if you even think about trying. Nobody is allowed to cross that line; haven't you learned that yet?"

Nicolas stood suddenly and went to leave. He turned at the back door and said, "It was Eve, wasn't it, because she was jealous and couldn't come up to anything Lilith was, so she had her set up, and blamed her. People have been blaming Lilith ever since, as the succubus; I know I read about it, and feeling sorry for poor stupid Eve instead. But it was her son who killed his own brother, not Lilith's children, because she was the one who made people feel so shameful and guilty about every little thing."

He stopped suddenly, distracted again, and frowned. He turned back then and said softly, "Is that's what's wrong with me, do you think? Is that what's happening? I don't feel guilty about anything, or ashamed. Why would I? Maybe, maybe . . . I can't think . . . it wasn't only Dionysus either, you know; Adonis and Hermes both came from human mothers as well, who made mistakes; they all did, and they were all beautiful, and they all copped it. How many more are there?"

He disappeared out the door. Jennie held Emma back, letting him go. After a moment she resisted, saying quietly, "Mummy, let me go after him. He's hurting and he'll be up there in the bush crying all afternoon if we leave him by himself."

Chapter Sixty One

"I'm not bloody talking to Marcus!" Nicolas yelled, frustrated. "What good is he? Bloody professor! He comes up here making out he knows something, not doing any work around the farm; says he'll be living off his investments, with all his friends, and now he won't help with the play."

"Well, no, he won't, Nicolas," Liz said patiently. "He can't teach you anything, and he's tired. He came up here to get away from teaching, and marking essays and assignments, and exam papers day after day. What do you think he does when he's not here? Besides, if you really want to grasp the essence of this problem he's trying to get you to address why don't you bone up on the argument between Saint Augustine and Pelagius, or on Cornelius Jansen's ideas perhaps?"

"Who?"

"There, you see! You didn't ask, did you, or discuss it with anyone. Why don't you simply write a whole new play and leave the other until later, perhaps when you've finished your undergraduate studies? You could write your doctoral thesis on Greek tragedy if you're still interested, or on the early Celtic Church, or on Germanic mythology, or the controversies in Rome."

She went on with a slight smile, observing him closely.

"I do know who'd interest you, Nicolas," she went on quietly, intrigued now, "Frederick the Second, *Stupor Mundi*; the Wonder of the World, and his relationship with the Papacy. His court introduced the Arabic number system and the foundation of mathematics into Europe, did you know that? He was excommunicated four times."

Nicolas stopped, staring out the window, "Is that right?"

He turned to her, alert now but watchful. "You're changing the subject. But if it's true, why are we talking about Marcus then? It's not even the same planet, is it. He and Karl, that's why they're friends, isn't it? They both say they're teachers but they never want to learn anything, not about this place anyway, and won't tell you anything except what they want. What the hell good is that? Why do they want to have anything to do with us anyway?"

He paced back and forth not looking at her, and head up suddenly dashed out the door. He strode down the hill past the sheds to the front paddock where he caught one of the horses and led it back over to the shed. Saddled up he disappeared over the ridge and out the back gate.

When he got to the farm Eric and Sarah were nowhere to be seen so he went through the gate and down the track to the house. They were inside having lunch.

He burst in, "Sair, you want to be in my play? I'm rewriting it, not a lot, just a bit, but you need to be in it, can you?"

"How much will you pay?" she wanted to know, but he broke up laughing.

"Ha! That's why, you and Robbie, but it's not; we're in the wrong paradigm," he retorted. "That's where the world thing gets confused. Can you play Freya for me? I want to change it, and get it out of that Classical thing, you know?"

Eric looked blankly at him, and when Chas rose from the table he followed him and both rinsing their plates left them to dry on the sink and walked out. Nicolas sat down.

"Why did you want to break up our marriage, Nic. You haven't explained that to me yet," she said quietly.

"What? No I didn't. What are you talking about?"

"I can't bear to be away from you, you know that, so what's going on?"

"Nothing, no, um, we were talking about farming, and you and Robbie being town people and not thinking the same way about organic living that we were; me and Em I mean. What she was worried about I think is if we all got married we'd be arrested again, so that was the best way to do it. I don't know what else, Sair; the grown-ups did that."

She looked at him. "Yes, slow down a bit. What do you want me to do now?"

"Freya, you know, if Em played Frigg who is more the Earth Mother, you could do Freya who's the Love Goddess. That'd resolve that whole business between Lilith and Eve, and that way we could bring things back to where they should be."

He rushed outside leaving her sitting at the table. "Chas, I need to talk to Eric," he called out before coming back inside. He sat back at the table, back in his chair, grinning until Eric arrived.

"What, Nic? What do you want?"

"Eric, I want you in my play as well. Pay's good, if we get a good crowd, but I want you to play Odin, who's king of the gods. It's not too hard; you get your eye dug out and a spear in your side, but that only makes you wiser and more powerful, and you get to have some hell good parties. I mean, you can fuck yourself silly, with anyone you like, because you're the father of everybody. That's about it, what do you think?"

Eric stared. "Nicolas, you are a very weird brother to have, did anyone ever tell you that?"

Sarah leaned over. "Who're you going to get to play Thor, Nicolas?"

"Marcus. Marcus can play Thor. He wouldn't do Pentheus for me, because he gets ripped apart, but Thor goes around with this big hammer keeping everyone in line. Bloody bastard he is; it'll be right up his alley. I'll make him do it, you'll see."

She looked at him. "So, what do you want Robbie to do?"

"He'll be Loki, the trickster."

"Who will you be then?"

"I don't know yet. It sort of seems all right 'til now, but I'll have to work on it. I'm not sure what happens next."

"Baldr, Frigg's son," she said. "I know that story too. Baldr, yes, I know what happens, be careful, Nic; we need to do it." She leaned forward. "Don't ask Robbie to play Loki, please, and not Eric either except you already asked him to play Odin. Get Karl, all right? He'll do it, he can be tricky."

She sat back thinking, and leaned forward again. "No, Robbie can play Odin, and Eric can play Baldr's brother Hod, or Hor; something like that."

"How do you know all that?" Eric wanted to know.

She glanced across at him. "Ha, you boys think I can work my pussy, and ride horses and be beautiful, but I've got a brain too, you know." She sat back, holding his gaze. "I qualified for Mensa the same time as Robbie but I didn't bother joining, did you know that? He's not so smart; I just let him think he is. Don't tell him, will you."

Nicolas stared at her, grinning a sheepish grin while Eric looked on curiously before turning to him, complaining, "Nic, you haven't told me what this play's about yet."

"Well, we've got this beautiful world you see, maybe not always beautiful but its alive anyway; organic, you know, and it gets invaded by all these pure and holy people who are actually dead, because they're jealous, and they bring with them a death cult that slowly destroys the life and turns everything into meat, and into machines, and well, sort of fucks everything up so nobody is allowed to feel anything. They've got this idea that you have to be dead here on Earth, not like zombies going rotten but beautiful plaster statues, so later you can become alive in some place called Heaven where you go when you die, except you're already dead because you're still alive here, and you can't ever get there."

"What?"

Nicolas gazed at him. "Don't worry, you'll get it. What I mean is, they scare the shit out of everyone by taking out some of the people and making an example of them, and beating them up and tormenting them until they confess to all these terrible crimes, so they all start walking around like statues in case anybody suspects they might actually have an erection under their clothes, or a sweaty pussy; something like that. Once we begin rehearsing and start doing it you'll see, all right, instead of me trying to explain. It'll be all right, you won't have too many lines to learn."

Eric rose from his chair and went back out to help Chas, head shaking in astonishment.

When he'd gone Sarah leaned across, frowning. "Nicolas, those plaster statue people are so pure and holy, they'd never stoop to violence; it's all part of their image they need to protect, so they get their Neanderthals to do all the roughing up, or troglodytes, or somebody like that; their followers, you know."

He looked at her in astonishment. "Yes, you're right! That's it! That's how all the people become so scared shitless they line up to confess, and pay their money, and get new statue masks to wear around so everyone looks the same, and suits and ties, so everybody else will think it works, and they're all saved and going to Heaven."

He leaned over and kissed her full on the mouth, lingering, then suddenly stood and rushed out the door. "I love you Sair," he called back, and mounting his horse broke into a canter and rode straight back up the track.

Chapter Sixty Two

Nicolas stewed for another whole week, taking long walks alone in the bush and refusing company, until Chas rode home with Eric and Sarah for a good break; they'd earned it, and to get ready for Christmas. Sarah promptly talked to Emma and together they went to see Liz. In the upshot Liz consulted with Marcus who the next night had a couple of beers with Karl, and a few joints, and with Sarah pointedly avoiding Karl in the meantime they all agreed finally they had a play.

It was a bit late to do anything more by then, so happy with the outcome agreed to shelve the project for a month or so until the festive season was out of the way. Robbie was unable to get time off work until Christmas Eve, while Eric was becoming fidgety about Sally and her family arriving and went into town with Chas to buy new clothes and some nice dress boots.

Jennie and Aunty Elsie decided they no longer wanted to honour Christmas the way it had been, but revert to the old tradition and start preparing Summer Solstice. Nicolas was curious about why they were starting so early when he thought it would be another week yet, and they told him. He disappeared for the rest of the day and came back arguing they had it wrong; it was all back to front, because here this was mid-summer not mid-winter. They couldn't have a Yuletide; it was the longest day not the shortest day, it's called Litha.

Jennie looked at him. "Let's just pretend for now, Nicolas. You go and work it all out for us, and if you want we'll all start changing over, maybe after Easter."

"But that's not Easter, either; it should be Mabon which is an autumn festival. Easter is the spring festival when all the little birds are laying their eggs, and all the wildflowers come out. I read about it, but I know it's true because I've been watching everything happen that way, you know, all my life. After Easter we celebrate Beltain, which honours all the beautiful boys and girls, and then each sort of person after that. Old ladies, and mothers, and fathers; we can include everybody if we do it that way."

"Yes, all right, before Easter. We'll make Easter Mabon."

"After Mabon we have Samhain. That's when Aunty Elsie can sit up there and we'll all love her, and bring her presents, but not now because it's the wrong time of year."

Elsie glanced across at him, scolding, "If you don't scoot, lad, I'll be giving you a present you won't forget. Be off with you, we have work to do."

"Yes, take the boys for a swim, will you," Jennie added. "You can all get out from under our feet."

Kennie didn't want to go swimming. He wanted to hang all the pretty lights up and join the conservatory of the big house with the old house, knocking down that old fence and lighting a walkway between the two so when all the people came to their party it'd be nice. They started walking over to the big shed to see where the lights were stored when Emma and Sarah came riding in. Dismounting they gave him the reins and walked straight over to the house, smiling back over their shoulder. He shrugged, unsaddled the horses and brushed them down before turning them out into the front paddock.

By time he was back Kennie had found the lights so they loaded the boxes onto the trailer and starting the tractor drove back to the house where he backed the trailer in to stand on while they strung the lights, moving progressively toward the old house, then back again to insert the light globes into their sockets.

"We could have knocked the fence down first, Kennie."

"No, why; we can put the lights up, can't we? Once we see where the lights are then we'll know which bits of the fence can go. Otherwise we have to do it all, and then it won't be two yards, will it."

"Funny kid you are, the way you think."

"Not, Nic, it's sensible. Mummy said she wants the food on this side, and Karl can do the music on that side, except now they won't have to climb over that broken bit of fence."

Owen broke in. He'd been watching from the conservatory door. "You think funny, Nic; you're a real strange super brain," he giggled.

He looked oddly at him for a moment, thinking about it. "Yes, I must be, you're right. I think you've got a good idea. I never thought about it like that." He paused for a moment. "So, where does Jen want the tables for the food, and where does Karl want the band? If we work it out that way, we might have to shift the lights a bit."

"No we don't, silly! We put the tables under the lights, and Karl can do whatever he wants himself."

That evening when Emma came to find him Nicolas was asleep on the old divan with the two boys beside him listening to the radio, so they decided to leave him there. When the boys went to bed finally Jennie came in and pulled a blanket over him, with a cushion under his head for a pillow.

Chapter Sixty Three

Nicolas stood around at the edge of things to watch as people began arriving, but once it was dark and the lights came on he withdrew into himself and stood there mesmerised by the patterns and noise and people moving about. He remembered being introduced to Sally, and smiling because she was really very pretty and Eric in his new clothes seemed to stand six foot tall, grinning from ear to ear, except after that it became something of a blur and he found himself back up at Edoras with his nose in a book.

His mind wandered again. After a while he sat up, and going outside walked back down to the old house where he browsed through Marcus's library until he found Descartes again, and disappearing out the back door took the book back up the hill with him.

Leafing through it he came back upon Descartes' idea of thinking, therefore he exists, and he sat contemplating that awhile before taking up his play script started making notes. But he was restless, jotting down thoughts and ideas then sat back frowning.

"But that's wrong," he said out loud. "They've got it wrong. The verb's wrong. It shouldn't be 'I think,' it should be 'I am thinking.' I am thinking. I am thinking. That's what Robbie was trying to say."

He put his pen down and closed the book, and standing stripped off his clothes and went over to the big mirror to look at himself. He turned at that and went naked out the front door and along the top of the ridge toward the swimming hole. He went slowly and cautiously in the semi-dark. There was a gibbous moon and the light was tricky, and when he was close to the dam saw some kangaroos grazing there on the grass. They all hopped a short distance and let him pass, and he stepped into the cool water until up past his waist he pushed himself off and swam a little way over to the other side.

"I'm alive," he murmured. "I'm thinking and I'm alive. Therefore I am, and I exist." But he pulled himself up there, head cocked curiously to one side. He went cold suddenly, and shivered.

"If I'm alive, I can die and go to Heaven. Those plaster statue people can't go to Heaven because they can't die; they're already dead. So are the machine people, and teachers, and the troglodytes."

Back at the party the last of their guests were leaving and Emma was going around asking everyone if they'd seen Nicolas. Nobody had any idea where he might be and she started to fret. She went out looking for him, and noticing lamps burning at Edoras hurried up the hill.

Nicolas was out of the water by this time and climbing back over the ridge wandered down through the amphitheatre, poking at the new pasture with his toes and gazing about looking at the sheep and horses standing quietly there in the moonlight, until he came to the stage.

He looked up. Noticing a rope dangling from one of the bearers he climbed up and tied it around his neck, then let himself drop.

Chapter Sixty Four

He became dimly aware of swinging to and fro, and kicking and trying to breathe , and his tongue filling his mouth, and of screaming from somewhere, and being held up, and more screaming, much closer this time and from beneath somehow, that reached a crescendo, filling him. The screaming gave way finally to a soft murmuring that seemed to emerge from a lot of noise and bustled and bumping around, and he opened his eyes. People were sitting around the bed he was in, and hushed suddenly as a hand reached over to flick a lock of hair from his eyes. He had a sore neck.

Emma stood and made everyone leave. Liz protested but Emma simply pushed her out the door then closed and latched it. She undressed and crawled into bed with him. She took one of the pillows and placing it against the headrest leaned back into it, gently placing Nicolas' head in her lap as she did so. She said nothing, but started crooning softly to him.

In the kitchen Liz was furious. She paced back and forth, speechless, until Elsie stood and sat her down.

After a moment the old lady said patiently, "He's still only a cub, Elizabeth. Pity of it is he never got licked properly. Sarah's not much different either. Better keep an eye on her too, I reckon."

Liz glanced up sharply, "By God, where are they? Where's Robbie?"

"We're out here," a voice came from the conservatory. "Leave us be, all right. Just shut up. Shut the fuck up, right!"

"You come in here with us, Robert, come in here this minute."

Robbie and Sarah came in through the back door, but instead of stopping went without a sideways glance through to their old bedroom. A moment later they came out with Nicolas and Emma, carrying her clothes and holding Nicolas up while he staggered unsteadily on his feet. The four disappeared out the back door and without looking at anyone made their way past the old house and up to Edoras where they tucked Nicolas with Emma into the big bed. Disrobing they joined them under the sheets.

The pleasant party mood had subdued quickly, with the screaming and crying, and carrying Nicolas into the house, though everyone relaxed as the four of them made their way through.

Jen shook her head, "Bloody kids, what next? Anyone want to adopt four tear-aways, by chance? They'd be very welcome," she chuckled.

Marcus leaned in close. "Be careful, Jen."

She glanced up at him. "No, Marcus," she said. "This is my family home. I'll remind you, you are guests here. All this has become far too complicated. We are simply not used to it, and I tell you here and now it's going to stop. God knows what forces we've unleashed, playing around with things that should rightly be left alone. It's going to stop, I tell you!"

She stood abruptly and went out, not looking back but following the path by the old house up to Edoras.

Up on the ridge Nicolas stirred. He sat up and shoving Emma gently aside got out of bed and went out onto the front verandah. He stood at the top of the steps gazing around in the bright moonlight, and turning saw Jennie making her way up the slope. He went down to meet her, until nearing a pile of rocks dug out from their house foundation he stopped to wait.

She must have noticed him up on the verandah, and losing sight of him scanned ahead as she came up the slope. As she came near then he stepped out to meet her. He took her hand.

"Jennie," he said simply.

"Nicolas. Are you all right? Tell me."

"Hmm, yeah, I'm OK. I sensed you were coming up, that's all, so I came to meet you. Can I talk to you a minute?"

She gazed at him a moment before indicating a sort of rough bench Emma or somebody had formed there among the rocks.

"Do you want to sit down?"

He turned around and still holding her hand sat and pulled her down beside him.

"Jennie, I'm not going to write any more. I don't want you to argue with me, or tell me it's a shame, just listen all right. It's too much trouble. I know it got me out of trouble, but in a lot of ways it's getting me into more trouble. I'm too young, and I can't deal with it anymore."

"What are you saying, son?"

"Well, I wanted to stop before, before I even came out here. But you wouldn't let me, you thought it was them trying to stop me."

He turned to her, earnestly, "Jen, I've got the opposite problem from most people. I don't get writer's block, I get possessed by all these characters and their stories, and there are too many of them. They go on and on. They're driving me crazy. If I keep doing this they'll kill me for sure, next time. I really just want to be a farmer, and get this place running properly, like we've said."

Jennie looked up suddenly to see Emma up there on the verandah, and stood waving to her to come down. Nicolas turned to see who it was, and as Emma neared he stood and stepped onto the track in front of her.

"We're here, Em, it's all right. We're just talking."

She held him close, not wanting to lose him, but he turned back to Jen and said, "Jennie, do you want to come for a swim with us?"

The three of them walked back up over the ridge in the moonlight and down again to the swimming hole. The two already naked waited while Jennie disrobed. Her breasts were heavy with milk and her nipples leaked slightly. In the water she stooped to wash them while Emma and Nicolas looked on curiously.

She watched their rapt faces, then smiling drew them both to her.

Chapter Sixty Five

The phone was ringing, and Liz hurried to answer it. She listened in growing alarm before replacing the handset and hurrying outside. She bumped into Karl in the doorway.

"Quickly, find Marcus and tell him to take his clothes and things up to Edoras. You do the same thing. Don't worry about the books, leave the school as it is. Then run up there and tell the rest of them to bring their clothes down here. Tell them to put them all in the cupboards in their old bedrooms, and hurry up about it."

She turned on her heel and down the corridor into her room she quickly gathered up her armfuls of clothing and threw them into a large suitcase. She swept her smalls and things in after them and banging the lid shut ran out through the conservatory.

Marcus called to her as she swept past the old house.

"That was the sergeant, telling us those dreadful *Bold Hearts* people in town have a search warrant," she called back. "They're coming out here to inspect the place. Get your things, quickly. When they get here we'll say we are living up at Edoras and the children are with their mother in the big house."

"Shit!"

Marcus ran inside and quickly packed his few things, leaving everything else in disarray as if the place had just dismissed a class.

Robbie was in town working with the builder, and Sarah was over on the new farm with Eric for the day, but neither of them had much to carry anyway apart from their spare work clothes and a few things for going into town. Nicolas stood around confused for a moment, trying to think why anyone would want to raid the property, until Emma called to him to help her with their things.

"It doesn't matter why, Nicolas," she said somewhat breathlessly. "Worry about that later."

He stared at her until she bundled a pile of clothes wrapped in a sheet into his arms, and he went out with it. He stopped on the verandah and cocked his head, then went back inside and dumped the sheet on the floor and started rifling through their belongings.

"What are you doing, Nicolas?"

"I've got it, Em. You take your girlie things and I'll take Robbie's things. I'll just take them to the old house, and you take your stuff down to Liz's room in the big house. OK?"

He started tossing her smalls onto the parquetry, and standing grabbed Robbie's work togs and wrapping everything picked the bundle up and hurried out.

By the time Emma got to Liz's room three cars were coming up the track from the main road. She quickly tossed their things into the cupboard and left a mess of clothes on the floor and on the bed before slipping on her panties and bra, and a loose summer shift.

She went through and picked up Gracie. Baby on her hip she went to the back door to gaze out at the commotion, with cars kicking up the dust as they pulled in convoy to a stop. Her mother was already there likewise carrying little Wally.

The sergeant got out and tipped his hat.

"Sorry to disturb you, Mrs. Larkin. We have a warrant to search the property."

Jennie made way for him but the moment the others tried to enter she blocked their way.

"Who are you people?" she wanted to know. "What are you looking for?"

"Ah, we are acting on a complaint that children living on this property are in a state of chronic neglect, and are in moral danger," one of them said politely.

Emma came up to stand next to her mother, eyes wide in innocent wonder. "What do they want, Mummy?" she said quietly.

"Oh, don't worry, daughter, they don't want anything."

Jennie turned to the group waiting there.

"This is my daughter Emma. She lives with me in the house to help care for the babies. Her friend Sarah shares her room, but she's working over on the other farm today."

"Where are the other children, the three boys?"

"Well, there are six boys. Who do you mean? Apart from little Wally here, there are my other twins Kennie and Owen. They live in the house with me. My husband is droving up north; he'll be back in a few months with another mob of cattle."

"The child protection committee here are interested in assessing the circumstances of the autistic boy, Nicolas Bruic, and his brother Eric McCallum. Have you seen either of them, by chance? We'd like to speak to them."

"Eric is over on the other farm today, working the cattle. Nicolas is here, he sleeps in the school house with his friend Robbie Ashcroft, and Eric when he's here."

"I'm not bloody retarded," Nicolas called across from the front porch of the old house. He'd pulled on a pair of clean shorts and a t-shirt and stood there like Emma, in bare feet. "Come and have a look if you want; see for yourself. I help the teacher with the littlies. We are going to University when we're old enough."

Jennie turned to the sergeant. "Go ahead with your search, if you want."

The policeman went inside the big house and after a cursory look around went over to the school and did the same thing there.

"Anyone up at the new place?" he wanted to know.

"Marcus lives up there," Nicolas said, "Professor Trent-Brown. They have a music school there for the time being, until we get our new studio built. Would you like to meet him? I doubt he'd appreciate being disturbed, there's a rehearsal on this afternoon."

The policeman stepped out onto the path and cocked his head up toward the ridge from where the clear sound of a flute wafted across the valley.

"Hhmmm," he glanced back at Nicolas and winked, "I don't think we'll worry too much, what do you reckon?"

Nicolas simply shrugged, eyes bright.

"The boys are tidier than the girls, Mrs. Larkin," the big policeman ventured.

No response.

"Anything you'd like to tell us about?" he persisted.

Nicolas simply gazed up at him until Jennie broke in, "They're all just kids, sergeant, you know that yourself. We were once like they are, messy, and willful I have to say, but nothing we can't manage. We are family. They'll grow out of it."

Chapter Sixty Six

As the crowd began to disperse back to the cars Nicolas came forward and making his way through stood in front of the fat woman who glared stone angry at him. He turned back to stand before the policeman, pointing at the woman.

"That's her," he said loudly. "I remember now. That's Dinky's Mum. That's the kid I was trying to think, who fucked me that time, you know, up the bum, that time when Simon got killed. They killed him, it was them who did it."

"That's Mrs. Kulinski, Nicolas. She's President of the High School P & C, and Convener of the *Bold Hearts* Child Abuse Advocacy. She drew this search warrant herself, on the basis of complaints she'd received about you."

"Who complained?" Nicolas turned on him. "No, if that's true she's definitely the one. She makes things up. I know, she abused me and assaulted me herself, when that old headmaster died. She's a child abuser herself. Wally was there, if he was still alive he'd be a witness. It's true."

He paused, frustrated, trying to find the words, then burst forth suddenly.

"She makes things up, I mean, she doesn't properly find out what's happening, only what she thinks is happening. And that Andy bloke she's living with, after she left Steve, he's the same. We know about him too, he wasn't a commando just a storeman at the SAS barracks. They say whatever they think will impress people, and get stuff in the newspapers to raise money so they can pay themselves, but only dumb people listen. Smart people can tell the difference, so they get their mates to beat them up. That's why nobody can solve anything, not really. That's why the school's full of bullies, because those people are in charge. She's a real serious bitch, you know. She's the child abuser, with the big mouth. She's got another child she abandoned, her own daughter from someone else, before Steve, we found out about that too. She did nothing to help me with Mum either, 'cause she's just the same; three kids from three different blokes. It's a small town, everybody knows that, but nobody's game to stand up to her. That's what's happening, nothing else."

He paused for a quick breath, then fired again, "What, is she going to have all these people here arrested too, as child abusers? They are the ones who helped me when I was getting the cuts all the time at school, and after her lot fucked me. They beat up Frank, and rooted me up the bum, and killed Simon . . . . and . . . . . "

"That's enough, son. We don't need the sordid details."

"By God, sergeant," the lady shouted, indignant. "Must we stand here listening to this? Do your duty and arrest that boy! I demand that he be taken into proper care."

The big man turned slowly toward her, frowning, then down again at Nicolas.

"Why didn't you tell me this before, young fella, when I came and asked you?"

Nicolas had his dander high up and stepped forward again to vent years of pent-up fury, but Jenny quickly took his arm and pulled him into her, smothering him against her breast until he settled.

"He's been terribly traumatised, you really have no idea," she said quietly, looking at nobody in particular, merely stroking his brow tenderly with her thumb.

After a moment she glanced up at the sergeant. "You have absolutely no tight to intrude upon his privacy, or ours for that matter," she said. "For the moment, I will tell you that it's only since last Christmas he's been able to start thinking clearly. We have all his diaries and writings from the time he was a small child, if you want to know officially where he's been all this time. We have expert diagnosis testifying to his condition, or can call on it if need be. So you go ahead and arrest him, and by God I'll see you in court!"

The sergeant nodded before gazing about him thoughtfully, then finally stepped over to the woman and taking her by the arm made her sit in the back of the police car. He went around to the front door and reaching in through the window picked up the microphone and called the station. When he'd patched through he gave explicit instructions for the apprehension of one adolescent Samuel "Dinky" Kulinski along with Sean and Lewis O'Reilly, and a list of their known associates.

When he finished he tipped his hat to Nicolas, and getting into the car turned it around spinning the rear wheels in the loose gravel, and quickly drove back out along the track.

THE END

ABOUT THE AUTHOR

Born in England in 1951, Tom Fisher migrated to Australia during the 1970s as an aspiring young teacher. Initially attracted by the legendary toughness and independence of the Australian bushman he soon started to notice perplexing anomalies. Eventually retiring from teaching he returned to university to complete a specialist degree in literature, and is now a full time writer.